Death in Brittany

Sandrine Perrot - Brittany Mystery Series
Book 1

Christophe Villain

Translated by
Terry Laster

Copyright © 2023 by Christophe Villain

A revised new translation of „Emerald Coast Murder".

All rights reserved.

No part of this book may be reproduced in any form or by any electronic or mechanical means, including information storage and retrieval systems, without written permission from the author, except for the use of brief quotations in a book review.

Christophe Villain

C/o Peter Bingel
Pettenkoferstr. 2
45470 Muelheim
Germany
author@christophe-villain.com

Coverdesign by HollandDesign
Translation by Terry Laster
Copy editing and proofreading by Elizabeth Ward

Directory of persons

- Sandrine Perrot: Police Lieutenant assigned to the police department in Saint-Malo
- Adel Azarou: Brigadier Chef de Police, partner of Sandrine Perrot
- Jean Matisse: Director of the police station in Saint-Malo
- Jean-Claude Mazet: Director of the forensics department
- Antoine de Chezac: Prosecutor in Paris
- Gerard Lagarde: Prosecutor in Saint-Malo
- Inès Boni: Office manager of Sandrine's division
- Charlotte Corday: Unknown woman killed on the Brittany Coast Path
- Isabelle Deschamps: Witness of a crime
- Thierry Kouame: Leader of a criminal gang
- Charles Carnas: Criminal in hiding
- Marie and César Treville: Owners of a public camping site
- Florence Morvan: Owner of the hotel 'La Baie' in Cancale

- Daniel and Sarah Morvan: Florence Morvan's children
- Léon Martinau: Owner of the club 'Équinoxe'
- Nicolas and Leonie Tanguy: Residents and witnesses
- Carine Fortier: Resident, witness and blogger
- Rosalie Simonas: Writer and Sandrine's best friend

Chapter 1

On the Brittany Coastal Path

Sandrine Perrot's alarm buzzed her out of a restless sleep one hour before sunrise. Her loud yawn was accompanied by a stretch, and she threw the duvet aside to sit up. A heavy storm had hit the coastline just after midnight, thunder ripping her from sleep, and for a while she had just watched streams of rain run down her skylight.

'Time to get going,' she murmured to herself. She stood up, shook the duvet back into shape and made her way into her tiny bathroom. Her adjoining office was barely any bigger. There simply was not much space in the top floor directly under the steep sloping roof.

Her shoulder-length dark hair was still wet from her shower when she made her way into the kitchen. The whole building had been lovingly restored, nothing remaining that resembled the simple stable it had once served as. She switched on the radio. The weather report promised a warm and pleasant spring day with some wind in the afternoon. Perfect for what she had planned. Her first job of the day led her to the shining, chrome espresso machine on the kitchen isle. The screeching grinder scared the cat from her sleeping position next to the warm fireplace. The stone stored heat for a long time, and therefore was the feline's favourite spot.

'Good morning, Pauline.'

The cat belonged to Rosalie, a famous writer who was renting the main building. Pauline claimed Sandrine's house as hers on a regular basis and had no trouble finding her way through the cat flap into the living room. Sandrine did not own any pets and had not wanted to get any as her job required long working hours. Since the beginning of this year her life had changed, though. She had been forced to take a leave of absence from her job with the police, moved from Paris to Brittany, and now had the time to spoil a pet. The cat stretched and jumped from the fireplace onto the oiled wooden floor. *Maybe a dog*, she decided. *But first I have to think about what I want to do with my future.*

To go back to her old job was not an option. She had written her notice weeks ago, and despite her move to Brittany, the envelope was still waiting to be sent. In the next few days, she would go to the post office, she told herself. Some people would be happy to get rid of her in such an easy way. It made the muscles in her jaw clench to think that she would make it that simple for her boss in Paris. The machine beeped, and Sandrine poured the warm milk into a ceramic bowl. She added the espresso and dusted the foam with some cinnamon and cocoa powder. The fridge was fairly empty, and she had to be content with a dry croissant from the day before. Dipped into the coffee, it was not half-bad. Maybe she would treat herself to lunch at the Pointe du Grouin. It was a hotel for tourists, but the food was said to be decent.

Sandrine held the bowl in both hands and relaxed with the warmth of the coffee. It was only the beginning of May and still chilly in the morning. She considered lighting the fireplace, but by the time the living-room warmed up she would be gone. In

45 minutes the sun would rise, and she planned to be at the Pointe du Grouin by then.

Her Aunt Celine had fashioned the room with a rustic flair; the wooden furniture was heavy and embellished with glinting copper tones on the shelves. The walls sported antique-looking kitchen utensils and dried herbs from the region. It was not really her style, but she would not be here long enough to justify redecorating the entire former stable. As a child she had watched Aunt Celine cook in the main house and had complained that she wanted to help. It had been in her aunt's kitchen that her first apple cake had burned to a crisp. Uncle Thomas had eaten the burned tarte aux pommes without any complaint, and Sandrine loved him for that to this day. Her culinary skills had improved since then. Now the problem was that she could not find the time to bake or cook. She made the resolution that this would change in the future.

She took her backpack, checked once again that her camera equipment was in it and that the batteries were charged. The tripod she fastened to the side of the backpack. Her sturdy outdoor jacket was hanging on its hook in the hallway. Even though there was no forecast for rain, Pointe du Grouin was famous for its strong winds. It was a headland reaching into the English Channel on the north side of Cancale, and with that it attracted its fair share of bad English weather. Sandrine slipped on her hiking shoes and threw the backpack over her shoulder.

From her house it was only a few minutes' drive to her destination, but on this day she decided to leave her car and motorbike behind. The old coast path ran just behind her house, and the prospect of a relaxing walk was too tempting to resist. She had learned quickly that movement lightened her spirits, and she had an inkling that she would not get much exercise or relaxation for the rest of the day.

She left the house through the backdoor and stepped into the garden. By now, nearly 20 years had passed since the death of her aunt. It had been just before her 15th birthday when she had left the stone house to Sandrine. The main house was rented out to Rosalie, while the adjoining building had been let to friends time and time again.

Sandrine had initially refused to set foot in the house after Celine's death, as the memories were too painful. It was only after everything that happened in Paris, she had decided to move here to clear her head and sort out her new life. So far, she had not regretted this decision. The calmness of the place made her forget the crime which had begun to haunt her in the big city. Here it was peaceful. She had found a good friend in Rosalie. She could even imagine spending her whole life here.

She locked the door and marched down the grass until a stone wall blocked her path. The GR 34 Brittany Coast Path started roughly two metres away from her land. The hiking trail cut deep into the embankment and a retaining wall protected it from falling dirt or large boulders. She took the time to pause and let her gaze drift over the sea below her. Dark lines were crisscrossing the turquoise water, marking the places where oysters were bred. Cancale was famous for its oysters. White sailing boats were rocking up and down on the waves. Most of them were only used during the weekends or the season. They carried their owners to the fashionable Saint-Malo or just along the coastline. A few skippers also ventured out to the British Channel Islands, just visible from the headland during clear weather. A narrow path led her down wooden stairs and onto the coastal path. The hiking trail started in the north, level with Mont-Saint-Michel, and snaked through the country 2000km before ending in Saint-Nazaire in the south of Brittany. One day she would take the time to walk the path completely.

A dog barked suddenly, tearing Sandrine out of her thoughts.

'Bonjour, Madame,' she greeted Florence Morvan who was taking her spaniel for a walk. She only received a curt nod as an answer. Florence was in her mid-fifties, and the owner of one of the most prestigious hotels in the port of Cancale, the La Baie, which was said to serve a good cuisine. So far, Sandrine had not had the time to visit and try the food for herself. Even though she had spent her vacations here as a child, she was nowhere near being regarded as a part of the community. It would take another couple of years until people accepted her. They counted her as one of the 'long-term' tourists. One waited to see how long they would make it far away from the city and the hubbub. Truth be told, there was not much that Sandrine missed from Paris – apart from her favourite bakery. She was still hunting for the perfect croissant in Cancale.

Madame Morvan did not deem her worthy of another look and hurried in the direction of the port. She had often noticed that the lady parked her car in one of the side streets, took her dog for a walk and then drove off again. Sandrine looked after her until she disappeared behind the next bend.

Sandrine checked her watch. 'Let's go,' she mumbled to herself. From her house it was nearly 3km until the Pointe du Grouin. It would take her more than half an hour. She was not someone to hurry along the path and enjoyed stopping at scenic spots to take in the beauty of the landscape.

The path led her down to the beach on two occasions and then back up the cliffs. She was able to walk quickly; from Cancale to the headland, the trail was in perfect condition. Thick shrubs grew all along the path and obscured any hikers from the eyes of curious leisure captains. That was not a coincidence. The path had been forged in the 17th century for the Gabelous, the customs officials of the *Roi Soleil*, King Louis XIV. They were careful to hide their whereabouts on the way to the shore while on the lookout for smugglers, looters or custom fraudsters. Right now, Sandrine was just thankful for the natural shield against the fresh breeze.

A car of the Gendarmerie Nationale was parked in front of

the closed restaurant. A policeman in uniform was leaning against the fender, his eyes trained on the Île, a small island which ran parallel to the headland. A metal thermos stood on the car's bonnet and a crumpled paper bag in his hand revealed the tip of an almond croissant. The man took a big bite and chewed.

'Bonjour, Monsieur Bertrand!' she greeted him.

The older gendarme turned in her direction. Judging from his raised eyebrows he had not heard her coming. The almond croissant disappeared back inside its bag, and he wiped powdered sugar from his chin with his sleeve. She had met the man twice, but only briefly. The alarm system of one of the neighbouring houses had called the police a few times. The owner of the house lived in Rennes during the week, and so they had decided to ask if any of the neighbours had noticed anything out of the ordinary. She had not lived long enough in Cancale to know what was included in 'out of the ordinary' but she had definitely not seen a burglar climb through one of the windows. She assumed that she had been asked not because she had a good view onto the neighbouring house, but simply because everyone had been curious to see who had moved in.

'Bonjour, Madame Perrot. Up so early and not even with a pet?'

'The air is wonderful today, and the morning haze will be gone soon. What would keep one in the house when such a view is waiting?'

He nodded in agreement.

'It's quite nice here,' he answered in the typical glib way of the locals. Still, pride for his hometown was glinting in his eyes. 'And you're only here for the view?'

She patted the side of her backpack which was holding the folded tripod. 'I want to take a few photos of the sea and the Île. I would like to catch the green of the water which gives the Côte d'Émeraude, the *smaragd* coast, its name. If I manage that, it was worth getting up early.' Last week she had agreed to contribute to a coffee-table book about the entire Brittany Costal Path. Her part was to be from Mont-Saint-Michel to the Pointe du Grouin. It was around 40km and a proper day tour for even a seasoned hiker. To catch all the best corners, she had planned in one to two weeks.

'Bonne jour.' He took a sip from his thermos. 'I like to come here before work to enjoy the calm and quiet, before the work starts.'

'I moved to Cancale because it is so quiet and peaceful here. Please, don't destroy my illusions.'

'Not because you own one of the pretty houses at the shore?' Laughter lines crinkled the corners of his eyes.

'That too, of course,' she answered, 'though I would prefer it if it was still my aunt's house.'

'I'm sorry,' he said. 'I heard of what happened.'

'You don't have to be sorry. It was a long time ago.'

'You're right, we don't have a lot of crime here. Maybe some teenagers with too much energy and tourists parking where they shouldn't, but apart from that ...' He shrugged his shoulders. 'Which is good because otherwise we wouldn't be able to close the station for lunch.' Judging from his bulging uniform he used the two hours of lunch break for a decent meal.

'I wish you uneventful work then,' said Sandrine as a goodbye. She had nearly reached the spot she had chosen a few days ago. Close to the steep cliff she unfolded the tripod and screwed the camera on. The whole trick with landscape photography was to be patient and to find the correct light. Nowhere in the world was light as clear and bright as in Brittany. She only struggled to find the patience.

The first few pictures had been taken and Sandrine spread her jacket on the grass. Soon the tourists would descend upon the scene. Some would come over the hiking trail, but most came in their cars and in coaches. It was not as bad as during the summer months, but the calm quiet, only interrupted by the screeching of the seagulls and the ruffling of the wind in the grass, would be over soon.

She lay down on her jacket, closed her eyes and enjoyed the warm spring sun on her face. She would stay here a while. It was unlikely that she needed to take more pictures, but it was never bad to have some extras. *If you want a good picture, you need to take hundreds*, had been the favourite lecture of her father. Some memories were rooted so deeply that one simply could not forget them.

A shadow suddenly fell over her face.

'Lieutenant Perrot?'

Sandrine opened her eyes.

'Monsieur Bertrand!' What was the policeman doing here again? The station could not have been open for long and it was unlikely that he was already taking a break. And why was he addressing her with her rank? She nearly corrected him, before remembering that she had lost her post as Capitaine. The Paris police prefect had insisted on demoting her before dismissing her from duty.

She sat up. 'Has something happened?' She hoped that he had just come back to give her some tips on where to set up her camera, but the wrinkles on his forehead told her that he was serious, maybe even concerned.

'Commissaire Matisse from the office of the Police Nationale in Saint-Malo sent me. You are needed, and you couldn't be reached by phone. They have been looking for you for a while.'

She knew the name of the head of the department but had not met him. Sandrine sighed. Did the man want to look at the investigator who had angered Paris? He would have been able to do that every day for the last two months, so why did he have to pick a Sunday morning?

'What is this about? Has someone broken into my house?'

'Not that I know of,' he answered and took out a notebook. 'We were asked to find you and bring you to him. We only get the bare minimum of information,' the man complained.

'I am off duty,' she responded adamantly.

'I didn't even know that you are part of the police.' The man sounded slightly insulted, as if it was protocol to identify it as soon as one happened upon a colleague.

She felt a sinking feeling in her stomach. They would not call her in if it was not necessary.

'Normally, they don't tell us why we pick someone up,' he continued, stressing 'pick someone up' as if he actually meant 'arrest someone'.

'Then please, show me to Commissaire Matisse.'

'No problem. It's nearly on your doorstep.'

From the sinking feeling in her stomach grew a premonition as to why she was being called. She pulled out her phone and typed a short message to Rosalie. The two had planned to meet for coffee in the afternoon. This was another aspect of her work that she did not miss in the slightest. She hated having to cancel her engagements. Murder and manslaughter had never cared much for her calendar.

Sandrine rose and let her gaze drift over the sea. The air was clear enough to see the coast of Normandy and the north of the Channel Islands. The view brought back some of the calm, which she would definitely need to survive the approaching confrontation.

Bertrand stepped back and observed her unscrew the camera, fold the tripod, and pack everything into her backpack. They went to the car together and she put her things in the boot. She had barely sat down when the policeman switched on the blue light and raced down the road.

'Is this necessary?'

'It's official business.'

'Switch off the siren at least. You'll only attract an audience and the press. The last thing I want is to start rumours just because I was seen in your car. My neighbours already treat me like a criminal.'

He switched off the blue light with a grunt, but his foot did not go any lighter on the gas. There was no way that he would miss out on the opportunity to race down the tight country roads. In theory she was his senior, but not his boss. He was part of the Gendarmerie Nationale over which she had no say, and so all she could do was hold on fast and hope for the best. *We'll be okay ... there is barely any traffic.*

After a few kilometres, the car stopped in a dead end. If she was not mistaken, they were between the Pointe de la Chaîne and Pointe du Hock. It was only a short walk to the port of Cancale, and with that also to her house. Several police and civilian cars were parked all over the unpaved footpaths. Residents were crowding around their fences and stretched their necks to catch a glimpse of the officers, or even better, the track down to the Brittany Coast Path which they were blocking. If so many uniformed officers were here, it could not be a mere accident. Bertrand had brought her to a crime scene. That was why they had called for her. The reason for her presence must be hidden behind the trees, most likely on the hiking path, and definitely dead.

'How bad is it?' she asked Bertrand.

'Philippe had to throw up. His first corpse,' the policeman explained, as if to excuse his colleague.

Sandrine doubted that Bertrand himself had seen more than a few victims of car accidents or drowned tourists. Capital offenses were as rare here as snow for Christmas.

'One doesn't get used to things like that easily, and once one is it's time to find another job,' she said. *And that's exactly what I am doing.*

The man murmured something unintelligible, and Sandrine got out of the car.

'Can I leave my equipment in your car?'

'No problem. I always lock it.' He jingled his keys. Sandrine marched down the street. Nothing moved behind the trees and the gawping residents turned their attention towards the new arrivals. She clearly stood apart from all the uniformed officers in her outdoor clothes. Some might even recognize her. Her house was exactly in this quarter of Cancale.

'That way,' indicated Bertrand, who stayed with the car.

At the end of the alley a uniformed gendarme stepped into her path.

'There's a police investigation going on here. Access forbidden for private persons.'

'Thank you. You saved my day. I had feared that I would have to look upon whatever happened down there in more detail than I wanted to.'

She turned away, but someone called, 'Where are you going? We're waiting for you. Down here, please.'

A man was standing between the trees and waving towards her. He was tall with a loud, stern voice, and short-cropped, graying hair. His appearance screamed military or police. His dark suit had a classic and timeless cut and looked quite expensive. *Monsieur le Commissaire*, was her first thought.

'Commissaire Jean Matisse,' he introduced himself and shook her hand. His handshake was like the grip of a vice, a premonition of what he planned on doing with her – to rip her out of her peaceful life and place her in this mess.

'Sandrine Perrot, Lieutenant de Police, off-duty,' she said.

'Then I have been misinformed. Paris told me that you were merely temporarily released.'

'That's a euphemism.' They had demoted her, suspended her and now she was waiting for the decision of the police department to fire her. Unless she could finally get herself together and send her notice.

'Anyway, you are police, and we want to use your expertise.

This is one of the most peaceful regions in the world. Violent crimes are an exception here, and now this.' The man shook his head. 'The only colleague who ever worked on a case such as this retired two years ago. Since then, we have been waiting for a replacement.'

'Even in peaceful places people die of unnatural causes. I am sure that your men have some experience.'

'Sure. Traffic accidents, affected manslaughter, sometimes a crime committed by a jealous husband, but incidents that can be cleared up quickly. This one is different.'

'How did you get the idea to contact me? Barely a soul knows that I moved to Cancale, and I doubt that Paris has given me a warm recommendation.'

The man, whom she judged to be in his mid-fifties, smiled. 'That's correct, but some people, whose opinion I cherish, were of a different opinion. You have been described as an extremely capable and dedicated investigator with a tendency to overshoot the mark at times.'

So, he has connections to Paris, she realized. There was clearly more to Matisse than just a simple police officer waiting for his retirement in the province.

'Still, I've been suspended and am not on active duty. Even if I wanted to, I couldn't help you.'

'I took care of that. The police director personally lifted your suspension and assigned you to us.'

I imagine he is still dancing around his ugly old mahogany writing desk. He got rid of his problem without any fuss, and I won't trouble him anymore.

'My notice has been written,' she retorted. She did not want to dive back into the swamp of murder and crime.

'I'm sorry to hear that.'

'If we've cleared this up now, I'll say goodbye.' She offered her hand to Matisse in farewell.

'It's sad that the police are losing such a precious colleague,' he said without taking her hand. 'But of course, all the more reason to use the time until your termination and solve the case.'

Sandrine lowered her hand. For a moment they held silent eye contact. She could not see any indication that he was enjoying his triumph. He really seemed to want her expertise and was clearly adamant enough to recruit her despite her wishes. There was no hole in which she could hide that he would not find.

'Are you always this well-prepared before a conversation?' she asked. He had won. She would have to work for him for the next three months. If she liked it or not.

'They warned me that you would not just swallow the offer.' He took a step closer towards her. 'Whatever happened in Paris, please treat this as a new start. If you still want to leave the force after this case, I will not stand in your way.' Without waiting for a response, he reached into his jacket pocket and pulled out a police ID card. He handed it to her. 'A weapon has been readied for you at the commissariat.' She eyed the new card. It seemed like another lifetime when she had felt happy after finishing her exam and receiving her first card. *It's only for three months.* Sandrine could curse herself for not sending her notice letter sooner.

'Please, let me introduce you to the team.' Her new boss gestured in the direction of the GR 34, the Brittany Coast Path.

'The team can wait. I want to see the crime scene first.'

'We can do both at the same time,' answered Commissaire Matisse. 'You seem like more of a lone wolf.'

'Is that a question or information from your sources?'

'We are a team here.' He avoided answering and stepped down the stairs onto the hiking path. Sandrine followed along but stopped in her tracks. Madame Morvan had gone this way. It had only been a few hours ago and the path had been deserted. *I hope she isn't lying down there.* Cases with people she knew personally were always much harder.

A rotund man with an impressive moustache was waiting for her. In his blue overalls he resembled a Teletubby, and his eyes were shining with barely contained excitement. Sandrine could tell already that he would not leave the crime scene before he had secured every last piece of evidence. Commissaire Matisse introduced him as Jean Claude Mazet, leader of the forensics department.

'Lieutenant Perrot.' She took his hand in hers. Somehow Sandrine was sure that she would be able to work well with the man.

'Do I get some?' She pointed at the disposable overalls.

'Not necessary. We have finished the track recordings. We documented what little evidence was left after the storm.'

'How long has the victim been here?'

'Judging from the condition of the clothes, I would say she was murdered during the night. Definitely before the rain started. The ground below her is nearly dry. Doctor Hervé will know more details.' He checked his watch. 'Our work here is done. We'll pack our things soon, and the corpse can go for examination as soon as you have had a look.'

She took a deep breath. So, it could not be Madame Morvan. 'Let's get this over with,' Sandrine said. The crime scene was only a few metres away but was obscured by the branches of a rhododendron. Sandrine caught herself taking another calming breath. Since she had left Paris, she had not been forced to lay eyes on the victim of a violent crime. Mazet's people let her pass, but she felt them eyeing her with a mixture of curiosity and suspicion. She did not blame them for it. She was new here and they could not categorize her yet. Of course, no one liked it when someone took a walk through the scene and destroyed possible evidence. *You don't have to worry, I know this very well*, she thought and greeted the forensic technicians while passing.

The dead woman lay on the ground with her back against

one of the walls supporting the path. She could have been mistaken for a resting hiker, simply watching the sea, if there had not been a hole in her chest. Sandrine stepped closer and squatted next to her. The woman was in her mid-twenties, maybe even younger. She was pretty, but no beauty. The dark, dyed hair made her face look ghastly pale. Her arms were hanging by her side, lifeless weights, with her hands resting in the mud. The rain had washed away most of her makeup. The rest of her mascara was still stuck to her cheeks as if she had cried black tears. She wore a red, tight blouse, jeans and a leather jacket. She had lost one of her high heels and her naked foot lay in a puddle.

After gaining a first impression, Sandrine was able to take a mental step back and regard her not only as a person, but as a corpse which would lead her eventually to the cause of death. It had not taken her much time to fall back into the long-practiced routine from Paris. She had gotten used to mentally sectioning the body into squares and examining each one individually so as to not lose herself in the details and miss a clue. *At least the woman was dressed.* Sandrine felt less like she was grossly violating the victim's privacy. *The perpetrator has already done that*, she thought.

'A rape gone wrong?'

She looked up to the man who had joined her. He paid Sandrine more attention than he did the corpse. Even in her squatting position she could see that he was tall and lean with broad shoulders. She judged him to be good at sports. His dark eyes looked at her with curiosity but also reservation. She wondered what stories the man must have heard about her.

'You are?'

'Brigadier Chef de Police Adel Azarou. I have been assigned to you as your assistant.'

'Good,' was her pert answer before turning her attention back to the corpse. 'You're wrong.'

'How do you know?'

Sandrine pulled a pen from her jacket pocket and pointed the tip at the gunshot wound.

'Not many rapists carry a gun with them. Knives are a much more popular choice. The fabric of the blouse is very thin but has no rips and she's still wearing her jeans. They are so tight that I don't think the perpetrator took the time to dress his victim again. If there had been a robbery it would look different. I assume that she was meeting someone and that they knew each other prior.'

'You mean the murderer and the victim had some form of relationship?'

'I don't see a murder yet. Do you?'

'The woman was shot in cold blood. What else could it be?'

'Murder is a legal classification. The court has to decide that and not us. At the moment, we can only assume that there is a perpetrator. We will find out what really happened here in the course of the investigation. There are several possibilities. You shouldn't decide from mere impressions.'

'What are you thinking?'

'Assumptions can lead us astray. I don't want to exclude anything at this stage: An amateurish suicide, self-defence, an accident while playing with a gun.' She looked up at him. 'But of course, it could also have been an intentional act.'

'It couldn't have been a suicide. The weapon would be lying here somewhere.'

He is testing me. Likely that he wants to know with whom he is working.

'The corpse was moved. We'll have to search for the weapon in different places.' She looked over her shoulder and at the forensic technician. 'Isn't that so?'

'Exactly.' Jean Claude Mazet nodded his approval and gestured towards the steep cliff opposite the path. 'Judging from the blood we found she was shot on the path and fell between the trees. She must have gotten stuck in the roots because otherwise she would have plummeted down to the rocks and into the sea.'

'So, the perpetrator shot her and placed her here?' Her new assistant took some notes on his pad.

'Someone shot her and moved the body,' Sandrine corrected him again. 'Most likely the perpetrator, but not necessarily.'

The brigadier nodded slowly. He seemed quite young for his rank. She judged Commissaire Matisse to be someone who would give her his best man, not only to help but also to monitor her. *He probably has to write a daily report detailing all the rules I have broken.*

'Did you find a handbag or any ID documents?'

'Nothing,' answered Matisse. 'Maybe we will find something down at the beach. We have low tide, but I am not very optimistic. If anything was in the water, the tide will have pulled it out by now.' He handed her several Polaroid images from an instant camera. 'The quality isn't great but for a first questioning they should be sufficient. The case files with the pictures will be on your desk by this afternoon.'

'Send them to Brigadier Azarou. It will be a while before I have my own desk.'

'I bet against that.' Jean Claude Mazet grinned. 'You haven't met our office manager, Inès, yet.' Her assistant nodded.

'Who found the corpse?'

'A lady walking her dog.' The brigadier leafed through his notebook to find the name.

'Madame Morvan with her spaniel,' Sandrine said before he could find it. From the corner of her eye, she noticed Jean Claude Mazet's surprised look.

'Yes, how do you know?'

'I met her on a walk around half-past six. Where is she now?'

'We questioned her and let her go home. She owns a hotel in the port of Cancale so she won't run away.'

'Any witnesses?'

'So far, none.'

The dead woman's handbag had vanished, and Sandrine could not make out the outline of a wallet in the pockets of the skin-tight jeans. Despite having little hope, she still asked for the identity.

'We don't have any ID documents. Unlikely that there will be a Missing Person Report yet. At the moment, we are in the dark.'

'Then it's our priority to find out who the victim was and where she lived. While forensics is working, we should start questioning the neighbours. Maybe she lived in the vicinity or had family here. We can safely assume that she didn't walk long.'

'Because of the shoes?' Azarou asked.

Sandrine nodded. 'No one goes hiking in such high heels. They have been bought for a club or a restaurant. The same with the skin-tight jeans. She probably had an appointment.'

'To run around the neighbourhood is more a job for the Gendarmerie, isn't it?' her new assistant interjected.

Sandrine offered her hand to him, and he pulled her up.

'There aren't that many. Maybe a dozen houses which are of interest to us. We can do that.'

'If you think so.' He did not sound very pleased.

She turned away from the corpse and studied the brigadier with more attention. His anthracite-coloured suit was very fashionable and looked expensive. It fit perfectly with the dark leather shoes but was definitely not the appropriate outfit for a crime scene.

'Were you about to take pictures for a dating website?' she teased.

'A family gathering. They picked me up from there, and I didn't have time to change.'

She shook his hand. 'We have to get along for the next three months. Until then we will solve this case together.'

'Only three months?' His eyebrows rose in surprise. Apparently, he had hoped that Commissaire Matisse had hired her long-term.

'That should be enough. Afterwards you can take over the job.'

'Capitaine Sandrine Perrot.'

She knew that strong voice and it made her freeze. What brought this man here?

'How's the former glowing star of the Paris' Police? You've found yourself a nice little spot here.'

She did not want to turn around and face him. He knew exactly how and why she had been suspended and degraded. Doubtlessly the man was up to his elbows in the process running against her. To address her with her former title was his typical condescending way of talking to people.

'Antoine,' she mumbled before she finally turned. 'What brings you into the province?'

'Work, as always,' he answered without offering a real explanation.

'Prosecutor de Chezac,' she introduced the arrival to her assistant. 'Or have you fallen up the stairs by now?'

They had worked together in the past and Sandrine knew that the man shied away from routine work whenever possible. He never got his hands dirty. It had been his relatives who had taken care of his ascension to the top. He would never have made the same mistake as her – he was too skilful for that.

'Not yet, but that should change very soon,' he said. Sandrine felt like he was talking more to himself than to her. But she did not have to care. What did interest her though, was what had brought the prosecutor from Paris to a crime scene in Brittany. *How has he learned of the corpse and what is his connection to her?*

'And what has your appearance to do with the case?'

'I wanted to take the chance to meet my former investigator again. Just a little chitchat between old friends.' He looked down at the dead woman who was about to be moved. 'Poor thing,' he said without any trace of sympathy.

'How long will you grace us with your presence?'

'Only a few days. The seafood is a lot fresher here than in Paris.' He waited for the body-bag to be zipped shut before he looked at her again. 'And I thought there would only be petty thieves stealing oysters or tourists' cars. What a surprise.'

Sandrine checked her watch.

'I have to go and do my job. Should you feel like more chitchat, you can call.' She did not think for one second about actually giving him her number. He knew how to find her and would not hesitate to do so if he smelled an advantage for himself. She made a mental note to find out how he had learned of her being drawn into the case and what he had to do with it. That this was no coincidence was obvious.

She left him there, and followed the path along with Azarou into the street in which Bertrand had parked the police car. At the top of the stairs, she looked back. Antoine de Chezac was standing close to the cliff and talking to Commissaire Matisse. She would have liked to know what they were discussing.

'There is more behind his appearance than just seafood, isn't there?' guessed Azarou.

'I don't believe that his love for oysters has led him to Cancale. This guy never leaves the city without having a proper reason. The reason can only be that he wants to help his career along.'

'That makes his sudden appearance all the more strange. Especially when he shouldn't have left the capital.'

'Why's that?'

'You don't watch the news?' Azarou looked at her in surprise. It was true; since she had arrived here, she had not opened a single newspaper or switched on the TV.

'You got me. What did I miss?'

'The government is putting more pressure on organized crime. Even here we have more raids and house searches than usual. All accompanied by a huge PR campaign. The public prosecutor's office is preparing a trial against Thierry Kouame and his gang in Paris.'

Sandrine whistled in appreciation. 'Thierry le Sauvage.' He had truly earned his title of 'the savage'. She had encountered a handful of his victims who had all been, like him, from the Ivory Coast. She had also interrogated him several times, but so far the police had not been able to prove anything.

'Is he in prison?'

'As far as I know he got out under strict conditions and is awaiting the start of the trial.'

'Has the guy made his way to Brittany?' That would explain why de Chezac was here.

'The press is camping around his flat. The man doesn't go anywhere without being caught on film or photograph. We aren't expecting him in Saint-Malo. Why should he come? His gang has never shown any activity here.'

'Then he has a flawless alibi for the time of the crime, and we still have to find our perpetrator.' She looked up the street. 'We will speak to anyone who might have heard the shot. The houses further off are for the Gendarmerie.'

Sandrine rang the bell of the first house on the left side of the street. It was made from stone and only slightly bigger than hers. The white paint was flaking from the windowpanes and corrosion marbled the garden fence. On a closer look, the garden seemed well-cared for in contrast. The lawn had just been mowed and a rhododendron had been planted along the crumbling cement wall. A bag with compost and a spade were resting against the house. It looked like more plants would join the rhododendron on a quest to hide the ugly wall.

'The garden runs all the way to the crime scene, but I cannot see any stairs leading down to the path. If the residents want to use the hiking trail, they have to leave their property and follow the street. I also don't think that they can see the path from the top floor. There are too many trees and high shrubs around,' Azarou noted. Sandrine nodded her agreement. Her assistant seemed to have a keen eye for details and patterns. She could have done a lot worse.

'I don't think we will find any eyewitnesses here. They might have heard the shot if we are lucky.'

Steps approached from the inside and a young woman with brown hair opened the door. She was made up as if she was ready to go out or awaiting visitors, with full makeup and an elegant outfit.

'I am Lieutenant Perrot from the Police Nationale and this is Brigadier Azarou.' Sandrine pulled out her police ID, but the woman did not even glance at it.

'Carine Fortier,' she introduced herself.

'Would it be okay if we ask you some questions?'

The woman looked her assistant up and down and hesitated before nodding. However, they did not receive an invitation to enter the house.

'Of course, I will help the police if I can.'

'I am happy to hear that. Did you notice anything out of the ordinary last night?'

'Actually, yes. Around 1:00am some guy raced up the street on his motorbike like a maniac. He woke up the entire street and of course the Tanguys' baby. The poor mother has her hands full with him crying all night. You can really pity her, and the husband too.'

'Did you see the driver?' Adel asked.

'No. When I made it to the window he was already gone.'

'You said he was male?'

'It was one of those high-revving racing machines. Isn't it usually men who buy such missiles to inflate their ego?'

'You are familiar with motorbikes?' Sandrine asked.

'My brother owns a Ducati. I would say it sounded similar to the one from last night.'

'Anything else?'

The woman tucked back a strand of her wavy brown hair. 'I woke up sometime before that as well. I don't know why though and directly fell back to sleep.'

'Do you know around what time?'

She rubbed her cheek and thought for a moment before shaking her head.

'I was still half asleep. It was definitely before all the noise started, but I don't know when exactly. Sometime around midnight.'

Sandrine searched in her pocket and pulled out the Polaroid pictures. The face of the dead woman could be seen well, without offering too many graphic details.

'Do you know this woman?'

Carine Fortier's eyes skimmed over the picture before handing it back.

'No, never seen her. Someone told me a corpse was found – is that her?'

Azarou handed her his business card, without confirming her suspicions. 'Should you remember anything else, no matter how trivial it might seem, please give us a call.'

'Of course.' She took the card and let it disappear inside the pocket of her beige-coloured trousers.

They said goodbye and made their way to the garden gate.

'Let's visit the Tanguys and their screaming baby,' Sandrine decided. Before leaving the property, she looked back over the shoulder. The curtain of one of the windows was moving.

'She wants to know where we're going next,' commented Azarou. He too had noticed the woman at the window.

'She's curious, but that doesn't make her a suspect.'

'Those people often see more than they tell us.'

'We will find our puzzle pieces one after the other. I'm sure that we will talk to her again. Maybe something will come back to her that she forgot to tell us today.' Sandrine was convinced of that. Carine Fortier had kept eye contact through every question. But when she received the picture, she had barely glanced at it and instead looked at the floor. She must have met the victim somewhere and was reluctant to admit it.

Sandrine was reaching towards the bell when the door swung open.

'The baby is sleeping,' mumbled a gaunt man, but he asked them to enter. 'Nicolas Tanguy,' he introduced himself without asking for their names or IDs.

'We are from the police.'

'Yes,' he answered. 'I'm not surprised. It's terrible what happened down there.' He noticed Azarou's questioning look. 'The whole neighbourhood is talking about a corpse which was found on the hiking trail. With so many police cars around no one thought that it was an accident. Or am I wrong?' He spoke quietly, and his eyes kept darting to the stairs leading to the second floor. Sandrine assumed the baby was up there.

'Did you notice anything out of the ordinary last night?' Azarou asked the routine question.

'Please, join me in the kitchen,' offered the man. 'We are just having breakfast.'

A woman with dark circles under her eyes was sitting at the kitchen table and looked up when they entered. Her hair looked oily and like it was long overdue for a visit to the hairdresser.

Sandrine felt a bit sorry for her. The baby must really be keeping her occupied. Her husband closed the kitchen door.

'We are questioning all the residents and don't want to take up a lot of your time. Did you see or hear anything strange on the street or on the hiking trail last night?' Sandrine had also lowered her voice. She knew that if the baby started screaming, she would not be able to get a word out of them.

'Claude, our son, woke up around midnight. I was carrying him around the flat when some idiot on a motorbike disturbed the whole neighbourhood. Afterwards, we couldn't even think of sleep. If I get my hands on that man ...' Nicolas Tanguy did not finish his sentence, but Sandrine could very well imagine where his fantasy was going.

'So, your son was already awake before the man on the motorbike woke everyone else?'

'Oh, yes.'

'Do you know what woke him in the first place?'

'Claude is a very light sleeper,' Madame Tanguy whispered with resignation in her voice. Unlikely that anyone had been speaking at a normal volume in this house for a while. 'He wakes up a lot during the night and no matter what we do he won't go back to sleep.'

'I had Claude on my arm when that man climbed on his bike and drove off,' the husband explained.

'You saw him?' Sandrine stood straighter. Could this be the first witness who was able to describe a potential witness or maybe even the perpetrator?

'The motorbike was parked at the end of the street, where the tarmac stops. It's easy to see from here. The driver came from the hiking trail, jumped on his bike and drove off. That was exactly at 1:00am.' He pointed towards a clock hanging over the door.

'Can you describe the driver?' Adel opened his notepad and held his pen at the ready.

'There are no streetlights here. I can only say that the guy was wearing a typical biker leather outfit and a black helmet.'

'Could you see his figure?' Adel asked.

'He was slim, roughly your height. That's all I can tell you. I'm sorry.'

'Did you see anything, Madame Tanguy?' Sandrine turned towards the woman.

'I was asleep for the first time in days. I didn't even hear the motorbike.'

'Then we don't want to take up any more of your time. Please give us a call if anything else comes to mind.' Sandrine placed her business card on the table, and they left the house. The questioning of the other neighbours gave them nothing new. All they had was a motorbike driver who had left from the direction of the crime scene just after midnight. It was less than she had hoped for, but it was a start.

Chapter 2

Port de la Houle

Azarou's phone rang. He listened, then ended with, 'We're on the way.'

'Good news, I hope?'

'I think so. Mazet's men found the victim's bag. As we thought, it slid down the cliffs and fell in the water. The tide pulled it out to sea, but lucky for us one of the straps got caught on one of the frames of the oyster farms. Jean-Claude is on site and securing the contents.'

'Hopefully that will help. So far, we don't know anything useful about the victim.'

Bertrand drove them to the port of Cancale. The Port de la Houle stretched in a wide arch along the high cliffs. Cancale was a split city. There was a picturesque quarter around the port in which the fishermen lived, and there was the quarter above where the merchants made their homes. Barely anyone still made their money in fish anymore. The days of the Bisquines, carb- and oyster-ships, were long gone. Out of the 200 ships that once called Cancale their home only one was still in existence, the Cancalaise. The sailing ship crossed through the bay of Cancale and kept alive the memory of former times.

It was the first weekend of May, and the sun was shining in

a beautiful blue sky. Tourists meandered along the promenade and queued before restaurants to study the menus and gawp at the towering seafood platters. Sandrine liked the smell of salt and seaweed which the breeze brought in from the sea. One of Jean Claude's men waved them towards him.

'Do you want to see the location where we found the bag or do you prefer to wait for Monsieur Mazet to return with it?' He looked at Azarou's fine trousers and leather shoes that would not survive the ordeal. She wore hiking boots, jeans and an outdoor jacket. Nothing that couldn't get dirty.

'Not necessarily.' Azarou was clearly trying to get out of the drive to the oyster farms.

'I would like to see the contents of the bag and the location. Can we drive with one of the tractors?' Sandrine asked.

'Sure. It's much faster and more comfortable than walking.'

Azarou shoved his notepad into his jacket and looked down at his expensive shoes with a sigh.

Sandrine turned to the brigadier. 'Would it be okay if you wait here for me?' It was not necessary that he ruined his clothes. They had taken him from a family party while she was wearing her hiking clothes and was better equipped for a walk on the mudflats. Besides, she didn't want to wait for Monsieur Mazet to come back to the port until she could take a look in the bag.

'If you wish.' He took the offer.

'Wait for me here or in the La Baie. We have to talk to Madame Morvan, and I would appreciate it if she knows we are coming.' Sandrine threw a quick look at her watch. 'I will be back in half an hour at the latest. Maybe we can make it before the restaurant opens for lunch.'

She climbed up on the waiting tractor. A road led down to the beach behind the small collection of blue and white booths selling oysters. The driver did not waste any time and pressed the gas pedal into the floor. Remaining water from the tide splashed to the side and the wheels catapulted silt into the air. The man was careful not to miss a single puddle. Sandrine laughed. This was better than any roller-coaster she had ever been on. A few minutes later, they stopped close to the oyster breeding grounds which stretched along the flat sand. Some of the wooden contraptions were still covered by the sea. It would take a while for the tide to free them from the water.

'There we are.' The driver switched off the motor and leaned over the steering wheel.

Jean Claude waved at her.

'Thank you for the drive.'

'I always help the police. Maybe one day it will help me when I get a parking ticket?'

'Only if you drive me back too.'

'Of course!'

She jumped down from the tractor. The wet sand below her squelched and water swelled around her boots. That would've been the death of my assistant's pretty shoes. The man she was now calling her assistant was clearly alert, clever and empathic, but their cooperation would not last long. In three months, I will be a civilian again.

She marched towards the forensic technician. Mazet held a clear plastic bag containing a small black purse, barely bigger than a wallet.

'Good work! I didn't even hope you would find it.'

The man's lips stretched into a wide smile.

'It was a lot of luck too.' He waved away the compliment.

'Anything interesting in there?'

'I think so. A key with a keychain, most likely from a hotel, her phone, a few banknotes, 30€ plus some coins, matches, makeup, and small bits and pieces. Also, a tiny plastic bag containing pills. From the look of them I would say Ecstasy, but the lab will check. Lucky for us no water got into it. Otherwise, they would have dissolved long ago.'

'But the oysters would have had a fun day.'

Mazet chuckled.

'This will help us. We should be able to find out who she was,' Sandrine said.

'The phone was submerged in salt water for a few hours. I am not sure if we can salvage any data, but I will send it to the lab in Rennes immediately. The memory card goes to Marie, our genius when it comes to bits and bytes. I already took a line-up and some pictures of the contents. I can send them to you if you want.'

'Of course.' The man impressed her. Sandrine switched on her Bluetooth and a few seconds later received the pictures. Mazet was right – according to her experience the evaluation of a destroyed phone could take a long time, if there was anything to save at all. It very much depended on where on the lab's waiting list one found oneself. Most likely the water had destroyed most other evidence. She shrugged her shoulders. There was nothing to do but play the cards that had been given to her.

Sandrine turned towards the cliff. 'You can't see the crime scene from here.'

'The engineers who created the trail wanted it that way.'

'I didn't really expect to have any accidental witnesses. It was dark around midnight, after all. No one would have been able to see more than maybe the glow of a torch.'

Sandrine made her way over the imprints of the tractor in the sand towards one of the wooden constructions holding the woven oyster baskets.

'That's quite a lot. I assume most of them go straight to the restaurants in the area.' She let her hand slide over one of the net-like baskets.

'Yes, you won't find any fresher oysters than these. Most of them go straight to the markets though.' The tractor driver had gotten down and joined her. He pointed towards some workers stowing bags of oysters onto a truck. 'Those have already been bought and will be on the plate of some fancy restaurant in Paris tonight.' Pride coloured his voice. 'Rock oysters,' he said and patted the bag. 'The best ones in all of Brittany. We in Cancale invented modern oyster breeding.'

'How many places claim that?'

'Oh no, it's the truth. It was a marine officer who caught oyster larva on a wooden plank at this place. Sometime in the middle of the 19th century, just at the right time. That was the start of oyster breeding in Brittany. Most oyster banks had already been emptied and many a captain sold his Bisquine. Now the city is living off oysters and tourism. You shouldn't leave before trying some of them.'

The man might very well be right about that. Cancale was famous for the oysters. Even Prosecutor de Chezac had used them as an excuse for his visit to the city. As if it had waited for the right time, her stomach grumbled. The last thing she had eaten had been the dried-out croissant and seeing corpses did not quell her hunger anymore.

'Then let's drive back. I would very much like a proper lunch.'

'The market stands are open. A dozen oysters is a proper meal.' The man grinned at her, as if he had already had just such a lunchl.

'Maybe later. I would prefer something warm now.'

'Later go to Laurette Bernier and tell her that I sent you. She will get the best oysters for you.'

'I will take your word for that.'

Her assistant was already waiting for her at the harbour promenade. To her surprise he was holding paper cups of coffee.

'I thought you might need something hot after the drive.'

'Thank you, that's very nice.' She took the cup and wrapped her cold fingers around it. 'Let's sit down. There's a free bench.'

'Madame Morvan is awaiting us.' He looked at his watch.

'We have 45 minutes until lunchtime starts at the restaurant. Afterwards we won't get a calm moment.'

'A few minutes won't kill her.'

Sandrine sat down and placed the coffee by her side on the bench. She pulled her phone from her pocket and scrolled through the pictures from Jean Claude Mazet. The keychain sported a green plastic sign with the number 335 and the picture of a stylised lighthouse.

'Do you have any idea what door this might belong to?' She gave him the phone.

'Number 335,' Azarou mumbled to himself. 'There are a few hotels here with more than three floors, but I don't know a single one with at least 35 rooms on each floor. Maybe it's from one of the big hotels in Saint-Malo. I will let Inès know. She was born and raised here. No one knows the area like she does.'

'Good, but don't limit the search to hotels. The cheap plastic bit looks more like it belongs to a camping sight or a youth hostel.'

'Consider it done.'

'What do you think of the pills?'

'I agree with Jean Claude. It looks very much like Ecstasy tablets. However, I have never seen them pressed into the shape of red skulls. They are either from a new dealer or the victim bought them from somewhere else. Do you think it could be a murder related to dealing drugs? Maybe she was a dealer and crossed paths with someone she shouldn't have.'

'It's just a few pills. Nothing she could deal with, more like what she might have used for a party. But you are right, we cannot ignore a single clue.'

Sandrine tilted her head back and closed her eyes. The rays of sunshine warmed her skin. She enjoyed the quietness of the place which was only interrupted by the cries of a few seagulls. She had moved here for moments like this, far away from the stress of the capital. And still, her past had closed its claws around her and again she had been pulled into police work, had kneeled next to the victim of a violent crime. If it was a murder. We don't even know that for sure.

The brigadier cleared his throat, and she opened her eyes. The moment of calm was over.

'You know the prosecutor from Paris well?'

'Antoine de Chezac. We worked together on a couple of cases.'

'You don't like him?'

'I've worked with worse.' But not someone as ambitious, who was ready to drop anyone who did not help to further his career.

'Is there something I should know?' he asked carefully. 'It felt like you were tiptoeing around each other.'

'Nothing that has anything to do with the case.' Sandrine finished the conversation and stood up. 'Madame Morvan is waiting.'

What had happened between de Chezac and her was not relevant to this investigation. Another three months and she would never have to see the guy again. What was left was only a memory which would fade with time. Sandrine threw away the empty coffee cup and marched towards the hotel. The brigadier jumped up and hurried after her.

The La Baie had been made up out of two houses of different heights. The right one had three floors and towered high above the left. Both timbered roofs had pointed dormers. A woman leaned out of one of them and took pictures of the harbour. That meant that the rooms directly under the roof were also rented out. Between the evenly painted light walls and the blue windowpanes with their bricked frames, the two buildings looked like they belonged together. On the ground floor and the annex towards the street was the restaurant. A huge etagere towered in the entrance and displayed seafood platters.

Sandrine threw a look through the windows. The staff was just laying out the last of the cutlery for the lunch. So far, no table was occupied but that would change soon. From 12:00pm onwards the place would be flooded by tourists. Everyone said that the hotel's restaurant was very popular.

They entered and were greeted by a waitress.

'We open in 30 minutes. If you want, I can make a reservation for you?'

Sandrine pulled out her police ID. 'We would love that, but unfortunately we are here for work.'

'It's a terrible thing that happened to Madame Morvan. A corpse, here in our little town? Incredible! And she found it.' She shook her head in disbelief.

'Where can we find her?'

'Most likely in the kitchen.' She pointed towards a swinging door left of the bar. On the right was the entrance to the hotel.

Sandrine put her head through the door and called, 'Madame Morvan?' The cooks looked up briefly but did not interrupt their work. Steam rose from the countless pots and fish filets sizzled in the pans. The smell reminded her that she had wanted to try out the restaurant. Maybe one day with Rosalie, she thought. Her neighbour and tenant was the closest thing she had to a best friend here in Cancale.

'Coming!' The female voice sounded too young to belong to Madame Morvan. The woman squeezing past the shelves resembled her enough to be her daughter. She was missing the strict aura of her mother, though. Sandrine judged her to be in her early twenties. Her white uniform had a few stains, so she must be working in the kitchen.

'I assume you are from the police,' she greeted the two before they could show their IDs. 'I'm Sarah Morvan. My mother is in the hotel and inspecting the rooms for this afternoon.' She looked around and nodded. 'All is running well here.

I can give you a few minutes. Please, sit down at the bar and I'll be there in a minute.'

Sandrine sat down on one of the barstools while Azarou remained standing and leaned against the bar. The counter was made from polished, red-brown wood and stretched nearly along the entire width of the room. Bottles and glasses crowded on mirrored shelves.

'The bar is well-stocked. There are some expensive liquors up there,' noticed the brigadier.

Sandrine nodded. Apparently, her assistant knew his way around spirits.

The young woman pressed open the door with her shoulder. With one hand she was carrying a tray with two plates, a cutting board, butter and a braided basket full of croissants.

'You don't mind if I work a bit while we wait for my mother, do you? I still have to prepare the restaurant for lunch.'

'They look delicious,' said Azarou, and pointing to the croissants.

Sarah Morvan put two cups in the espresso machine behind the counter. 'When it lands on the table it looks perfect, but back in the kitchen it is created with blood and tears. We like our work though. Otherwise, no one would go through all of this stress.'

She placed the cups in front of Sandrine and Azarou, followed by two little spoons and several packets of sugar which proudly sported the logo of the hotel.

'That makes waiting easier.'

'We appreciate it.' Sandrine ripped open one of the sugar bags and poured its contents onto the dark foam covering the black coffee.

The woman took out one of the croissants and positioned it on the cutting board.

'Leftovers from breakfast. We started baking them ourselves, but I am not 100% satisfied with the outcome. We still need to adjust the oven properly.'

She cut straight through the croissant. Crumbs from the first layer spread over the counter.

'They look perfect to me,' Sandrine commented.

'They are crispy enough and the structure is how it should be.' She pointed the knife at the cut she had just made. 'The bubbles have nearly the same size which is what we want. The problem is that the base is a bit too hard. I need to reduce the bottom heat of the oven.' Finally, she pushed the basket in their direction. 'Please, help yourself.'

'Is that not a lot of work? You could make your life easier and maybe even save money if you bought them from one of the bakeries in town,' Sandrine asked while topping her croissant with a dollop of the slightly salted butter. She took a bite. 'Delicious,' she mumbled with her mouth full. They were the best croissants she had tried since arriving in Brittany. She assumed that only a trained palate would notice that the base was too hard. For her they tasted divine.

'Most likely you are right, but that,' she gestured in the direction of the kitchen, 'is my passion. Don't you want to be the best in your profession?'

Sandrine nodded slowly. It had not been long ago when she would have agreed with the woman without a moment of hesitation. But now, she was having her doubts.

'There is one thing you might be able to help us with.' She searched for her phone and showed Sarah the picture of the key. 'Do you have an idea what hotel this key might belong to?'

She studied the key for a moment, but then shrugged her shoulders. 'No idea. It's definitely not one of ours. Maybe someone at Tourist Information will be able to help you.'

'Thank you. I guess it's worth a try.'

Next, Sandrine put one of the Polaroids on the counter.

'Have you seen this woman before?'

Sarah took the picture and looked at it but shook her head. 'I haven't seen her in our restaurant.'

'How booked out is the hotel?' Azarou asked.

'From now to the beginning of the season. We only have a few rooms available during the week. The La Baie is very popular.'

'Also expensive for Cancale. I had a look at the price list at the entrance.'

'The hotel and the service are worth the price, and our guests are happy to pay for the quality.'

He raised his hands in defence. 'I am sorry, I didn't mean to imply anything.'

'No problem. High quality is important to us. It has been since my grandfather founded the hotel. He was the one who bought the neighbouring house as well. You could call it the life's work of the Morvans. Most likely my grandchildren will still be running the hotel.' She laughed. 'My mother lives for this house. It's the centre of her life.' Her smile dimmed ever so slightly before vanishing. 'Maybe a bit too much.'

Before Sandrine could ask what she meant, Madame Morvan entered the restaurant.

'We met this morning,' she stated without any greeting. 'You are the niece of Celine Perrot, right?'

'That's correct.'

'And now you live in the sheep's stable? You should move into the main house.'

'It hasn't been used as a stable for a long time. I don't require much, and it's perfect for me.'

The older woman now turned her attention to Azarou, and the corners of her mouth dropped even further. He did not seem to match with her idea of a perfect customer. She placed her slender hands on the counter. Florence Morvan wore no jewellery apart from her wedding band. Her fingertips began to drum onto the polished wood. She didn't look like she appreciated having police officers sitting in her restaurant.

'That will change as soon as you have children.'

Sandrine did not plan to discuss her thoughts on family planning with a stranger and turned the conversation back to the actual topic.

'When did you find the corpse?'

'Shortly after I met you on the trail. Might have been less than five minutes. My dog found her.'

'Did you touch her? Maybe to make sure that she was really dead?' asked the brigadier.

She threw an ice-cold look at him, and her mouth drooped further.

'Are you out of your mind? Why would I touch a corpse? That's the job of the police. It also looked very obvious that the woman was dead.'

'Did you know the deceased?' asked Sandrine.

'She does not look like the sort of people we have business with.'

'I thought so,' she replied. 'Did you notice anything out of the ordinary this morning? Foreigners acting in a strange manner?'

'Apart from you? No. It is always very quiet on the trail at that time of day. That's why I walk the dog there. I park in the Rue des Rimains and start my round from there.'

The restaurant's door swung open, and an older couple entered. Madame Morvan threw a look at the waitress who hurried directly to the guests.

'I assume there is work to do in the kitchen or are they managing everything without you?' said the woman to her daughter. Sarah Morvan had been quiet since her mother arrived.

'Of course. Forgive me.' She took the plates and wiped the crumbs from the spotless counter. 'It would be a pleasure to have you here for dinner. You're always welcome,' she said as a goodbye and disappeared into the kitchen. Her mother looked after her as if she was judging every single step. Sandrine noticed that the young woman was slightly dragging her left leg.

'Children,' muttered Florence Morvan, 'they are still lacking seriousness and a purpose. You will one day understand what I mean.' She tidied the two cups into the sink. 'I assume that you are busy catching the murderer and that I should not take up any more of your time.' It was not the smoothest way to point them towards the door, but Sandrine could not really blame her. No one wanted to have the police sitting at the bar.

'One last question. Do you recognize this key?' She offered the picture to the woman.

'Never seen it,' she answered without even looking at it.

'Then we don't want to take up any more of your time.' Sandrine put her phone back in her pocket and stood up. 'We will see ourselves out.' She left the woman at the bar and stepped outside followed by Azarou.

'Wow, what a dragon,' he mumbled on the way to the police car.

'We are bad for business. This will happen to you again. People prefer to see us leave.'

'Did you notice the daughter? She seemed quite intimidated as soon as her mother made an appearance.'

'The woman intimidated me too. I fear that Sarah Morvan didn't have the happiest childhood.'

'Not enough "purpose"? Feels very unlikely. Her daughter makes croissants from scratch for breakfast. Do you know how long that takes?' Azarou asked.

'No idea. I normally just buy mine from a bakery.'

'With all the resting times two days. Minimum two days.'

'That's a lot of work. But admittedly you only get your first Michelin star like that.'

The brigadier had surprised her again. Not only could he

tell expensive liquor from cheap booze, he also knew about the production of croissants. The man had hidden talents.

Azarou's phone vibrated, and he took the call.

'It's a message from Inès. She's on the way to bring us my car. It should make it a bit easier to be independent from the Gendarmerie.'

'I have heard much praise for Inès already. Who is this very talented woman?'

'She is the most efficient office manager we've ever had. I think you will like her.'

'First, we get something to eat. Half a croissant was nice but doesn't replace lunch.'

'There is a brasserie over there. There should still be a space at this hour.'

Someone honked their car behind them, and Azarou turned. 'Damn, there she is.'

A white Peugeot 308 stopped at the side of the road, followed by a forest-green Mini Cooper. A surprisingly young woman with chestnut-coloured hair left the car. She had spotted the two of them and waved at the brigadier. Inès was a petite woman and at least a hand smaller than Sandrine. Her top was a screaming cacophony of colours, falling down to her hips. Together with the washed-out jeans and the trainers she wore, Inès definitely had her own style. White bluetooth-EarPods sprouted from her ears and her gait was bouncy.

'I really imagined her differently,' Sandrine whispered. 'Has she finished school?' This woman did definitely not resemble any office manager Sandrine had ever met in her life.

'Most people react like that. She might not look it, but she was born and raised in Brittany. Believe me when I tell you that she knows every crack in the street.'

'Inès Boni,' she introduced herself. Her handshake was a lot firmer than Sandrine had anticipated. 'So, you must be the disgraced genius from the city of love?'

'You can't just ...' Azarou started, but Sandrine waved him away. She was warming to this woman.

'You could say that, Mademoiselle Boni. Though I would say I didn't see much of the rosy, lovey side of the city. I was more in the darker parts.'

'Ah,' she warned Sandrine. 'No one calls me Mademoiselle Boni. My name is Inès and that's that.' She pulled a note out of the back pocket of her tight jeans. 'Your workstation has been prepared. These are your login details for the police-net and your laptop. There is also your work-phone.' She handed a new smartphone to Sandrine. 'If there's anything missing just let me know and I will take care of it.'

'That's very nice of you, but I don't think that I will be staying that long.' The woman's eyebrows twitched up in surprise. Apparently, she didn't know everything about her yet.

'We will see. Most people like it here so much that they don't want to leave. Like our brigadier boss.' She grinned impishly at Azarou.

'As you already know so much about me, do you have any news about the case or the identity of the corpse?'

'I'm working on an identification, but so far without much success. At least we know where the key came from.' She opened a notebook. 'It belongs to a campsite north of Cancale. Camping Côte d'Émeraude. Not a very exciting name but easy to remember. The owner's name is Marie Treville. She runs the site together with her husband, César. The office seems to be closed at the moment, or at least I wasn't able to reach anyone over the phone. Otherwise, we would already have the name of the victim. We also found the club from which she must have gotten the matches. It's in an industrial area in Saint-Malo and will open around 10:00pm.'

'Good work.' Sandrine's new colleagues had clearly not exaggerated. This woman was very efficient. Especially considering that the pictures of the handbag could have only reached her moments before she started driving.

'Your gun is in the car. I need a signature for that.'

Sandrine followed the woman to her assistant's car. Inès handed her a gun in a shoulder holster. 'I hope it fits.'

'I can work with that.' She pulled out the gun. It was a SIG Sauer SP 2022, the standard weapon of the Police Nationale. It rested well in her hand and was not too heavy.

'English police manage without,' Inès noted. Her aversion to weapons was clearly written on her face.

'It can be very helpful,' Sandrine replied. She had shot countless paper cut-outs but thankfully only had to aim at a few humans in her life. She signed for the weapon and her badge. After the paperwork was done, the office manager said her goodbyes, climbed into the Mini Cooper and left Adel and Sandrine standing.

'I am sorry. She's very outspoken and very direct,' the brigadier excused Inès.

'No problem. She seems to do excellent work and that's what matters.'

'Then we make our way to the campsite?'

Her stomach grumbled in protest, but it was more important to find out the identity of the corpse. Afterwards there would be time for a snack.

They parked close to reception. The barrier in front of the campsite had been lowered. No one was in sight. They got out of the car and took a look around. From here it would not even be a 30-minute walk to the Pointe de Grouin, where Madame Morvan had found the corpse.

'There's someone inside,' Azarou said, 'the curtains are moving.'

'Do we scare people that much?'

'I don't think I do.'

'Then there's someone hiding from us. People who don't want to be noticed normally have some very interesting things to tell.' Sandrine stepped onto the veranda in front of the wooden house and gave a sign to her assistant to go to the back. She knocked against the doorframe.

'Police. We would like to ask you some questions.'

Someone walked through the room, and she heard a door slam, followed by the voice of Azarou. Seconds after, the brigadier escorted a skinny man with thinning hair and a shaggy beard around the house. What caught her gaze was a laceration under the man's eye and his limping gait. She was very curious what story he would tell them.

'He wanted to leave through the backdoor.'

'That's wrong! I didn't hear you coming and just wanted to get to work. There's repairs to be made.'

'You are Monsieur Treville?' Sandrine asked.

'Yes, I own the place.'

'I thought your wife was the owner?'

The man only muttered, 'Little details.'

'Is this one of your keys?' She showed him the picture on her phone.

'Looks like it, but I'm sure there's tons of these.' He avoided meeting her eye and instead focused on the bungalows stretching in a straight line away from them. A cylindrical dome in the background seemed to be marking the location of a little pool.

'Who rents the house 335?'

'I have to check that. My wife does all the bookkeeping.'

'Come on,' the brigadier interrupted. 'It's the first weekend of May. How many guests do you have, a dozen, maybe two?'

'Yes, yes, alright. Her name is Charlotte Corday and she's from Caen in Normandy, as far as I know.'

'Charlotte Corday from Caen. Are you sure?' Sandrine

asked. Even before he nodded, she knew that they had found where the dead woman had been staying, but most likely not her true identity.

'What is a woman from Caen doing here at this time of year?' Azarou asked, astonished. 'The beaches of Normandy are basically on her doorstep.'

'It's nicer here with us.'

'How did the woman pay?' He was clearly hoping for a credit card and the details that came with it.

'Her friend paid for her in cash.'

'A friend? Is the friend still here?' Sandrine asked.

'No, he never stayed here. He left the girl here roughly three weeks ago and came to visit every few days. You know why.' He winked at Azarou and grinned from ear to ear. 'Charlotte spent all the money and afterwards went around asking for cash, until he came back and gave her more.' The man rubbed his cheek and flinched when he touched the laceration.

'Did she have any other visitors?'

'No, I didn't notice anyone. Only Daniel spent some time with her. They made some excursions along the coast.'

'Who's Daniel?' Sandrine asked.

'He works here, but God know where he is right now.' He shrugged his shoulders. 'No idea.'

'Where can we find him?'

'Outside the season I let him live here. In the house over there.' He looked at one of the bungalows. 'His Ducati is gone so he isn't here.'

Adel threw her a look when the man mentioned the motorbike.

'Was he here on the campsite last night?'

'No idea. I didn't notice anything. He's been out all night recently with the girl. She's a bad influence, I tell you.'

'Why do you think that?'

'The girl is pure poison. Pretty sure that she's just after his mother's money. Daniel is Madame Morvan's son.'

'Why does he work here if his family has money?' Azarou asked.

'Doesn't care much for hotels, I assume.' He crossed his arms in front of his chest. 'Not a nice woman, that old Morvan.'

'We will have to talk to him. Please tell Daniel to come to the police.' Sandrine made a subtle sign towards Azarou. He pulled out his card and handed it to the man. They had no reason to believe that Daniel had anything to do with the death of the young woman, but the chances of two people from the same family being involved could not be a coincidence. Sandrine had the feeling that there was more behind this.

'He won't like that,' grumbled the owner. 'What's this all about anyway? Did the boy do something?'

'It's just routine. He might have witnessed something that could help us with a case.' A friendship, a strange coincidence and a motorbike waking the neighbours. It was not enough to accuse anyone.

She took out one of the Polaroids from her pocket and showed it to César. 'Is that Charlotte Corday? The girl who lives here?'

The man stared at the picture, and the remaining colour drained from his face. Only when she cleared her throat, did he take his eyes from the picture. His Adam's apple bobbed when he swallowed.

'That's her. What happened?'

'We are trying to find out,' said Sandrine. 'May we have the key for the house?' It was more a demand than a question.

'I'm sure she won't like that.'

'I think it will be okay, she's dead and can't object. In case you didn't understand us, we are from the police and authorized to look at the bungalow.'

'I don't have the key. Someone stole it. Charlotte has the

other. She never leaves it at reception even though I asked her a few times.'

'We will look at the bungalow. Maybe she forgot to lock it,' Sandrine said. 'You wait here. We still have some questions.'

'There's lots of work to do on the campsite. The season's just about to start. I can't just sit here on my behind and let time pass. My wife won't like that.'

'I am sorry, but that will have to wait for a bit. We might have some more questions.'

'Alright,' muttered the man and slumped onto a bench positioned next to two planters.

Brigadier Azarou took out his phone and typed a message.

'If you're looking for her in the system, I wouldn't bother,' said Sandrine.

'Why? We know her name now, and Inès can find out more details while we look at her bungalow.'

'No use, it's the wrong one.' She climbed up the three stairs that led to the mobile home 335.

'Why do you think that?'

'She was brought here by a man who paid her bills in cash and looked after her every few days. And the name, Charlotte Corday. That sounds suspicious to me. Something is rotten here.' Sandrine leaned against the railing of the veranda. 'I am just wondering who invented her identity. I assume it was her mysterious chaperone.' And she had more than just an inkling who that person was. The case was getting more and more intriguing.

'You think he is the perpetrator?'

'Not necessarily. Charlotte trusted him enough to find lodging for her. They knew each other and it doesn't look like an act of passion. The man could have gotten rid of her at a less conspicuous place than a busy hiking trail. We still need to find out the real identity of the woman and the man who paid her bills, and the reason why she was here. With some luck we will find the motive as well.'

'That will be difficult. Apart from Monsieur Treville no one has seen him. He was careful enough to not leave anything behind. We don't have a license plate or credit card details. Maybe Jean Claude can find his fingerprints in the house and check them with the database. Hopefully he is in the system.'

'I bet that we know his identity by this time tomorrow.'

Azarou looked at her with a surprised expression. 'Why are you so convinced by that?'

'The man will come to us of his own accord.'

'Do you have a secret crystal ball somewhere, or are you just guessing?' His eyebrows rose even further. She grinned. Most likely he thought she was crazy. She would not deprive herself of this little pleasure. 'A little bit of both, but it will prove correct. Wanna bet?'

'Surprise me!' He rattled the door, but the wood did not budge. The curtains had been drawn and obscured the inside.

'What now? Forensics still has the key. Shall we drive to the commissariat?'

'All the way to Saint-Malo?'

'What other choice do we have?'

'Let me try.'

He moved aside and Sandrine stepped close to the door. From one of the pockets of her jacket she produced a little box.

'You carry a box for lockpicking around with you?'

'It's an old habit of mine. I tend to be clumsy and keep forgetting my housekeys.' She threw in the quick lie. It took seconds for the door to click and swing open.

'Where did you learn that?' His surprise had morphed into suspicion.

'Has your family not taught you anything?' She brushed the curtain aside and entered.

'Well, yes, but not how to pick locks and break into someone else's home.'

'Come inside. I want you to look at this.'

It was one of the typical little houses that could be found on most campsites. It was just a living room with a simple kitchenette, and a bathroom and doors to the bedrooms on the other side. Everything was functional, clearly intended for a small family staying here for a week. Why was the victim hiding in such a place under false identity? Who had been looking for her? It was obvious that someone had searched for her or maybe something she had in her possession.

The shelves had been wrenched open, and the contents spilled all over the floor. Glass shards were clustered before the dishwasher, and the smell of olive oil hung heavy in the air. Only a quick glance into the bedroom proved that similar chaos was reigning there. Someone had turned the mobile home upside down and had not tried to hide it.

'Madame Corday had some enemies.' Azarou wanted to enter the room, but Sandrine held him back.

'If there was anything in here, they found it and took it with them, or it's hidden so well that it would take us forever to find. Who knows what evidence we would destroy if we started searching.'

'The stains on the bench look like blood.' A few red lines were dragged over the grey, fake-leather cover. 'Was she killed here?'

'There's not enough blood for that. The crime scene was on the coastal path. We don't doubt that.'

'Maybe they dragged her away from here whilst she was still alive.'

'Yes, we can't exclude that. It doesn't feel likely for me, though. Why would they destroy the house if they had Charlotte? It would be much easier to threaten or beat her until she told them what they want to know.'

'Possible that she wasn't here and only came back after the guys had come to her house.'

'It's possible.'

'I will call forensics, okay?'

'Do that. We already ruined their Sunday anyway. Jean Claude Mazet can bring the key to the bungalow too.'

'How did the burglars get in? The lock looked new. One key was supposedly missing and the other one was with the victim.'

'I'm sure I'm not the only one who can open a door without a key. The owner of the campsite might have also lied to us when he claimed that the key is missing.'

'Judging from his face he is somehow involved in all of this.'

'We'll ask him before he runs off.' Sandrine left the bungalow and walked down the steps. Adel closed the door behind her and called forensics. She hoped that the men had not made plans for the evening.

'Monsieur Treville,' she called to the man, who was still sitting on the bench close to reception. He had watched them like a hawk on their way to and from the mobile home. She assumed that he knew exactly what they had found in there.

'Did you find something?' he asked, trying to sound genuinely interested. She did not answer. The man pulled a handkerchief from his pocket and wiped beads of sweat from his forehead. 'It's quite warm today.'

'Not hot enough to sweat though,' she replied and shrugged out of her outdoor jacket to drape it over the bench. 'A very nice place you have here. Some houses even have a sea view. That's quite rare.' She pretended to admire the campsite and turned her left side to the man. His eyebrows began to rise, and his gaze twitched to her shoulder holster.

'What happened to Charlotte?'

'Are you that invested in all of your guests?' she asked quickly.

'No,' he stuttered, 'only in the regulars.'

'Madame Corday was a regular visitor?'

César Treville did not answer.

'She's dead,' Sandrine said without any emotion. 'Someone shot her and left her dead body.'

'Murdered?' He wiped his forehead again and his eyes seemed to bulge from his face. 'But I saw her just yesterday.'

'When was that?'

'Just after noon. Before …' The man stopped as if in shock. He had said more than he wanted to.

'Go on,' she encouraged him.

'Before I drove to Leclerc for shopping,' he lied. That's obvious.

'Do you have a receipt to show us?' Sandrine turned the vice on the man.

'I don't keep every receipt. Don't have it anymore. Do you keep all receipts?'

'I don't have a business and the tax office isn't on my back. Enough with all of this now. What happened here yesterday?'

'Why do you think something …?'

'Do you want to tell us that you ran into a door? We are talking about a murder, and if you refuse to cooperate and tell us the truth, we have to put you on the list of suspects.'

'Murder.' The blood seemed to drain from his cheeks. 'I've got nothing to do with that,' he stammered.

'What else?'

'But I told the truth.' His eyes darted between Sandrine and Azarou.

'I am sorry. Please, forgive my suspicion,' she said in a much more forgiving tone of voice and sat down next to him on the bench. 'It's been a long day and corpses don't help. I tend to get a bit sharp.'

'It's okay,' murmured the man under his breath. His shoulders drooped back down in relief. Sandrine ignored the confused, but imploring, look of her assistant.

'Just a little thing and then we shall leave.'

'What?'

'The mobile number of Madame Treville.'

He jumped up as if she had given him an electric shock.

'Why do you need that? She hasn't seen anything. Marie spent yesterday in Dinan with her mother.'

'How many vehicles do you own?'

His eyes twitched to the park's exit. Azarou stepped between him and the barrier. César Treville fell back on the bench like a ragdoll. He covered his face with both hands.

'It looks like you only have one car, which was used by your wife. How else would she have gotten to Dinan?' Adel stated the obvious.

Sandrine fixed the man with piercing eyes. 'We are looking for a murderer. So spit it out. Who did you fight with?'

The man sighed in his hands before he lifted his head.

'They came in the afternoon, around 4:00pm.' His eyes were fixed on the gravel-covered ground in front of him. 'Two guys, black and with muscles like bodybuilders. They were looking for her, but they only had a picture and didn't know her name.' He turned his head and the corners of his eyes fell in sadness. 'I don't talk about my guests with strangers. But ...' His hand touched the wound in his face. 'What should I have done? I also knew that she was away with Daniel.'

'And then?'

'The guys grabbed the key and dragged me with them. They punched me again in the house, and then they started to wreak havoc on the place. She must have hidden something that they wanted.'

'Did they mention what they were searching for?'

César Treville fell quiet for a moment. He reached into his pocket and produced a packet of cigarettes. 'One of them talked about a book.' He lit a cigarette and took a deep breath. 'As if Charlotte had been reading.' He gulped a bitter laugh.

'Did they find it?'

'Judging from how much they were cursing I don't think they did. One of them was so angry that I thought he would pulverize my ribs. I was down on the ground, gasping for air like some fish, when they left. The key they simply took.'

'Why didn't you tell us that from the start? As far as I can see you haven't done anything wrong.' Adel seemed to be trying his best to calm the man down. Sandrine could not help but admire him. After a few years in one homicide division after the other cynicism ruined most people's empathy. And still, her instincts told her that there was a lot more that Treville was not telling them.

'They warned me and told me to keep quiet. They know where to find me.'

'Don't worry about that. They must have been professionals and they knew that you wouldn't be able to keep quiet if it came to real questioning. It's very likely that they left the area.'

'Can you describe them to us?' Adel asked.

'Most likely,' he answered, but seemed unsure.

'Then please accompany us into the station and we will write a report. You will look at a few pictures and maybe you'll recognize them.'

'If you insist.' The man had given up his defence. Whether he would actually be able to give a helpful description remained to be seen. He had taken several hits and had been under a lot of stress. Sandrine did not feel very optimistic.

They packed César Treville in the back of the car and drove to the commissariat in Saint-Malo.

Chapter 3

Saint-Malo

Sandrine Perrot entered the open plan office in which she would be working for the next three months. The office of the Police Nationale was housed in a modern, four-story building on the Boulevard Theodore Botrel, barely five minutes away from the most beautiful beach of the city, the Grande Plage du Sillon.

'Lieutenant Perrot.'

She turned around, surprised to find anyone in the office on a Sunday afternoon. Inès Boni hurried towards her.

'Still working?' Sandrine greeted her new colleague.

'Of course. Normally we have to worry about burglars, drugs, bar-fights, or drunken teenagers driving a stolen car down the port and into the water. How could I just abandon the office and go home during my first interesting case? That's not an option. Most of all, you need a functional workstation and an efficient backup.'

'I just need a quiet corner. I don't plan on staying long.'

'We will see. Please, follow me.' She made her way towards a desk in front of a window, providing a view into the courtyard. On a first glance everything she needed seemed to be there;

laptop, telephone and some drawers with keys. A box held some basics like pens, notebooks and office bric-a-brac.

'Thank you very much. It can't have been easy to find all of this on a Sunday.'

'That's my job. The business cards will take another couple of days, and the company car another two weeks, but you can just take a car from the car-pool.'

'I'll manage. Until then Brigadier Azarou will have to play chauffeur for me.'

'One of our best colleagues.'

'Seems like it. I assume there is no news from forensics?'

'There is news, but we aren't sure how to work with it.' Deep wrinkles stretched over the office manager's forehead. That could not mean good news.

'What happened?'

'They stole the corpse.'

'What? She's gone?' She stared at Inès Boni. This had not happened before.

'Gone is not the right word. We know where she is but have no access.'

'Paris,' Sandrine said and sat down on her chair which creaked in response.

'Correct. They took over and are doing the autopsy.'

'What reasons did they give?'

'Since when do Paris' people give reasons? They waved a judicial decision at Doctor Hervé and gone they were with the unidentified corpse.'

'Fits the picture.' The assumptions she had made so far became all the more likely. That did not mean anything good. Again, she would be sliding into dangerous depths, depths which she had tried to avoid with her move to Brittany.

'You want to enlighten me?'

'As soon as I have a clear picture. Could I ask you something? I should warn you; it might be a bit of work.'

'I already cancelled my plans for this evening.'

Sandrine wrote instructions and names on a piece of paper and handed it to Inès.

The woman whistled. 'It's getting more and more interesting. For that I will even work overnight.'

'You think you can find something?'

'If you know the right people you can get many things done.'

'Thank you very much.'

'Where is Adel?' asked Inès.

'He's talking with Monsieur Treville, the owner of the campsite the victim was living on.'

'Is he a suspect?'

'At the moment only a witness.' Sandrine rubbed her chin between her fingers. It was a habit that she caught herself doing whenever she was not able to understand a problem 100%. Some men had attacked César Treville at reception. They had taken the key from him and dragged him along so that he would not be able to call the police. She was sure that he had not tried to fight, so why had they hit him again in the bungalow? To relieve their anger because they had not found what they had been looking for? The worse he looked the more likely it would be that he would go to the police after they had left. It did not make much sense. There were still some questions the man would have to answer, but first she had to gain more information. Once the time for questioning came, she would not be so friendly anymore.

'What's your plan?' The office manager had sat down on a swivelling chair and looked at Sandrine with curious eyes.

'I'll take a walk and think about our case. There are many things that do not fit together, and we have gaps that are big enough for a train to drive through.'

'The weather is beautiful and it's only a few metres to the beach. The Brasserie du Sillon is very nice in case you want to grab a bite to eat. The job is so busy, I doubt that you have been able to eat much today.'

'I will remember that.' It was true that a tasty meal sometimes helped her think. 'Do you know the Équinoxe?'

'Of course. It's in an industrial zone outside of the city.'

'The victim had one of their matchboxes in her pocket. Have there been any illegal activities in the club?'

'Less so than in other clubs. A few small drug dealers, drunk drivers, some guys so full of themselves that they pick fights with bouncers. But nothing out of the ordinary. You want to visit?' Inès looked her up and down. 'Not in this outfit, surely?'

'I wanted to go on a calm hiking trip along the coast this morning. For that these clothes are perfect. But I will change before I go, so the bouncers don't notice me.' She grinned at her colleague and patted the pocket under which her gun was hidden. 'I also have an entry ticket.'

Inès rolled her eyes. 'What do you want to do? Shoot your way through?'

'I thought more about my police ID.' Sandrine smiled. Flashing the weapon had worked with César Treville.

'Shall I come along?'

'Thanks for the offer, but I am old enough to go without a chaperone.'

'I didn't want to come as your chaperone. I know the owner so that would make a lot of things easier.'

'I need you here. That's more important.' She tapped the folded paper in Inès' hands. 'Commissaire Matisse already gave me Brigadier Azarou. That should be enough help for now. Would you be so kind as to reserve a meeting room for tomorrow morning? We have to coordinate everything internally.'

'Adel is a good policeman.' She leaned forward to rest her arms on the desk. 'Some say he is too ambitious as the youngest general of the brigadiers, and some colleagues make sure that he doesn't forget his lack of experience with capital crimes. I am sure that he sees working with you as a great chance to learn things.'

'I can imagine that,' Sandrine said thoughtfully. She had once been the ambitious youngster herself. De Chezac's little allusions had also aimed at that fact. She had reached her rank as a Capitaine de Police in record time. What she was missing was an antenna for the political intrigue in the force. Because of that she was only a former glowing star. Nothing that I mourn.

'Try your best,' she said and stood up.

'I always do.'

'And I want to talk to Daniel Morvan. Maybe the Gendarmerie can help us to find him.'

'Consider it done.'

She had only known Inès Boni for a few hours, but she was sure that all she had asked for would be ready tomorrow on her desk.

It was not even 300 metres to the Grande Plage du Sillon. Sandrine turned to the left in the direction of the old town with its defensive walls. To her right lay the Fort Nationale, clustered on a rock in the bay. The water was low enough to walk there without getting one's feet wet, but she decided to save that for another time.

A staircase led from the Chaussee du Sillon down to the beach. The stone wall reminded her of the one against which she had seen the corpse that very morning. The only difference was that this one was built to protect the city from floods and was thicker. She slipped out of her shoes, stuffed her socks in them, tied the laces together and folded up her trouser legs. With the hiking shoes swinging in her hand like a bag, Sandrine strolled over the warm sand which felt like it had absorbed the spring sun. In early May, the water of the Atlantic was too cold for swimming, and so she simply enjoyed the fresh waves lapping at her feet. The wind blew through her hair, whipping it from left to right, and emptying her thoughts of the dead body for a while. The first few days of an examination were the most crucial ones. The police school had made sure they understood that, and it had proven to be a reality. Sandrine had also seen enough police officers who got stuck in small details and pulled into the stress of the investigation. Whenever she felt like this would happen to her, she stepped back and looked at everything from an objective distance. If she had to write a report today, there would not have been much to record. She was not able to identify the woman or to present a suspect. All she had to show for this first day of work were some vague clues that led to the campsite, the Morvan family and Paris. There was no motive yet. She would have to find out more about the dead woman or they would keep searching in the dark and stumbling over their own feet.

Her feet began to tingle from the cold, and she decided to turn back. Adel Azarou was standing on the wall and looking towards her, as if he was waiting for her. She doubted that he had been missing her already, so something must have happened that she needed to know.

'Are you looking for me?'

'Inès said you wanted to go for a walk. Where else if not the beach? Someone has to bring you home.'

'I can take a taxi.'

'That's not an option.'

'Thank you.'

Sandrine climbed up the stone steps and rubbed her feet against her trouser legs to at least remove some of the sand. Adel's car was parked only a few metres away. She put the shoes in the boot, which already contained her backpack, and made herself comfortable in the passenger's seat.

'Did Treville say anything of interest?'

'No, he's still sticking with his story. Now he's at the station and is looking through the pictures of the archive.'

'Maybe we'll be lucky and he'll recognize someone. That would help us quite a bit.'

'I doubt it. He's constantly muttering that black people all look the same. An experienced defence attorney would rip his statement into shreds in seconds.' Judging from his voice he did not value the owner of the campsite too highly. Sandrine could understand that. The man was lying. Maybe not everything was a lie, but he was clearly keeping an important detail to himself.

'I can't think that far into the future at the moment. Until we make it to a court, we still have lots to do. At the moment I am thankful for every piece of information we can squeeze out of him.'

'I fear we won't be able to squeeze much out.' The brigadier started the car and zipped into the traffic.

Adel Azarou stopped in front of the main house.

'This is yours? You live in an exquisite place. Bertrand didn't exaggerate.'

She pointed at the former stable. 'My flat is down there.'

He stretched his neck to see where she was pointing.

'Smaller, but still first class. What an amazing view from up here! To gaze upon the sea while having breakfast is a dream.'

'True. My Aunt Celine owned it. As a child I spent a lot of time here during the summer holidays, but I never thought that I would move to Brittany one day.'

'What changed your opinion?'

'Long story.' She evaded his question.

'Has it something to do with the prosecutor who showed up at the crime scene today?'

'It was more because of my own stubbornness. But most of all it was an unhealthy mixture of arrogance and stupidity.'

He looked at her, waiting for an explanation that she was not ready to give.

'Another time.'

'I'll collect you tomorrow morning. An unmarked car is not available at the moment.'

'I'll take my own car or drive with you. I prefer that.'

'Whatever you like.'

She took her things from the boot and the brigadier drove off. With her shoes in hand, she carefully made her way over the gravel path to the main house. The sound of the car faded away behind her.

She had barely made it to the entrance when Rosalie opened the door and beamed at her.

'Come in.' She grabbed Sandrine's arm and pulled her inside. 'I heard about the dead woman when I was in town. You have lots to tell me.'

'Actually, I just have one question. Won't take long.'

'Sure.' She gave Sandrine a small broom. 'Scrub the sand from your feet and come in properly.'

Sandrine did as she was told and put the socks on just to be sure. The shoes she left in front of the door. Rosalie was very adamant about keeping everything spotless.

'Get comfortable,' she called from the kitchen. Sandrine walked through the hallway and into the library. She knew her way around the place. Most of the furniture had been Celine's or Celine's parents', that was how long the house had been in the family, even though they lived most of the year in Paris. It felt to her like this was her true home, not the shining villa in Paris in which she had grown up. She nearly expected to see Celine preparing dinner in the kitchen, or Uncle Thomas who was always carrying tools in his pockets to hunt for something that was in need of repairing. He had hated nothing more than sitting idle. She had many beautiful memories of her holidays in the countryside. However, living in Paris had also taught her many things about life.

Uncle Thomas had gained the reputation of being able to open or switch off any safe or security system. When she was twelve, he took Sandrine along with him to a burglary. Aunt Celine had been furious. She found it difficult to bear the idea of her niece standing guard at night, but Uncle Thomas insisted on teaching her his trade; after all, she was to receive a sound education and his profession was always in demand. That was at least what he thought. At thirteen she was allowed to try her skills on the lock of an old villa in one of the suburbs. Uncle Thomas had boasted with pride how fast she had been with the lock and with what ease she had disabled the security system. To his honest surprise, Celine did not share his passion. She packed her things and moved back to Brittany. It broke his heart. It did not stop him though, and he kept taking Sandrine on his nightly excursions. Uncle Thomas was only interested in pieces of art, especially paintings and small sculptures. Sandrine remembered this time as one big adventure, climbing up walls, making her way inside the houses of strangers and leaving undetected. At that age she had not really understood what was actually going on. Nor the fact that most of the items they took found their way to new owners through her parents' art galleries. Sandrine's family had lived outside of the law. Only Aunt Celine had been very careful to not let a single piece of loot come into her house.

It was tragic that it had been her who died during a burglary. She found burglars in her house, one of them shoved her out of the way and she had fallen backwards down the stairs. One of the steps broke her neck. On that day, Sandrine decided to switch sides. She concentrated on her school, studies and the police. All the knowledge she had gained under her uncle's tutelage, she now used to find criminals. Despite all her work, she had never been able to catch the burglars who had been responsible for her aunt's death.

In the last few years, she'd had to learn that there were areas in which it was impossible to tell one side apart from the other. Even though the state printed Egalité on every coin, not all people were equal in the eyes of the law. Some of them were untouchable, as she had to learn the hard way. And now she had returned to her old home in Brittany to lead her life outside of the police force.

The door hinge squeaked, and the dark brown wood floor creaked under her feet. She sunk into one of the big Chesterfield-chairs, with their high backrests from buffalo leather and let her gaze drift through the garden, through the trees and out to the sea. Books filled the shelves and some of them lay opened on the cherrywood-table. Rosalie's writing desk was the centre of the room. The screen was lit up and she could hear the quiet humming of the machine's fan. She must have been writing when I arrived. A shelf at face height was reserved for Rosalie's own books. Novels about the cases of Commissaire Hugo Delacroix, the protagonist of her novels, and a few Brittany travel-guides. Sandrine knew that Rosalie had tried her hand at writing a cookbook recently, but she had no idea if she had finished by now or given up.

'Voilà. Potage de légumes,' her friend said and placed a tray with a bowl, cutlery and a few slices of baguette over the armrests of the chair. Rosalie had crumbled some herbs and croutons over the soup. Sandrine appreciated it that she always took out some of the cubed vegetables before she pureed the rest.

'With something warm in your stomach, the world looks better right away.'

'Thank you, but ...' she started.

'Not a word! You eat now.' She did not let Sandrine finish. 'And afterwards you tell me in detail what happened today. The neighbours say you were somehow caught up in the murder of a woman on the coastal path.'

'Somehow, yes. But not in the way that the gossips from the neighbourhood think.' She slowly ate her soup. It was hot and hearty, exactly what she needed after this long day. While she was eating, she started to recount what happened. Rosalie was an excellent listener who did not interrupt her or spoke her own opinion until she had heard all the relevant facts. One of the most important requirements of a top author.

The shadows began to lengthen. Soon the sun would disappear behind the house. Sandrine maneuvered a last piece of carrot with her baguette onto her spoon. With a sigh she leaned back into the wide armchair and stretched her legs. Darkness began to filter into the room, but she did not switch on the light. Both women enjoyed the cosy semi-darkness.

'Another three months and then you want to end everything?' Rosalie asked, deep in her own thoughts.

'I have to make it until then.'

'You've been here since February and had enough time to send the letter.'

Sandrine stayed silent. She knew exactly what her friend was hinting at.

'I will end it. A life without death and crime will be good for me. Maybe photography can be my new job. I always dreamed about travelling more, and now I have the time for it.'

'We will see.' Rosalie stood up and took the tray. 'And this de Chezac just showed up at the crime scene without any explanation?' She brought the tray into the kitchen and loaded the dishwasher.

'Definitely without a sensible explanation,' Sandrine called after her.

Rosalie returned and handed an espresso to her. For herself she had made tea. By now she had learned what her visitor enjoyed.

'You don't have a suspect?' she asked. Her curiosity was totally professional. She made her living writing crime novels, and with that the two of them were basically colleagues and soulmates. They were both women whose life it was to solve crime.

'No, so far we don't have much.' Sandrine carefully placed a sugar cube onto the brown foam watched the liquid sink into the sugar and dissolve it. 'Florence Morvan found the corpse.'

'Poor woman. She's really suffered enough already.'

'You know her well?'

'Well, the way people know each other here. She took over the La Baie from her father. The old August was a very strict man. She didn't have much fun.'

'Is he still alive?'

'No, he died a few years ago. He was already quite old when she was born.'

'But she seems to love the hotel.'

'I am not sure if its love or duty which she has been trained for all her life. The old Morvan had a strong hand.' She took a sip of tea. 'She rebelled only a single time, when she married a man her father hated. No one was good enough for his daughter, or adequate to run the hotel after him.'

'I didn't meet a husband. He doesn't work at the La Baie?'

'Sebastian died last year. Poor man. Must have been some time in spring.'

'How did he die?' Every unusual event was worth her curiosity.

'Heart failure they said. But no one really believes that. He was suffering from the rejection of his father-in-law. We watched him transform from a happy-go-lucky man into a deeply sad man developing depression. There is talk that he had a drug problem. Painkillers, they say.'

'Then they falsified the death certificate?'

'Or all stuck to the story and didn't want to talk about the real reason. Doctor Marais is an old friend of the Morvans. I don't think that the friendship would be deep enough to falsify a document, but they knew each other enough to not make the whole thing public. Maybe he even helped to spread a few false rumours.'

'I met her daughter today. It looked like she had total command of the kitchen. Her croissants were out of this world.'

'And her mother has total control of her,' said Rosalie. 'I remember that she already worked in the restaurant as a child. She came home from school and there was the hotel waiting for her.'

'She wants a Michelin star.'

'If someone has earned it then its Sarah. I'm sure that she'll get one sooner or later. She has ambition and skill.'

'Her mother seems to be less optimistic.'

'There is a rumour that the La Baie has had some financial troubles in the last few years. On top of the early death of her husband. We can only guess at what Florence wanted from her life. She must be a bitter woman, and clearly lets her daughter feel her frustration.'

'Daniel has left the business?'

'After his father's death he pulled out. Allegedly, he lives on a campsite at the Pointe du Grouin and helps as some kind of jack of all trades. That's all I know though.' Rosalie looked at her over the brim of her teacup. 'You think Florence is suspicious?'

'She doesn't seem the type of person who grabs a gun, sneaks around the Brittany Coast path at night and shoots people.'

'You never know. The more innocent they look the deeper are the clefts in their souls.'

'Maybe that is true for your books, but I have to deal with real-life criminals and that is different. That's something else.'

'True. My readers want less reality and more exciting fantasy.'

Sandrine downed her espresso and put the cup back on the fragile saucer with a chink.

'At least we know the victim's identity by now.'

'Which you don't want to tell me because it's a running investigation?'

'I would make an exemption in this case.'

Rosalie sat up straighter.

Sandrine had her full attention and was just waiting for the right moment to pull the rabbit out of the hat. 'Our victim goes by the name of Charlotte Corday.'

'Heard that before.'

'Not only that, she is also from Caen.'

The woman's eyebrows moved a millimetre closer together. 'You are pulling my leg, aren't you?'

'Not in the slightest.'

'Then you won't be able to catch the murderer. They will already be out of this world.'

'I agree with you.' Sandrine chuckled and Rosalie joined in with her own melodious laugh.

The motion sensor clicked, and the outdoor lighting switched on. Sandrine pressed her eyes closed for a moment. Maybe she should install something a bit more discreet than this 200-watt halogen spotlight. Her aunt had built it in many years ago.

It was only a few steps to her garage. She pulled on the lever, and the door opened with a creak. In front of her stood another heirloom, a burgundy and black Citroën 2 CV. The car, which was often called *ugly duckling*, was from the model series 'Charleston' straight from the 80s. Aunt Celine and Sandrine celebrated their birthdays in the same week, and when Celine had received the car, Sandrine had been gifted her first bicycle. Back then a lot of her friend's parents had driven one of the little Citroëns, but nowadays only sentimental romantics seemed to own an old-timer like this one. So far, she had not used the car. *Let's see if it even turns on.* Uncle Thomas had loved it and given long talks about the history of the vehicle while screwing around on the engine. She remembered it as if it had been just a few days ago. Supposedly, it was designed to offer enough space for two farmers in boots, a 50kg sack of potatoes, and a barrel of wine. Moreover, the Citroën 2 CV was supposed to be very economical, have an amazing suspension so that a basket full of eggs could be transported over a bumpy road without a problem, and be so easy to steer that even the most novice of drivers would be able to swerve around potholes. Sandrine smiled. Strangely enough, when her uncle had told her the story he had always spoken about female drivers. Male novice drivers did not seem to exist. She let her fingers slide over the fender. Dust floated to the ground, and she blew a thin layer of grey from her fingertips. For all that the car was not supposed to be overly pleasing to the eye, she still thought the bendy lines looked very aesthetic.

But not today. She walked past the car and pulled up the zipper of her leather jacket. She had never owned a car in Paris. The Boulevard Périphérique, the highway leading around the 20 Arrondissements of the city, was notoriously clogged. It was much easier to get around on a motorbike. Even once one had reached one's destination, finding a parking space was a miracle. She pushed the BMW F750GS out of the garage and closed the door behind her. A press on the starter and the motorbike whirred to life. It should not take her more than 15 minutes to make it to the Équinoxe. It was a few minutes until 10:00pm. She did not think that there would be a lot of traffic, and the club should also be quiet. It was still too early for the party people.

Should make it easier to find someone who has time to talk. She put on her helmet and drove slowly up the driveway. Most likely her neighbours were already in bed, and she remembered all too well the displeased comments about the bike driver who had woken up the whole neighbourhood.

Sandrine pulled into the car park of the Équinoxe. The club was not more than a simple hangar in an industrial zone and looked absolutely deserted at this time of night. The bouncer looked in her direction. She pulled the clutch and revved the engine briefly. Bouncers usually liked motorbikes and the showiness connected to them. Childish, but it would make it easier for her to get into the club if she could make friends with the guard dog at the door. Maybe she would even get around pulling out her police ID.

She stuffed her gloves into her helmet. The helmet would come with her. If Inès had been right, it could not hurt to have something hard with her in case she needed to defend herself. She had not taken her gun. If the bouncer saw it, it would only cause unneeded attention.

The man at the door nodded at her and let her in without any questions. As soon as she entered the club, she was hit by a 180-decibel wall of quick beats. She stopped and looked around. The dancefloor was empty. There were only around two dozen people milling about. On the room's long side, a bar was stretched out. Sandrine made her way towards it. If there was any information here, she would find it there. She lay the helmet on the bar, pulled over a barstool and sat down. It did not take long for the barman to come over. He was tall, dark-haired and with trained muscles showing clearly under his white t-shirt. He leaned his underarms on the bar nonchalantly and smiled at her.

'A grown woman in my place? I'm delighted to see that.'

She took out her badge and showed it to him.

'And a dangerous woman on top. Drinks are on the house, of course.' His smile seemed to deepen.

'Your place?'

'Bien sûr. This is my club.' He nodded. 'Léon,' he introduced himself and shook her hand. His grip was strong, but not in the way that many men chose to impress their counterpart. She felt like his face was somehow familiar, but she could not pinpoint where she might have seen him before. Most likely she would remember it once she got home. That was what usually happened.

'If you showed me your ID, I fear it is not a private visit.'

She pulled out one of the Polaroids from her jacket pocket and put it in front of the man on the bar.

'A box of matches from the Équinoxe was in this woman's pocket.'

'We make sure that many people carry them. It's an excellent advertisement.'

'Do you know the woman?'

The man picked up the picture and looked it over for a moment.

'She looks dead.'

Sandrine nodded without a comment.

'To say I know her would be an exaggeration. She turned up two weeks ago and has become a regular. No idea what her name is or where she lives.' He gave the picture back to her. 'What happened to her?' He was either an excellent actor or he really had not heard what had happened.

'If she was a regular, I am sure you can tell me a bit more about her.'

'She was one of the kind of people I don't like to see in the club. Wherever she went, trouble followed shortly after.'

'What type of person was she?'

'The type that abhors boredom. We had our eyes on her.'

'Why?'

'There was talk that she was dealing. I have no proof, but she would definitely have been capable.'

'Something like this?' Sandrine took out her phone and showed him the picture of the pills with the skull-shape.

'You don't really assume that I would admit to knowing these things? I don't want your colleagues to turn my club upside down or make me lose my license.'

'I am not interested in drugs.'

'What are you interested in then?' He leaned forward and tried to establish eye-contact.

Sandrine leaned forward too, until their faces nearly touched.

'Murder.'

'What?' Léon twitched back abruptly and straightened. 'I have nothing to do with that.' He lifted his hands in defence. She had provoked the reaction, and her gut feeling told her that the man was telling the truth. He had passed the test. His surprise looked authentic, and he really had not heard of the whole incident.

'I didn't say you did.'

He poured himself some schnaps and downed it in one. 'I didn't like the girl much, but to be murdered ... I don't wish that end for anyone. I don't even know her name.'

'Can we now agree that a few pills are not important to me?'

'Yup.'

'Out with it, did she deal?'

'One of the staff thought she had seen a bag with pills on her. She didn't want to vouch for it though. They looked like the ones you showed me on the picture.' He rubbed his neck. 'The woman was always broke, which doesn't really speak for good business. Every few days she showed up with money, threw it around and then asked anyone she met to help her out.'

'Who was she indebted to?'

'Many people. The girl wasn't shy. It wasn't amounts that would justify killing someone, though. I would assume she owed Daniel the most. The two normally turned up together, and he paid the bill in the end. As far as I could tell the girl used him from the start. He was a means to an end and nothing more.'

'Did you warn him?'

'I run a club and not a couple's therapy.' He looked towards the entrance. 'You can ask him yourself.'

A young, skinny man, not older than his early twenties stood in the doorway and stared over at them. Sandrine got up, but in that moment, he whirled his body around and bolted out of the door.

'Damn it.' She grabbed her helmet and sprinted after him. One of the guests staggered into her way and collided with her. She roughly pushed him aside and ran outside.

A motorbike roared, and seconds later he raced from the parking lot. The driver accelerated, shifted up several gears and disappeared into the darkness. Sandrine cursed. It was no use chasing after him. He was too far away already and knew the area way better than her.

'He's gone?'

The barman had followed her and looked in the direction Daniel Morvan had disappeared. The sound of the motor was fading in the distance. Judging from the reaction, César Treville must have warned him. She would not be able to meet the man at the campsite. He was not that stupid. She would have to write out a search for him, which she would have liked to avoid.

'Tomorrow is another day,' she mumbled.

'Then it's the right moment for a drink,' Léon suggested.

'Another time. After I solve the case.'

'Fingers crossed. I hope you catch the murderer soon. You know where you can find me and a strong drink. It would be my pleasure.'

'Once I have him, we will clink glasses over it,' Sandrine replied. The man was not unsympathetic, and she had not gone out in a long time.

'I think, though, that you are barking up the wrong tree with Daniel.'

'Why?'

'He's harmless. The guy was besotted with the girl and couldn't tell left from right. There is no chance that he did something to her.'

'Most murders are relationship acts.'

'Not Daniel.'

'We will see.' She left the man, went to her motorbike, and drove off. In the mirror she saw that Léon was looking after her.

Chapter 4
Charlotte Corday

The barrier rose and Sandrine drove into the parking lot of the police department in Saint-Malo. To her surprise, and happiness, the motor of the Citroën had started on the first attempt. Rosalie had used the car now and again and kept it in good condition. She had enjoyed the slow drive along the small streets past the farms, the fields, and the long stretches of wood so typical for this area. Now, however, she could already feel the case dragging her back into stress. The team meeting would begin in 30 minutes, and she did not have any clues or concrete answers which could lead them closer to the perpetrator.

Letters, sticky notes and files were towering on her desk, and she scanned over them quickly. On top of the pile was a note from Commissaire Matisse informing her that Paris had offered support and had brought the corpse into Paris' forensic department for that reason. The staff there worked on the weekends so that waiting time would be greatly reduced. It was an advantage, but it still made her gall rise to think that she had to work together with de Chezac. Her suspicions became more and more certain, and should they prove right, he was in this case up to his neck. Under no circumstances could she let the direction of the investigation be taken out of her hands, otherwise he would bring too much politics into play.

'Good morning,' Inès greeted her.

'Here again or still here?'

'Was a short night. How could I have slept with such a case on the table?'

'Did you find anything about my suspicions? Maybe I am completely wrong, but my instinct tells me it will be worth the work.'

'It already was worth the work.' She handed a small folder with a few sheets to Sandrine.

'Lieutenant Perrot,' Azarou waved at her. 'We can start.' Her assistant had switched his elegant suit for a pair of Calvin Klein jeans and a dark jumper which looked like cashmere. He really paid attention to his appearance.

Sandrine checked her watch. 'Is everyone so punctual here?'

'Normally not,' Inès answered. 'But in this case, you will see how motivated the team is.'

'I don't have the time to read through this. You know the contents so please come inside.'

'Really?' The young woman rocked onto the tips of her toes in excitement. 'I am not usually invited to these meetings.'

'With me you are. How did you even gather all this information on a Sunday?'

'I know people from the training for office managers. One hand washes the other. After all, we have to stick together.'

'Let's go then.'

'Read this.' Sandrine pressed all the documents she had received from Inès into Azarou's arms. The man looked a bit shocked. 'That may take us a good step further.'

She entered the simple meeting room. Around a long table waited Jean Claude Mazet, the boss of forensics, two policemen in normal clothes, and a Capitaine of the Gendarmerie. The door opened again. Commissaire Matisse had decided to join the meeting. He was followed by Antoine de Chezac and a man whom Sandrine had never seen before. His face was round and soft as if he still had his baby-fat and he wore a dark suit. Most likely his personal valet, was Sandrine's first thought. Azarou threw a questioning look her way. He was surprised that a prosecutor from Paris would get involved in this case and be present in this meeting. Sandrine was not. She had anticipated that he would show up.

De Chezac sat down on a chair away from the table, playing a mere visitor. Meanwhile, Matisse greeted his colleagues with handshakes and finally sat down next to de Chezac.

'Most of you already met Lieutenant Perrot at the crime scene yesterday. She will lead the investigation of this case.' The Commissaire introduced her to all the assembled. 'Capitaine Jenaud has been so kind as to coordinate the activities of the local Gendarmerie and keep in contact with the homicide division.' The uniformed man nodded his agreement. Normally his office would have been responsible for a case in a city as small as Cancale, but he did not seem interested in taking it for himself. Or he was simply lacking knowledgeable staff.

'The brigadiers Dubois and Poutin will work together with Lieutenant Perrot.' Dubois nodded at her, while the older Poutin did not let an emotion cross his face. 'They have been freed from all their other duties. I think we have a good line-up with that.' He turned towards his guest. 'Doctor Hervé will not join our meeting today. Prosecutor de Chezac, who happened to be in Saint-Malo, was kind enough to grant us the help of the Paris' office. As we are running out of time, I took his offer, and the corpse has been brought to Paris.' He smiled at de Chezac. Sandrine wondered if the next talk between the two men would run in a much less harmonic way. 'Monsieur Lagarde represents the public prosecutors of Saint-Malo.' That must be the guy with the suitcase.

Sandrine stood up and went to the whiteboard which took up most of the wall.

'We are still at the beginning of the investigation. Every one of us has brought some puzzle pieces, and we have to assemble them into a nice picture today.' She had never been one for long speeches, so she just went straight to the case. Sandrine took one of the round magnets and stuck the picture of the woman to the board.

'The victim lived on the campsite Côte d'Émeraude close to the Pointe du Grouin. Monsieur Mazet was able to procure the key to her mobile home.'

'A tourist?' She was interrupted by the man whom Matisse had introduced as Dubois.

'I don't think so. She was involved in the club scene, supposedly dealt a small amount of Ecstasy and apart from that, barely left the campsite. She met Daniel Morvan on the campsite and the two were seen together many times.'

'Then we should talk to him,' the Commissaire suggested.

'I tried that last evening, but he fled on a motorbike as soon as he saw me.'

'And you didn't jump in your race car to follow him?' Renard grinned like an alligator. Her arrival in the little Citroën had clearly been noted and commented on by her colleagues.

'I'll save car chases for suspects. We are not there yet,' she retorted.

Dubois grinned. 'I would love to see that.'

'Where did the woman go who, no matter rain or shine, came on the motorbike to the crime scene? You got yourself a car?' De Chezac cocked his head to the side and examined her for a moment. 'Are you getting soft here in the countryside?'

'I enjoy the luxury of a reserved parking spot in front of the office,' she replied to his sarcastic comment, then returned to the case at hand. 'Daniel Morvan had a close relationship to the victim and fled a questioning. We also know that residents heard a motorbike near the crime scene. All of this makes him a potential witness, but not a suspect.'

'Shall I create a search for him?' Capitaine Jenaud asked.

'Yes, but be gentle with him. We don't know yet if he's really connected to the woman's death.'

'Did we identify the victim?' pressed the Commissaire.

'Not officially, but I am quite sure whom we are dealing with,' Sandrine confirmed.

'Charlotte Corday. That's the name she signed in with at the campsite,' said Renard. 'Shall I ask the office in Caen for help?'

'No, better not. We don't want to look like fools,' she said. For the first time since he had entered the room de Chezac lifted his head in interest and looked in her direction. *Maybe he has an idea what we found out.* 'The name isn't real, that's for sure,' she continued. 'What is important for the investigation is the name of the man who accompanied her and paid her bills. He wanted to make sure that she wasn't found, but obviously that didn't work.'

'Could that be the perpetrator?' Dubois asked.

'We don't assume that at the moment,' she replied.

'If it's a fake name, do we have any idea who the dead woman really was?' Commissaire Matisse seemed to lose his patience.

'The woman is from Paris, and her real name is Isabelle Deschamps.' She let the bomb explode. The prosecutor's eyes might have burned into her skull. 'I am sure that Monsieur de Chezac will be able to tell us why he was hiding her on the campsite.'

All eyes turned towards him. He dropped the file he had been leafing through on his knees. 'Why on earth do you assume that I have something to do with this Isabelle Deschamps?'

'Who would choose the name Charlotte Corday except someone who is well acquainted with the famous women of the

French Revolution and who at the same time assumes that everyone else is too uneducated to read the clue correctly? I would have given the name little meaning and overlooked the connection, but to say her place of residence was Caen, where the real Charlotte came from, was too much of an exaggeration,' said Sandrine.

'Charlotte Corday, the one who murdered Jean Paul Marat and ended under the guillotine?' Matisse's eyes fixed on the prosecutor. 'Explain this to us, please.'

'How do you get to Isabelle Deschamps?' De Chezac ignored the commissioner's question and directly asked Sandrine.

'We found out that she is on the internal list of witnesses in the Thierry Kouame case. It wasn't very hard to get a picture of her as she has a pretty thick police file.'

'Respect,' he said and nodded, then caught himself quickly. 'The Home Office insists that the true name of the victim stays secret.' He turned to Matisse. 'To not influence your investigation, I was forbidden to inform you of her background.'

'Charlotte Corday stabbed a knife through the Jacobite's leader's, Jean Paul Marat's, heart and killed him. I assume Isabelle Deschamps was supposed to get rid of Thierry Kouame.'

The prosecutor stood up and joined her at the whiteboard. 'Damn clever of you,' he whispered.

'I learned from the best,' was her answer.

De Chezac turned to the investigators watching him.

'Nothing of what I am about to say is permitted to leave this room. Do we understand each other?' He looked from one member of the meeting to the other until they all nodded. 'Anyone who speaks against Thierry Kouame and his gang puts his or her life in danger. Because of that we brought the witness to the campsite. We assumed that no one would search for her in this area.' He took a pen and drew a circle around the woman's picture. Then he drew an arrow pointing at her and finished with writing the name 'Kouame'.

'In our fight against organised crime, Isabelle Deschamps was an important witness to help find Thierry Kouame, the head of a gang. So far, we haven't been able to find any concrete proof strong enough to send them to court, and now it looks like years of policework were swept away with her death.'

'We should have been informed about the woman's identity.' It was as if a shadow had darkened Matisse's face. 'All this secrecy was not helpful.'

'The prosecutor's office has decided to wait for the first investigation results. Perhaps we were wrong in our fears, and it is an accidental act unrelated to Kouame's trial.'

'But?'

'I made sure my people worked through the night and were given priority in reconciling the databases. That's why we are attending the meeting.' He gestured at Prosecutor Lagarde. 'We don't want you to suspect that we are intending to withhold information.'

'And what did you find out working through the night?'

'The woman was shot from a distance of roughly two metres. Judging from the angle the bullet entered, the perpetrator stood opposite her. The gun used has a calibre of 9mm.'

'That would match the shell we found at the crime scene,' Jean Claude Mazet added. 'So, it was definitely murder.'

'The weapon is registered in the national database. Roughly a year ago, the gun was used at a bank robbery in Créteil. One of the drivers was shot, and nearly 1 million euro were stolen. We weren't able to catch the culprit.'

'Do we have suspects?'

'Yes, all men from Kouame's gang. The head of the operation seems to be a certain Charles Carnas. We keep finding his name in connection with organised crime. We can trace the gun to him as well.'

'Where is he? Likely in Paris where he knows his way, right?' Dubois asked. 'It would be too easy if he just happened to be on a holiday trip in Saint-Malo.'

'He vanished after the robbery. The last place he was seen was a hotel in Calais. Most likely he took the ferry to England and is lying low. We know he has connections there too.'

'And how does Isabelle feed into all of this?' She tapped on the picture of the woman.

'She was his girlfriend, in on the game and sold drugs in clubs. We assume that he took the money from the robbery to get to England and left her behind. He will try to build up a new life in England now. He can't start new with old ballast from Paris. Isabelle was certain though that he wouldn't leave her. She was one hundred per cent convinced that Kouame's men had killed him and taken the money. It would explain how they got the gun with which Isabelle was shot.' He circled the name of the gang-leader.

'What proof did she have against him?' Matisse asked.

'Isabelle said she had information which would send him to jail for a long time. That's why we got her out of Paris and found her the most unassuming place we could think of.' He tapped the pen against the board. 'No one would profit more from her death than him, and we have a direct connection from Kouame to the murder weapon. The man is our prime suspect in the case.'

'An indirect one,' Sandrine threw into the room.

'Excuse me?'

'It's based on the assumption that Thierry was responsible for the disappearance of Carnas and took the gun himself. None of this is proven. Let's not commit too quickly or we will lose sight of other aspects of the case.'

Brigadier Azarou raised one hand. 'Monsieur Treville identified the men in our database. He wouldn't swear on it but was quite sure. Forensics also found many fingerprints. It will take a few days, but after they have been there and checked the mobile home, we will be able to say if it was really them.'

'Who is it?' Sandrine took the two photographs Azarou handed her and fixed them to the board with more magnets.

'Their names are Ibrahim Gradel and Lago Zaha.' He looked up after reading the names. 'To print out their criminal record, I would have to put in a stack of paper: drugs, racketeering, assault, prostitution – these guys leave nothing out.'

'And they are part of Thierry's organisation,' said de Chezac.

'Then we should talk to them as soon as possible,' Sandrine decided.

'They will lie low for a bit after getting rid of the witness. I am sure we will find them sooner or later in Paris.' He left her and went back to his chair. 'By now we have enough indicative against Kouame. I will request that the case be referred to the Public Prosecutor's Office in Paris.'

'You can't do that.' Commissaire Matisse jumped up. 'First you leave us stumbling in the dark, and then you rip the case from us as soon as we find suspects?'

Sandrine leaned back against the wall and hooked her fingers into the pockets of her jeans. She was used to this banter about responsibilities. It always happened as soon as someone smelled the opportunity to gain laurels. As always, she stayed out of it. In fact, she should be happy. A day after the murder, the team had been able to present two suspects. Not a bad achievement, considering the circumstances. Besides, she had never wanted this case. De Chezac could take it if he really wanted it. It suited her just fine. Maybe he is happy enough with the way the investigation is going and can do something about my notice period, then Matisse will have to let me off the hook sooner. The letter was in the inside pocket of her jacket, and all she had to do was hand it in.

A woman opened the door and waved at Inès. Inès looked at

Sandrine as if to ask permission and left after Sandrine nodded. Shortly after she reappeared with an edition of the Quest-France in her hands and cleared her throat.

'What's up?' One could tell from the inspector's voice how annoyed he was at the prosecutor's sleight of hand.

'Secrecy is over,' said Inès, putting a copy of the newspaper on the table. The headline was bold enough for Sandrine to read from across the room: Murder on the Brittany Coast Path.

It had been obvious that an article like this would appear on the front pages today, but Sandrine had not expected the journalists to get a picture of the crime scene and print it. Damn it, she cursed inwardly and went over to Inès. The picture showed the woman how they had found her, sitting against the wall with a blood-smeared blouse.

'Where did they get the picture from?' She leaned over the newspaper. She did not care that she obscured everyone else's view.

'Not from us,' Jean Claude Mazet was quick to assure them. 'Maybe Madame Morvan took it. Who knows? Everyone always has a phone with them nowadays.'

'It's all the more urgent now that we take on the case and ensure that it is handled professionally.' Antoine de Chezac gave a curt nod and left the room. Lagarde jumped up and hurried after him while Commissaire Matisse clenched his hands and stuffed them into his jacket pockets.

Sandrine grabbed the newspaper, sat down and looked at it closer.

'Shall we question Madame Morvan about it?' Azarou sat down next to her.

'The picture wasn't taken by her. I am sure.'

'How do you know that?' The forensic technician stood behind her, craning his neck to see over her shoulder.

'It rained a lot during the night, but the woman's hair is dry.

Someone must have taken the picture before the rain. Which means at or around the time of death.'

'And her makeup hasn't run over her face yet.' Her assistant took out one of the Polaroids and held it next to the newspaper. The black traces of mascara on her cheeks were missing from the newspaper. Sandrine nodded; it had reminded her of black tears.

'The picture might have been taken by the murderer then?' Jean Claude exhaled at length. 'Why would he do something like that and send it to the media as well? To make us look foolish?'

'No idea, but we will find out.'

'The case isn't ours anymore,' Commissaire Matisse noted.

'De Chezac may act like a little god, but I am not part of his theatre. Until I get my hands on an official letter from the district attorney's office, this is ... our investigation.' I almost said 'my' investigation. I need to keep my distance.

Sandrine looked at Inès. 'I am not convinced that the prosecutor is right about the two suspects having returned to Paris. Would you be so kind and call the hotels in the area to check if someone who matches the suspect's description has checked in? Chain hotels should be best as they offer some anonymity. Put the ones with an automatic reception, at least during the night, on top of the list. The suspects should feel right at home there.'

'No problem,' she said and hurried off.

'What's your plan?' Commissaire Matisse leaned forward with both arms on the table.

'Maybe de Chezac is on the right track and those guys are the murderers of Isabelle Deschamps. It's definitely possible, and I would have followed this approach myself. However, that doesn't necessarily mean that they went back to Paris and are hiding.'

'It would be the cleverest thing to do. They are home there.

Here they are just strangers who will get noticed,' Matisse retorted.

'Isabelle Deschamps claimed to have information which would send Kouame to jail for a long time. That gives weight to Monsieur Treville's testimony. He told us that they were searching for a book but couldn't locate it. The victim only had a small handbag with her on Saturday evening, definitely not big enough for a book, notepad, or something similar. She will have hidden it somewhere safe. I bet that's why Thierry sent those two men to Brittany, to take care of Isabelle and find the papers. If I was one of them, I wouldn't return to Paris and risk my boss' wrath before the job was finished. So, I suspect they are still around, and we should do our best to track them down,' Sandrine said.

'Do that. In the meantime, I will talk to the chief prosecutor. Maybe he will support us. Lagarde doesn't have the nerves for that.' Matisse turned and left the room. For a man who had to assume that an important victory had been snatched from his hands, he was coping well.

'As long as they don't take the case from us officially, we will keep searching.' She waited for everyone to agree. 'Any news from forensics?'

'We found footprints on the path. Close to the corpse we have a perfect imprint of a boot's sole, possibly a motorbike boot. The trees shielded the print. Otherwise, the rain would have washed it away. Apart from that we found what we expected to find, tracks of hiking boots, different running shoes and holes from hiking sticks.'

'The phone?'

'Is still with the technicians in Rennes. The memory card is in our lab, but I wouldn't get my hopes up on finding anything useful.'

'As soon as you hear something let me know. We need all we can get.'

Sandrine added the name Daniel Morvan to the whiteboard. 'We have to talk to him. Too many members of this family are involved. Adel, please talk to the newspaper's editor-in-chief. Don't let him go before you know who sent in the picture. It's either from the murderer or a witness who can help us.' She looked around the room. 'Any questions? If not, let's get to work.'

One after the other left the meeting room. Sandrine stayed behind for a while and let her eyes wander over the whiteboard before she also left.

Inès held a phone in her hand and looked up at Sandrine who entered her office.

'Would you be able to put this letter into Commissaire Matisse's P.O. box?'

'Sure.'

Sandrine pulled out the notice from her inner jacket pocket and handed it to her.

'Thank you for letting me stay during the meeting. It has been my wish for a while to help at the front and not always just do magic in the background. Also, it was a pleasure to watch you deal with that arrogant little prosecutor.'

Sandrine took a chair and sat down next to her.

'It's one of those pleasures that are amazing for a moment but will come back to bite me one day. De Chezac will wait to get his revenge. He always gets his revenge.'

'Still, he earned a little shake on his pedestal.'

'When I heard the name, I remembered my history lessons from school. But without your connections we wouldn't have been able to identify her in time. I need to be the one who is thankful for your help.'

'It was a pleasure to feel like a real policewoman.'

'You are a real policewoman.' Probably more than me. De Chezac would most likely agree with her on that point.

She stood up and walked in the direction of her desk.

'Madame Perrot.' She looked back towards the young woman. 'I hope you stay here with us.'

'We will see,' Sandrine answered. What else could she say? Policework and she had drifted apart. She was not good at dealing with people like Antoine de Chezac, and she did not care to learn how to improve.

Adel Azarou had offered to show her the cafeteria, but she had refused politely. Instead, she decided to head down to the beach. On the way she bought a baguette and a café au lait. She sat down on the wall above the Plage du Sillon and let her legs swing. The sun was high in the cloudless sky, and she discarded her jacket. The SIG Sauer was in the locked drawer of her desk. She would hopefully not need a gun during lunch.

Sandrine enjoyed the warmth on her skin and the soft breeze from the sea. The screeching of the gulls and the rolling of the waves helped her to relax. The meeting with Antoine de Chezac had cost her more nerves than she would have thought. The man is part of my past. Most likely I will never see him again, she tried to convince herself, but every time someone said his name, she felt her heartbeat quicken. His mere existence made it easy to say goodbye to the police.

'Now it's break time,' she mumbled and took a sip from her café au lait, still nice and hot. She poked her finger into the foam and licked it clean. Even as a child she had loved the milk foam more than the actual coffee. I should have bought a croissant too, and not only the baguette.

A wave rolled over the flat sand. Little sandpipers ran after the receding waves and the quiet crackle of air-bubbles trapped in the wet sand filled the air. One woman dared to venture into the sea. Sandrine felt her skin break out into goosebumps just thinking about going into the cold water. Watching the swimmer, she took another sip of hot coffee. The smell of the fresh baguette wafted from the paper bag. She held it up to her nose and took a deep breath. Her stomach grumbled in response, and she freed the baguette's tip from the brown bag. Before she could take a bite, her phone rang. With a curse she took the call.

'Brigadier Azarou, what an unpleasant surprise ... No, it wasn't irony.' She was quiet for a few seconds. Then she placed the baguette on top of her folded jacket. 'Bring my gun with you. Top drawer on the right. Inès has a spare key. I will wait at the Brasserie Le Sillon.'

The car stopped at the side of the road, and she got in.

'You should take this thing with you. That's why they gave it to you.' He gave her the gun in its shoulder holster.

'Why? To scare small children at the beach?'

'To be ready when there is an unexpected mission. Like right now.'

'Unlikely that we will chase after some armed criminals. This is the province of Brittany, not Mission Impossible.'

He pressed the gas and Sandrine fastened her seatbelt. 'You had the right feeling. The guys are still in the area. Inès found them in an Ibis hotel.' He evaded a small transporter and cursed.

'Is the task force on the way?'

'Yes, on the way.'

'Then there is no reason to drive like a maniac. Or do you want to play the hero? We will arrive early enough to be present at the arrest.'

He took the foot from the gas begrudgingly, and Sandrine relaxed her shoulders a bit more. She hated it when she could not drive and had to blindly trust another human. It would never be an option to drive with someone else on the motorbike.

The idea of being completely at someone's mercy gave her stomach cramps.

Ten minutes later, they stopped with squealing tires in front of the Ibis hotel. It was a two-story building, resembling an elongated cube with a glass annex housing a restaurant. It was an unassuming little hotel which was normally used by tourists or businesspeople who did not plan on staying longer than one to two days. Sandrine checked her watch. Most guests should be out of the hotel at this time which would make their job easier. They drove into the parking lot. The task force had already arrived, and police cars and a squad van were parked in front of the Ibis.

Three policemen in dark combat gear and machine guns were posted close to the entrance.

'Lieutenant Perrot.' She showed her badge to one of the men. 'Have the suspects been located?'

'They have been secured and will be escorted outside very soon. The building is safe. You can enter.'

They entered the lobby at the same moment a group of policemen brought down the two suspects. The hands of the two men had been secured with handcuffs, and they did not pose any resistance. According to their files this was not the first time they had been in handcuffs. They knew how to act to not get into even more trouble. Sandrine did not doubt for a second that these two men were professionals. Whether they were the murderers of Isabelle Deschamps, though, that was another question.

They went up to the room and the guard stepped to the side to let them enter. It was a normal room with two single beds. They were made but showed the outline of someone who had been lying on them. A few greasy pizza cartons, and a couple of empty beer bottles were strewn over the floor. A soap opera was blaring from the TV.

'Looks like they were waiting for something.'

'Maybe they wanted to lie low until the excitement dies down. It would have made it easier for them to leave,' Azarou guessed.

She pulled out a pair of plastic shoe covers and slipped her feet inside. After that she put on plastic gloves. Surely forensics was on the way, but she could not resist a quick glimpse into the room. Slowly and carefully she opened the drawers of the nightstands. The brigadier watched her from the door. Sandrine shook her head.

'No gun to be found.'

'They will have hidden it.'

'If I owned a gun, it would be close enough to grab anytime.'

'I would have thrown the thing into the sea after the murder.'

She nodded. She would have done exactly the same thing. Without the murder weapon a sentencing would be a lot harder.

'Let's get out of here. We have to question them.'

'Shouldn't we leave this to the people from Paris?' asked the brigadier.

'It's still our case. As long as we think that those two men could have committed the crime we need to investigate.'

'Is this what you believe, or do you only want to do this because you have to settle things with this prosecutor?'

She halted in her movements, but then left the room and the hotel without giving him an answer.

'Is there any news from forensics?' Sandrine asked as soon as she had stepped into the office.

'They're still working on salvaging the files from the phone and are praying for a technological wonder,' Inès reported.

'Do you have the details of the connections, phone calls or anything?'

'The request is out. I assume we'll get some answers tomorrow afternoon.'

'Maybe the colleagues in Paris can speed up the process a little. It's their witness that has been murdered.'

'I already asked. They said they would take care of it, but it didn't feel to me like they were very interested in collaborating with us.'

Sandrine slumped down into her chair and stretched her legs. 'I'm not surprised to hear that.'

'Shouldn't de Chezac be motivated to find Isabelle Deschamp's murderer? She was the main witness after all.'

'He just wants the fame and glory of sending Thierry le Sauvage to prison. With his witness and all his leverage gone he can only still get him if he proves that Thierry was somehow involved in the murder. He will be convinced that he doesn't need our help. He doesn't like to share his fame.'

'What does he actually have at the moment?' Inès leaned back in her chair. 'Barely anything.'

'He gets the men arrested by the task force as soon as the case has officially been signed over to Paris. With that he should also get some useful clues which he can use to put pressure on them. If I were him, I would step up the heat on these two guys bit by bit, hoping that a murder charge would make them cave in and testify against their boss.'

'Will he be successful with that?'

'I have seen the corpses of people who have been accused of treason by Thierry. It wasn't nice. No, the men will stay quiet and simply go to prison for burglary and assault. It will be impossible to prove that they were connected to Isabelle's murder in court.'

'And what will you do now?'

'What law tells us to do. I will question them before they go to Paris.'

Sandrine looked at the door as Azarou entered the office. 'How are the suspects?' she asked when he sat down at his desk.

'They are sitting in interrogation rooms. No one has said anything. They didn't even ask for a lawyer.'

'Their boss will send two from Paris. One for each of them. If they don't talk until then we don't stand a chance.'

'Do you think they will tell them to stay quiet?'

'They are not just lawyers but also their nannies. Every word they say, Thierry will hear it.'

She turned towards Inès. 'Did you find out who sent the pictures of the crime scene to the media?'

'No, so far I haven't been successful. The editor hides behind shouting that we have freedom of the press and are not a police state. The usual talk.'

'We haven't made any progress,' she mumbled more to herself than to the others in the room.

'We found something,' Inès interjected. 'Daniel Morvan is in the last free interrogation room.'

'The Gendarmerie got him?'

'No, he turned himself in. His sister accompanied him.'

'Then we shouldn't let Mademoiselle Morvan wait. If she's gone too long there will be chaos in La Baie's kitchen.' At least some good news today. She took off the shoulder holster and locked it in her desk. 'I won't need this here. Will you come with me, Azarou?'

'Of course.'

'Please, keep checking in with forensics and the phone lists,' she told Inès on the way out.

'Without those we won't go anywhere.'

Adel opened the door to the interrogation room and let Sandrine enter first. The young cook and her brother looked up. Daniel

Morvan's eyes dropped back down on the tabletop while his sister held Sandrine's gaze. She pressed his hand as if she wanted him to know that she was here with him, and all would be well.

'Bonjour, Sarah,' Sandrine greeted the woman. 'Thank you for convincing Daniel to come for a little chat with us.' Her eyes landed on his black and red motorbike boots. They looked new. His jacket was hanging over the back of his chair, but she could not see a helmet anywhere. Most likely he had left it with the motorbike.

'I didn't have to convince him. He came by his own accord. He didn't know that you wanted to talk to him, and he also didn't know that suddenly half of France and the Gendarmerie were searching for him. Mother is very angry. Police in the hotel is not a good advertisement. All of this only because she was unfortunate enough to find a corpse on her walk.'

'It didn't have to come to this. He evaded questioning last night.'

'I didn't know who you were and I was scared,' Daniel said in a mere whisper. He still did not look at her and kept rubbing his hands against each other. He noticed her eyes and placed his hands on his thighs. She believed that he was scared. The question was just what he was scared of.

Sandrine sat down at the table while the brigadier leaned against the wall, forcing Daniel to look up at him.

Sarah's brother did not look much younger than the chef, but he was lacking her maturity.

'The first thing we can change in seconds. This is Brigadier General Azarou, and I am Lieutenant Perrot.'

'Daniel Morvan,' he mumbled as an introduction.

'May I?' she asked while placing her finger on the button of the recorder standing on the table. Sarah nodded. Sandrine switched on the recorder and dictated the necessary formalities.

'What were you scared of?'

'After ...' he took a deep breath, 'what happened to Charlotte I feared that the people who did this to her were also looking for me.' He looked up briefly. 'And you didn't look like a policewoman in the dark motorbike clothes.'

'What relationship did you have with Charlotte?'

'We were friends,' he said.

'Did she sleep with you?' She did not give him time to think.

'Yes ... sometimes. Why is this important?'

Sandrine did not ask who had initiated anything. After she had seen Isabelle's file she did not need to ask.

'Charlotte knew that her life was in danger?' For the time being she abstained from telling him that the woman had used a false name. She believed Daniel when he said that he was scared and did not want to throw him any more off balance. That would have to happen later.

'We often went on little trips during the weekends. Charlotte is ... was a night owl. To get her out of bed during the day was difficult, but she always liked our trips. When we came back from Cape Fréhel and stopped at the barrier, she saw two guys she knew march up to her mobile home. She panicked and we drove off as fast as we could.'

'What did she say about the men?'

'I never saw her like that before. She was very scared. Normally she was a very tough woman, and much cooler than me.' His voice broke and his hands were shaking. Sandrine gave him a moment to calm down.

'From where did she know the men?'

'From Paris. Where else?' He wiped over his eyes with his sleeve. Sarah placed a hand on his shoulder.

'You have to tell them everything, okay? You are not involved in any of this.' She must have noticed how close her brother was to a breakdown and did not mention the word 'murder'.

'An acquaintance of hers had some problems with the guys.

At least that was what she told me, that he stole something from them. She didn't know what it was, but she said that the guys were convinced that she had it in her possession or knew where to find it. They definitely wanted it back.' He searched Sandrine's eyes with his for the first time. 'They are capable of anything, Charlotte said, even murder.'

'You think that the strangers murdered her?'

'I wouldn't know who else.' It burst from him. The answer had been so fast that Sandrine believed him.

'Daniel has nothing to do with this,' his sister interjected. 'Are you accusing my brother? You must see how much her death has hurt him.'

'We're only asking him as a witness,' she said to calm them down. 'Everything else we will see afterwards.'

'I have no idea what happened with Charlotte during the night. You have to believe me.' He stared at her with wide eyes. Fear was written all over his pale face. 'I told her that we should leave but she didn't want to. Instead, she called someone whom she believed would protect her.' His tense shoulders shook. 'But that was not the case.'

'Do you know with whom she talked?'

'No idea. She made it quite a secret.'

Sandrine threw a quick look at Azarou. He nodded. She must have asked the prosecutor for help. That was why de Chezac had appeared at the crime scene so quickly. Instead of informing the local police he had taken his car and driven directly to Brittany. As if he was a guy who could take on Thierry's henchmen!

'Where were you on Saturday evening?'

'She wanted to clear up some things and sent me away. I was supposed to pick her up just after midnight. We wanted to disappear for a while.'

'In the street leading to the coastal path?'

Daniel nodded. 'Exactly. At the end of the Rue du Port Mer. I waited but she never showed up. There was no one around at all. Just a quiet, boring area for all those old people and families. There was only a light on in the two front houses and a baby was crying.' He swallowed. 'She must have been lying a few metres away from me, maybe dying as I was standing there, and I didn't notice. I could have saved her.'

'Even an experienced doctor wouldn't have been able to help her. The shot was deadly. She didn't suffer.' Sandrine knew that it was not much to console the boy, but it was all she could offer.

'Still.'

'And then?'

'I was angry because she was toying with me and drove off.'

'Fast or slow?'

'As I said, I was angry and didn't care about the people there. I raced the bike through the street. The neighbours must have fallen out of their beds.'

The residents had confirmed that as well as the time.

'Is that enough?' Sarah Morvan lay an arm around her brother's slim shoulders. 'Can't you see how hard this is for him?'

'Just one more thing. We found boot prints in the mud. Can we check them with yours? If they don't match, we can cross you off the list of suspects in an instant.'

'You want my boots?'

'Unfortunately, yes.'

'And how will I get home?'

'We can lend you some shoes. But I fear none for driving a motorbike with.'

'It's okay.' He leaned down and took off the boots. 'I'll manage.'

'Let's go.' Sarah stood up and pulled her brother along with her. Sandrine opened the door of the interrogation room for them.

'That reminds me, how did you know that we were talking about Charlotte?' Sandrine asked him.

'I am sorry, but I told him yesterday after your visit,' his sister confessed.

'Who else could it have been?' he replied. 'Also, the picture was in the newspaper. Who does something like this? It's disgraceful.' It was the first time he had raised his voice.

'So, you lied to us, Mademoiselle Morvan, when you told us that you didn't recognise the woman in the picture.'

'That's true. I had to talk to Daniel first. I wanted him to hear it from me, and not from the police or the newspapers.'

'And your mother thought the same?'

'I don't know if she ever saw Charlotte. Even if she had, it wouldn't make much of a difference. She didn't like the woman. If she doesn't like someone she simply turns around and ignores their existence. It was always like that.'

'Obstruction of police work is not a trifle. You know that right?'

She nodded slowly. 'If you want to file charges, I will accept the punishment. I had to protect my brother.'

'Brigadier Azarou will show you the way out.'

Both went through the door which the brigadier held open for them. A weak smile sat on Daniel's face. He seemed relieved to leave the office a free man.

'Charlotte's real name was Isabelle Deschamps,' Sandrine called, 'and she was the girlfriend of a guy named Charles Carnas.' Daniel froze in his movements. Sarah threaded her arm in his and pulled him along as if she wanted to drag her brother to safety. Sandrine watched them leave.

'He didn't know her real name. Otherwise, he wouldn't have been that surprised,' said Adel Azarou and joined her.

'I am not so sure about that. He only looked shocked when I mentioned Charles Carnas.'

'What would someone like Daniel Morvan have to do with a criminal like him? I cannot imagine that a boy like that would have any contact with a man like Carnas.'

'Why would the name throw him off like that though? There must be some connection.'

'I don't see one.'

'Neither do I, at least not at the moment.'

Adel held the boots in his hand. 'I'll hand them over to forensics.'

'Thank you, but it will be work for nothing.' Daniel had handed them over without any protest, and they looked like they had come fresh from a shoebox that very morning. The likelihood that they matched the prints they had found was close to zero.

Sandrine returned to her desk and picked up her daypack.

'Are the two men from the Ibis still in the interrogation rooms?' she asked Inès.

'No. They refused to say anything and are now under arrest.'

'I'm not surprised. They know what they are doing.'

Azarou joined them a while later, boots still in hand, and dropped onto his office chair.

'Delivered?'

'Yes, wasn't much work. One look and Jean Claude knew that they weren't the same boots.'

'Would have been a shock if they were.' She took a boot and looked closer. 'This is not the kind you get at any old shop. How many shops are there in the area who specialize in motorbike gear?' She only knew one.

'You can count them on one hand.'

'Then please send Poutin or Dubois to have a look at the

shops. It shouldn't be hard to find out if they were purchased this very morning. He may have thrown the old ones away.'

'Will do. What will we do in the meantime?'

'We will take the information received from Daniel and try our luck with the guys in the cells.'

'They won't say anything. No chance. I already tried all my tricks.'

'We don't have time for both of them. It won't take long for their lawyers to show up or for them to be transported to Paris. Which one would you bet on if you had to?'

His gaze trailed out of the window. 'Lago Zaha, I would try that one. He should break easier under pressure. Ibrahim Gradel is a prison veteran. We won't be able to intimidate him.'

'Then let's give it a try.'

'Alright, but he will be as silent as an oyster.'

'It's worth a shot. What do we have to lose?'

'It's your choice, but my prophecy is that we are wasting our time.'

'Most likely you are right but that's how the job is. Take something to read.'

'Really?'

'Best would be this morning's newspaper with the picture of the victim. Let Monsieur Zaha see the front page, but don't even react.'

'As you wish.' He grabbed a newspaper from the desk and followed her.

The arrested man sat at the table and looked at the door when they entered. When he beheld Sandrine the corners of his mouth drooped down. A woman would not make him talk, was very clearly his message.

An armed police officer sat in the corner and rose when they entered.

'You can go. We will manage.'

'Very well.'

The suspect placed his handcuffed hands flat on the table. Both feet were squared against the floor like he was an immovable statue.

Sandrine judged him to be in his late twenties, maybe early thirties. He was tall with wide shoulders, and according to the files, from Ivorian decent, like all of Thierry's gang members.

'Nothing without a lawyer,' he said.

'Your choice,' she answered simply.

Two microphones jutted from the middle of the table. Adel Azarou leaned forward to start the recording.

'We don't need that.' Sandrine stopped him while pulling a chair close. She sat down with some distance to the table. Both men looked at her with eyebrows raised in question. 'If he doesn't want to talk, we should respect his wish.'

The suspect watched her with open suspicion but also confusion. He had clearly expected a harder questioning with the police putting him under pressure. At least that must have been what he had experienced in the past.

'If you think so.' The brigadier took one of the remaining chairs, sat down and opened his newspaper.

'Just one little question, your name is Lago Zaha?'

The man nodded but stayed silent. It was obvious that he would be unable to hide his identity. His fingerprints were in the system. 'Your family is originally from the Ivory Coast, is that correct?' She waved her own question away with a dismissive gesture of her hand. 'I am sorry. You didn't want to say anything. I forgot for a second.'

She placed her daypack on her thighs, unzipped it and reached inside. The man sat still with only his right foot tapping a bored rhythm onto the floor. The other foot was pointing at the door. He did not want to be here. At least the cell had a hard bed he could lie on.

'There it is,' she said and pulled out a brown paper bag. 'My breakfast,' she said to Azarou. 'It's a strange job, isn't it? You either sit around all day and stuff your face with fast food or it's so busy that you don't get a bite to eat at all.'

'The back office has an easier job in that regard.' He sounded bored and flipped a page of the newspaper. 'Here's an ad from Dafy Moto. They have motorbike jackets and boots on sale.'

'I'll go there on my way back. My jacket has a ripped seam at the shoulder.'

'What is this bullshit?' the suspect hissed at her. 'You drag me here to read me some garbage from the newspaper? Take me back to my cell.'

Sandrine took the baguette from her bag, and then proceeded to fold the bag and place it on her legs.

'I'm afraid law dictates that we must give the suspects time to talk. That's why the three of us are wasting our time now. Though, in your case, time isn't very important.' Now he has a chance to think about that.

She put the baguette on the bag and used it like a tablecloth. 'It's from Mullière,' she explained to her assistant.

'Those are the best in the area, but also a tad more expensive.'

'It's not very crunchy anymore.' She looked at the suspect. 'That's thanks to you.'

He looked at her as if his face had turned to stone. Sandrine could guess very well what was going on inside the man's head. He was confused. How was he not the centre of attention, but a lousy baguette instead? The bored tapping of his food sped up a bit.

She opened the baguette. 'I like the combination of slightly salted butter and Paté de Campagne.' She lifted one of the cornichons between thumb and pointer finger, pushed it into her mouth and her face twisted into a grimace. 'Super sour.'

'I want you to take me back,' demanded Lago Zaha.

'I don't give a damn what you want,' she snapped at him. 'You will stay here until I've had a proper break and time to eat my breakfast. You should get used to this. The next few years you will always have to wait for someone to tell you when you are allowed to go where.' When she mentioned 'next few years' his eyebrows twitched up, but he regained his composure quickly. He had to be aware of the assault, the break in and the property damage. He would not have shown any reaction if he had known of the murder.

She bit into her baguette. 'It's really good,' she mumbled.

The investigation room lay in nearly complete silence. The only sounds were the tapping of the suspect's foot on the hard floor, a ruffling of newspaper from time to time and Sandrine eating, not even trying to be quiet. The break was good for her, and during eating she could think best. There was no reason to scream at the guy or threaten him with violence. She had known that before entering the room. He had grown up with crime and the rules of the street and the gang. Nothing she could threaten him with here would be even half as bad as what Thierry would do to him if he talked.

There was only a sliver of baguette left when the man turned towards her.

'Can I go back to my cell now?'

She ate the last bite, got a Coke can from her bag and washed down her food.

'Yup. Done. I really needed that.' She looked at her assistant. 'Are you done?'

'Only sports left. The moneybags from PSG Paris are out shopping again. They have to come first with all the money they spent.'

'Money shoots goals,' noted Sandrine.

'You are lucky that you are even allowed to play, you peasants from the provinces.' The suspect grinned condescendingly at Azarou.

'He's not a fan of Stade Rennes.' Sandrine smiled.

'I preferred the guy when he kept his mouth shut,' replied the brigadier.

'Football is one of those man-things. Every idiot thinks he knows best.' She squished the paper bag into a ball and threw it at the bin. 'Got it.'

'Maybe you should play basketball,' commented her assistant.

'I want to go back to my cell, you idiots.'

'You can go now.'

She made a sign at Azarou, and he pressed the doorbell to let the police officer know they were finished.

'As you gave me a calm lunchbreak, I will tell you how we will proceed.'

'So friendly all of a sudden?'

'You are part of Thierry de Sauvage's gang. I don't care if you rot in prison.'

The sass that had shown in his eyes dimmed. His eyes turned dead while he looked at her. His foot kept tapping the ground in the same rhythm. Most likely he was hoping to annoy her.

'Your lawyers will get here soon.'

He nodded and the corners of his mouth lifted into the shadow of a grin.

'You won't get to see them though. As soon as they set foot in the building, you will be brought out the back and driven to Paris to prison. Prosecutor de Chezac is already waiting for the two of you and has great plans.'

A small twitch in his shoulders showed her how little he liked the man.

'He will get you for murder.'

He stared at the wall.

'You were at the mobile home of Isabelle Deschamps and left us lots of little fingerprints. The owner of the campsite has identified you. You won't get out of this.' She leaned back and watched him intently. 'You think that's not enough for a conviction? We will see. You aren't very clever and made an important mistake.'

Sandrine fell silent. There was only the tapping of the shoe on the floor. 'You shouldn't have shot the girl with the gun you got from Charles Carnas.'

For a breath the prisoner did not move. When he continued to tap the ground, his foot was faster.

'When did you steal the gun from him? After the raid on the money transporter or only when you didn't want to share the money and got rid of him?'

'Lawyer,' was all he said.

'Ah.' She waved the word away. 'It's just a question of politeness. The people from Paris took over the case. De Chezac wants you to talk about Thierry, or he will make sure that you will never leave prison again. Both is fine for me. This is no longer my case. We only have to finish with the dirty work and find Carnas' corpse. That's thanks to you idiots. The next few weeks we will not leave a single rock in all of Brittany unturned until we find his remains. Thank you very much.' She stood up and went to the door.

'Isn't this the moment where you offer me a safety rope or something?' Lago Zaha was grinning at her again. 'Isn't that how you normally do it?'

'There is no safety rope for you.' Without another word she left the room.

Sandrine fell into the chair, folded her hands behind the nape of her neck and rocked back and forth. The office chair squeaked with every movement.

'He didn't smile much in the end,' said Azarou.

'That's not important. We learned what's of interest to us. That's enough.'

'We did? What was it that interested us? The guy didn't say more than three words.'

'It would help you to remember a few of the things they throw at you during the training sessions. Over 90% of human communication is non-verbal. In this case I absolutely agree with psychology.'

'I couldn't read much from his pokerface.'

Inès joined them with a pile of files in her arms.

'Sit down,' Sandrine said and pushed a chair in her direction. 'Have you had an older relative you never liked?' She turned to Azarou.

'Sure, who doesn't? Aunt Naima. I was really scared of her. She was a terrifying woman.'

'What did your mother teach you? Smile when your aunt enters, don't stick out your tongue at her when she isn't looking and so on.'

'Yes.'

'Forget the face. We are trained from childhood onwards to lie with our faces.'

'The guy sat there like a monolith. Only the constant tapping of his foot was getting on my nerves.'

'That's why he did it.' Sandrine smiled. 'But he gave himself away with it too.'

'When he stumbled in the rhythm.'

'Well spotted.'

'When you mentioned Carnas' gun.'

'Those things are very important if we want to figure out the motive of the case. We have to find both, the gun and the man.'

'You think it's that Carnas, don't you?'

'Zaha and the young Morvan both reacted to his name. It feels a bit too much to be just a coincidence.'

Inès cleared her throat. 'Commissaire Matisse wants to talk to you.'

'Come, Azarou, the boss is calling.'

'He only wanted to see you,' the office manager interjected.

'We're a team. Shared suffering is only half as bad.' She waved him along, and the brigadier followed her to the office of the boss.

'Commissaire Matisse, you wanted to talk to us?'

'Sit down.' He gestured at them to come inside. Only one chair stood in front of the desk, and she left it to her assistant. For herself she pulled one over from the round meeting table.

'I want to give my thanks to you. You have done exceptional work during this case. The local chief prosecutor and the mayor are very impressed by how quickly you found and arrested the criminals. Brigadier Azarou, this case will be very important for your future career.'

'Thanks, Monsieur le Commissaire.'

'We have two men in custody. We can present them to court for coercion, assault and damage to property. The murder ...' Sandrine raised her hands. 'We are still missing solid proof.'

'The prosecutor from Paris is convinced he has enough for a conviction.' He slid a fax over the desk and tapped his pen on the paper. 'A formal request has also been made to send Lago and Gradel to Paris. Prosecutor Lagarde's boss has approved everything. The case is out of our hands.'

'Then we only have to finish the paperwork. There's nothing else left to do.'

'Lieutenant Perrot, are you sure that you don't want to reconsider? It would be a shame to lose your expertise in the police. We could very much use you in our little town. I am missing an experienced team leader.'

'We only met yesterday, but I can already say that you are

one of the better bosses I have had the pleasure of working with. I want to be very clear and open – my time with the police is over. This case only made it clearer to me.'

She pointed at the fax in front of the Commissaire.

'Politics is not there to help the police force but to hinder and break its bones. I believe it's a mistake to hand over the case.'

'I am sad to hear that. At least you still have some time in our commissariat. I hope my people will learn a few things from you.'

'You have an excellent team.' Sandrine said her goodbyes and returned to her workstation. The brigadier followed her.

'De Chezac will never get the guys behind bars with such thin evidence.' He rested his underarms on the tabletop.

'Maybe he is hiding findings behind his back. That would fit his character and the way he's approached everything so far.' Or he fabricates evidence to put the prisoners under a lot of pressure, that would also suit him.

'I don't think we should give up that fast,' he said, trailing after his thoughts. 'The young Morvan might spit out something else.'

'No.' Her voice sounded harsher than she had intended, but she had to stop this. The clearer the better. 'The case has been given to Paris. We will take care of the paperwork and that's it. You should also call back Poutin and Dubois. Daniel's boots don't matter to us anymore.'

'If those are your orders.' She had angered him, and he didn't try to hide it. She hated it when she had to play out her higher status, but in this case, it was for the better. The brigadier was a competent policeman with a bright future, and she would hate to see him ground under by the bureaucracy just because he had searched in places people did not want him to.

'Until tomorrow,' she said as a goodbye. It was still rather early to call it a day, but the case was gone and the paperwork would wait.

Sandrine packed her workout clothes. Not too long ago, she had found a boxing studio in Saint-Malo in which she could train. Her mother had taken her to her first kickboxing lesson on her fifth birthday. Since then, she had been training whenever her job allowed her some time to breath.

The doorbell rang. She was not expecting any visitors. As a matter of fact, apart from Rosalie no one had ever been inside her apartment. Her gun was in the safe in the bedroom. She halted. Maybe I should get it. Finally, she decided against it.

In front of the door stood a man she had met in Paris. In his cashmere coat, elegant suit and polished shoes he looked like a serious businessman which he definitely was not.

'I hope my visit is not at an inconvenient time.'

'It's a surprise. To claim anything else would be a lie.'

'May I still come inside?'

Sandrine hesitated but then stepped aside and let him in.

The man placed his hat on the little table next to the door and made his way into the living room and kitchen.

'Furnished very nicely. The view on the sea is priceless. I'm a bit jealous.' He pulled a bottle of wine from the pocket of his coat. 'Do you want to sit outside and enjoy the light a bit? The golden hour, as photographers call it.' He turned to her. 'It's said that you are a passionate photographer.'

'You wouldn't mind if ...?' She lifted her phone.

'Not in the slightest. I understand.'

She typed a number and waited until the call was answered.

'Commissaire Matisse? I would like to inform you that Monsieur Kouame has found his way to my home.'

She listened, then looked at her visitor.

'My boss asks if he should send a special task force for my protection?'

The man chuckled. 'No, we won't need that. I'm only here to help your investigations and explain some unfortunate misunderstandings.'

'You heard him, Monsieur le Commissaire? If it helps to make things clearer, he will visit the commissariat tomorrow and give his explanation for a protocol.'

'Tell your boss that I will definitely be there. It's a shame, but I'm forced to pay a visit to the police every single day. An annoying condition, which I owe to our mutual friend at the prosecutor's office.'

Sandrine opened the door leading to the veranda. Thierry le Sauvage opened several drawers in the kitchen until he found a corkscrew. Without looking back at her, he went outside.

'We will see each other tomorrow,' she said to Commissaire Matisse and hung up the phone. Sandrine took two glasses and followed the man.

'There's no reason to feel alarmed by my unannounced visit.'

'A policewoman who has a visit from someone like you and does not tell her manager makes herself suspicious. I have no intention of making myself susceptible to blackmail in any way. You do realize that, don't you?'

He sat down in the small, iron chair which stood on her flat terrace. With a plop, the cork jumped out of the bottle's neck.

'I hope some wine doesn't count as blackmail. It should rest a moment before we enjoy it, but,' his eyes wandered over her workout clothing, 'I assume you have plans for this evening.'

'What brought you here? Why didn't you come straight to the office? Commissaire Matisse is a pleasant man.'

'I prefer to stick to the people I know.'

'De Chezac left not too long ago. He would have liked to talk to you.'

'I was forced to spent much too much time with that man recently. He's nothing but a bore who clutches at every blade of grass to find something to accuse me of.' He grinned and white teeth blinked between his dark lips. 'He really thinks I'm a criminal.'

'Stop the games. We both know what you are.'

He poured wine in the glasses, placed the bottle to the side and took a sip from one.

'Exquisite. A Château Margaux from 2005. My favourite wine from the Médoc. They say Ernest Hemingway's granddaughter was named after the winery.' He chuckled again. 'Sometimes love goes too far.'

She knew exactly from which criminal activities the money for the wine, which had most likely cost a sum with many zeros, was from. His manners and the small talk were only a costume to hide the wolf. She knew it was nothing but theatre, but she wanted to get as much information out of him as possible, and so she played along.

'Get to the point, Thierry.'

'You arrested my men. That was a mistake.'

'Are you threatening me?'

'Not at all. The two idiots deserve a few days in a cell. To think that they murdered Isabelle Deschamps though, that's the mistake you're making. It will only distract you from finding the real murderer of that poor girl.'

She let him believe that she thought his two men were the culprits. There was no way she would give him anything about the case that he did not already know.

'No one has a better motive to get rid of the woman than you.'

'Is that so?' he asked, stretching every vowel.

'Isabelle Deschamps was to testify against you in court.'

She took a sip of wine and savoured it in her mouth before

swallowing. His eyes wandered to the sea foaming against the cliffs just below her house.

'She was ... I think if you want to say it politically correct nowadays, a sexworker. On the side she was dealing for her boyfriend and pimp. I wouldn't believe anything the woman said. She was only interested in money.'

'Isabelle tried to blackmail you?'

'I'm not someone you can blackmail. Especially not a cheap slut like her,' he answered sharply, but caught himself in seconds. 'Excuse me, one shouldn't talk ill about dead people. But then I wouldn't be able to talk about her at all.'

'How much did she want to draw back her testimony?'

'When there's a crime in Paris, I'm the one they point at, and I'm the one they blame. From time-to-time success-hungry delusionists like this de Chezac try to get me in front of a court. But,' he sat up straight and looked at Sandrine, 'I have never been sentenced.'

'The public prosecutor is convinced to change that soon.'

'With the help of someone like Isabelle Deschamps?' he laughed. 'My lawyers are worth their money. From the woman's credibility nothing would be left after the first day. You are correct, Capitaine Perrot, blackmail was her favourite little thing. Dozens of her customers had to bleed to make sure that her pimp didn't send some very interesting pictures to their wives. And then she was going to charge me with a trumped-up testimony if I didn't pay a nice sum of money. A really lousy witness, considering her police record. Is that all our friend de Chezac has to offer the court? That will never do. Especially now that she's deceased. She probably messed with the wrong guy.' He had addressed her in her old rank which had been taken from her by de Chezac. She hid her smile. It was a childish attempt to make her feel like they were allies. After years in the police in Paris she had thought that she had seen everything one man could do to another, but when she had beheld Thierry's last victim, she had thrown up at the crime scene. There was nothing they had in common, not even their dislike of de Chezac and his methods.

'What interest would the murder of that woman have been to me? Her death made my position worse. Now the prosecutor office tries to blame me with contract killing.'

'Why were your men in Isabelle's mobile home? We have a witness, and their fingerprints are everywhere.'

'Zaha and Gradel are not the brightest. I assume it was their plan, without my permission, to scare the woman a bit. It was a stupid move and completely unnecessary.'

'They came all the way from Paris by themselves to trash Isabelle's home? What were they looking for?' She did not expect an honest answer, but it would not hurt to give it a try. Maybe he will say something about the book Treville mentioned.

'They didn't search anything. To cause a bit of chaos inside the four walls that people consider safe often does wonders. As I said, it was a stupid mistake, and they have to sit for that.'

She did not believe a single word which came out of his mouth, but she did not have to let him know that.

'A very good wine,' she said and took another sip from her glass. 'Is there anything else you want to tell me?'

'I simply wanted to make sure that you don't waste your time with a lead that isn't one. It's my tax money too, you know.'

'It's always welcome when tax-paying citizens give us a hand and help to maintain order,' she replied flatly.

'Then we understand each other.' The look on his face was nothing less than a threat to not come any closer. Sandrine held his stare until the man blinked.

'What brings you to Brittany if it's not Isabelle Deschamps' murder?' she asked.

'I'm a businessman and am looking at a few interesting properties in the area. The prices in Paris are ridiculous by now, but here there are still places with a lot of potential that are very much a steal.' He checked his golden Rolex. 'It's time to say goodbye. I have a dinner engagement.'

Sandrine led him through the garden to his car. She did not plan to ever let this man inside her house again. She watched as he left the property, got in his car, and drove off around the next corner. Afterwards she tidied up the glasses and poured the rest of the wine down the sink. Thousands of euros vanished down the drain, but she could not stand the idea of drinking even another drop of the liquid. Sandrine packed her sports bag and threw it on the passenger seat of her car.

Sandrine bombarded the punching bag with hits. She had to get her defeat by de Chezac and the meeting with Thierry Kouame out of her head, and there was no better way than physical exhaustion. Panting heavily, she rested her forehead against the punching bag. Her muscles were burning and shaking, and her clothes were bathed in sweat.

'Enough for today.' The exhaustion made her sway slightly as she went to one of the benches and sat down. She took off her wet gloves and let them drop to the floor while watching two women sparring in the ring. A tall, red-haired fighter used her superior reach to keep her opponent at bay, only occasionally breaking cover for a quick hit. It was only a matter of time before she would win the fight.

'Don't even think about it,' she heard a familiar-sounding male voice behind her say. She turned her head and saw the owner of the Équinoxe.

'Ah, it's you.' What was he doing here?

'So we meet again. My pleasure.'

'Saint-Malo is a small place,' she replied.

'Working again?' He sat down next to her without an invitation.

'Does it look like it?'

'You didn't look like the typical policewoman in the club either.'

'Touché. I'm here for fun.'

'You like Martial Arts?'

'Wouldn't be here otherwise.'

Sandrine wanted to train and be left alone. That was it. She was not too keen on a chitchat with the man.

'Lilou is training for the national championship. A killer. Don't enter the ring with her. It wouldn't end well.'

'Why should I want to do that?'

'I noticed the look in your eyes. It's the way people look when they want trouble. I very much remember it from my time as a bouncer.'

'Then you must be out of practice. I am not looking for trouble. In general, I try to avoid it.'

She stood up and made her way to the changing rooms. The guy did not seem like the type to spread harmony and peace. She decided to avoid him.

Sandrine lay sprawled on the sofa, too tired to switch on the TV and too exhausted to bother holding a book. Someone knocked at her door.

'I'm coming,' she called.

Rosalie pushed the door with her shoulder. She carried a tray with two large soup-bowls. 'Am I interrupting?' Without waiting for an answer, she entered the kitchen. There was not enough space in the house for a hallway.

'The new novel came back from the printers today. I signed a copy for you, as you are my favourite detective.' She put the book on the table. The Oyster Murderer. Sandrine smiled. Rosalie's novels were equal part crime fiction and equal part cookbook. Maybe that was her secret to success. Or maybe it was the sex scenes.

'I am Lieutenant de Police, not a detective. You should remember that for your next book.'

'If you were Madame le Commissaire you would at least have time for a proper lunchbreak.'

She sat up and stretched her arms. The overworked muscles hurt. It was obvious, if she got pulled down by laziness and didn't take the time to stretch tonight, that she would be unable to walk tomorrow. However, the thought of more movement did not feel very enticing.

'I had a very tasty lunch.'

'What? A sandwich with flat ham and a cheese that barely deserves the name from the cafeteria?'

'An excellent baguette with paté from Mullière.'

'Okay, that's good enough for once. But now I need someone to try my Cotriade bretonne. It's also much nicer to eat together. You should come over more often and tell me about all your cases.'

'It was a long day,' she said, apology swinging in her voice.

Rosalie handed her a bowl of the fish soup which had been filling the kitchen and living room with its delicious smell. Sandrine always liked that Rosalie did not douse her dishes in garlic.

'I threw in a few shrimps and mussels too. I feel like it gives an extra kick to everything.'

Sandrine fought her way into the kitchen and returned with glasses and a bottle of Sauvignon Blanc. It was not a 1000€-wine, but good enough.

'What's happening in the case?'

'Finished.'

'You caught the murderer? That was really fast in the end. Even my Commissaire Delacroix isn't that fast.'

'How could he be? You have to fill 300 pages, so he takes his time.'

'Tell me.' Rosalie pulled up her legs and made herself comfortable in the armchair. She listened to Sandrine, enraptured, but reminded her now and then to eat her soup. Cold shrimps were not for her.

After a bowl of fish soup and two glasses of white wine, Sandrine yawned loudly.

'You let them take the case from you just like that?' Rosalie asked in surprise. 'That's not like you.'

'This is not a novel but reality. De Chezac submitted an application, and the Saint-Malo Public Prosecutor's Office approved it. It's that easy. Lagarde can dismiss the case as closed and join the mayor for an interview. We will see it in the Ouest-France regional section tomorrow. De Chezac has two guys he can press until they give him something on Thierry. Everyone wins.'

'Everyone apart from you.'

Sandrine looked at Rosalie. Now it was her turn to be surprised. 'Why do you think that? I never planned to go back to the police. I am too much of a simple person for the job. Someone murders someone else and I search until I find the murderer.'

'Like Commissaire Delacroix.'

'But he's not dealing with politicians and their campaign donors interfering in his police work. This is not my world. It takes a different kind of investigator for that.'

'Like your brigadier?'

'I fear it will break him as soon as they ask him to look the other way or let a person go just because they are rich and influential.'

'Isn't that a reason to stay and work for justice?'

'I am too tired for that fight,' Sandrine retorted. 'And they knocked me out.'

'That's your own fault.'

'True,' she yawned again. 'My eyes are dropping. We'll talk another time.'

'Sure. I'll leave the dishes with you. Just bring them over clean. A bit of housework will clean your head as much as hitting a punching bag.'

'I will and thank you for the soup. Tomorrow I will go shopping, promise. Then it's my turn to cook something for us.'

Sandrine went to the door with her friend and watched her disappear into the second house. She cleaned the bowls and placed them in the dishwasher. She liked fish soup, but there was no reason for the smell to linger in her house for the next few days.

Chapter 5

Unexpected Turn

Sandrine rose early the next morning. She stretched her stiff muscles and forced herself to do some stretching before going down and taking the car key from its little box. It was not far to the centre of Cancale, and the bakery she liked to frequent was already open. She ate a croissant and a Chausson aux pommes in the cafe and then drove to the office.

Azarou sat at his desk and was busy typing a protocol into his computer.

'So early at work?'

'It looks like I will finish the paperwork today. It's not a lot.' He patted a small stack of files. 'It was only two days of investigation.'

'Did the reports from forensics arrive?'

'Commissaire Matisse slowed everything down. Jean Claude and his team can concentrate on other cases now.'

'Good morning.' Inès joined them.

'Did the telephone records arrive?'

'They should be here in the afternoon. Are they still important?'

'Of course, maybe we'll find some new evidence,' said Azarou.

'No, they are not,' Sandrine decided. 'The case is closed. We will just put them in the files and then it all goes to the archive. We don't want anyone to accuse us of not working properly.'

'Are we really giving up that quickly? I know you are also doubting that those two guys are the murderers.'

'The case was taken from us, and the Paris' police is competent enough to find the real murderers of Isabelle Deschamps. We stay out of this. If you want you can prepare a charge of assault, coercion and damage to property on the campsite, and send it to the public prosecutor's office. Maybe they will also send it on to Paris.'

'You're giving up?'

'I follow orders, which is something entirely different. I would suggest you do the same,' she said with a harder voice than she had intended. She had learned from experience what it meant to refuse an order.

'If you think so.' Azarou drew back and continued writing the reports.

'Commissaire Matisse is right. You did an excellent job. You have to learn when it's time to let go.' She tried to sound amiable, but the brigadier kept typing without reply.

Sandrine took a file and began to sort through it. It would not be a fun day. She hated paperwork in the office and the eyes of her co-workers drilling into the back of her head.

The rest of the day went by without any incidents. The last report had been typed in the early afternoon and handed to Inès Boni. It would be her job to ask for the missing files and archive all of them together. If the colleagues from Paris did not request the files, and Sandrine was very sure that they would not, they would just end up in the archive of the commissariat.

'See you tomorrow!' she said goodbye to her assistant who would stay longer as he was on on-call duty.

Back home Sandrine changed into sweatpants and running shoes. She ignored the red blinking light from the answering machine. After a whole day behind a desk, she had to get out for some fresh air. She only wanted to run a short round, no more than one hour. Afterwards there would still be enough time to check who wanted something from her. Most likely it was just someone from the press who had found her phone number.

She stepped out of the door and looked from the garden to the sea. The sun was low already and drew long shadows on the grass. With a little luck she would be back home before it was dark. In a slow jog she made it to the wall and down the steps to the Brittany Coast Path. Her eyes twitched to the right. A few hundred metres away was the crime scene. That's not your job anymore, she chided herself and turned away. Once to Pointe du Grouin and back would be enough for today. The path was too uneven, with roots growing all over the ground, to run there during darkness.

She ran past the campsite of the Trevilles, and out of a small forest onto the open plain which led to the tip of the headland. A policeman stood on the trail and waved at her. Not again. She slowed in front of him and kept jogging in place. The wind had freshened, and she did not want her muscles to cool down. The last thing she needed now was a cold.

'Monsieur Bertrand, please tell me you aren't looking for me again.'

'I'm sorry. You are an important person, like a VIP,' he tried to joke.

'What's it this time?'

'Someone broke into a vacation home.'

'In Cancale?'

'Not far from here. Just around the corner basically.'

'Is that not part of your duties?' A sinking feeling crept up her throat. The Gendarmerie would never ask the Police Nationale for help for just a simple break in. There would be more behind this.

'In theory yes, but Capitaine Jenaud asked for you.' She

remembered the quiet, gaunt man who had been present during the meeting. The Police Nationale was normally only involved in crimes which happened in bigger cities while the Gendarmerie cared for peace and quiet in the provinces. Cancale was definitely part of the province.

'Can I change before?' she asked even though she already knew the answer.

'Capitaine Jenaud was clear: It's urgent.'

'How did you know where I would be?'

'Madame Rosalie was so kind as to inform me.'

Sandrine made a mental note. She would have to talk to Rosalie about this. She would very much prefer it if Rosalie did not tell everyone who asked where she was going. Otherwise, she could wave goodbye to all her free evenings.

The gendarme stopped in the Rue du Chatry, a little street above the youth hostel which offered a wonderful view over the beach and the harbour with its boats. He parked opposite a two-story building. Several police cars had already arrived and secured the area. A lot of drama for a break-in, was her first thought. A bad feeling crawled up the back of her neck. Her assistant was already here. Adel Azarou was giving instructions to two uniformed officers. When he noticed her, he came over.

'Why are we being called to a break-in?'

'It's connected to our case. Follow me.' Without further explanation he entered the house and Sandrine trailed after him. Whatever was waiting for them, certainly would not be a pleasant surprise.

He held the door open for her. The apartment was furnished very simply and with a focus on convenience. There was no personal touch to be found, no bookshelves, and the pictures on the walls were cheap prints depicting the surrounding landscape. A vacation home, she thought. The owner isn't living here, but probably in Rennes or Paris.

'We have to go upstairs.' The brigadier interrupted her thoughts. Reluctantly she ascended the stairs.

At the door to the bedroom, she stopped. A man was lying on the bed, staring up at the ceiling with dead eyes. Blood from a wound in his chest was soaking the white sheets. It dripped down the bedframe and onto the wooden floor. It was Daniel Morvan.

Her stomach cramped. She took a few slow breaths until she calmed down. What she could not calm was her conscience. She should not have let him go while it was still unclear if the murderer was also looking for him. Her gut had screamed at her that he knew more than he had told them, but she had decided to ignore it. She had shied away from the fight with de Chezac. She had run away like a coward and now the young man had paid with his life for it. It's not your fault, she tried to convince herself. Think only about the crime scene. Find his murderer, you owe Daniel that much.

She entered the room and stepped in front of the bed. He must have come here on his motorbike. He was wearing leather clothing and a pair of old, worn boots. His helmet was on a nearby chair. She looked around. The room was as simple as the others had been below. Everything was in its place. There had not been a fight here. The perpetrator had either surprised him, or they had known each other, and Daniel had trusted him or her.

'How did the marksman enter?' she asked Azarou.

'Neither the entrance nor the backdoor have been broken open. The windows were locked and aren't damaged. He must have had a key or Daniel let him in,' the brigadier informed her. 'There's a backpack with groceries in the kitchen. It looks like he planned on staying here for a while. But why? Inès contacted him today so he could collect his boots. He knew he wasn't a suspect anymore.'

Sandrine pulled the plastic covers over her shoes and

stepped closer to the bed. She kneeled down, careful not to touch the pool of blood. Daniel Morvan was dressed in the same clothes he had been wearing in the commissariat. It did not look like he had been to his home or the campsite to change.

'He was scared and wanted to hide here.'

'But what or whom was he scared of?' Adel squatted next to her. 'The guys who beat up Treville are behind bars.'

'I assume he knew Isabelle's murderer and thought he would be the next target.'

'If he had told us the truth he wouldn't be lying here now.'

'You had on-call duty?' She made sure.

'Yes.'

'Make sure that Paris doesn't steal this body from us too.' She rose and looked down at Daniel Morvan. She bit her lower lip until it hurt. She had an inkling who had left a message on her answering machine. Most likely it would not have helped; judging from the clotting of the blood, he had been dead for more than two hours, but that did not quieten her conscience. 'Damn,' she hissed out and kicked the bedframe in fury.

Azarou looked at her in silence.

'Let's leave the crime scene to the forensic experts,' she decided. 'Send someone to fetch me tomorrow morning.'

'Consider it done.'

Her quick steps echoed from the wooden floor. She had to get out of there as fast as possible.

'Shall I give you a ride home?' Bertrand offered.

'No, it's not far and I prefer to walk.'

Sandrine started jogging. The air had cooled down, but it did nothing to soothe the hot anger bubbling inside her. She was angry at the narcissistic prosecutor from Paris, but also at herself as she had put her head in the sand. In this case she hated to be right. If she had stayed on the investigation, Daniel Morvan might still be alive.

. . .

The sun shone through the window, and the rays left a painful sting in her eyes. Sandrine lifted herself up. Pain shot through her head. With a sorry groan she sunk back into the pillows. Her tongue felt like an old, dusty cloth that had just been used to wipe a blackboard, and her stomach twitched in cramps. Damn. She had only needed one strong drink after the crime scene, but clearly more had followed. Definitely more than had been good for her. She remembered only finding wine in the house and so she had driven to Saint-Malo. She was still wearing her workout clothes. Only the shoes she must have taken off. Slowly her memory returned. After a few drinks she had decided to go to the gym and get rid of her frustration.

The alarm rang and she covered her ears with her hands. That thing was just too loud on a morning like this. She threw a pillow at the clock and sat up again. Adel Azarou would pick her up very soon, and she had to look halfway presentable.

'Come on,' she tried to motivate herself. For a moment, she stayed sitting on the bed until the dizziness and the pulsing headache abated a bit. At least she had remembered to put a bowl next to the bed in case she got sick. *I couldn't have been that drunk.*

In front of the bathroom mirror she stopped in surprise. On her cheek spread a purple bruise. She patted it with her fingertips and sharply pulled in the air between her teeth. *I must have fallen or run into something.* The next quarter hour she spent in the shower and scrubbing the terrible taste from her mouth. She kept adjusting the shower from hot to cold until her spirit returned. First a double, or triple espresso. As much as fits in the cup. And two aspirin. She wrapped the towel around herself and climbed down the steep stairs. One hand she kept clamped around the rail. Dishes rattled and Sandrine froze. An intruder. She looked around for a weapon. A baseball bat was close to the door, but she would not be able to get there undetected.

'Already up?' someone called.

'Who's there?'

Steps approached, and a man came into her view. Léon, the owner of the Équinoxe.

'It's me. Who else?'

'What are you doing in my house?' She held tight to the towel while accessing him with suspicion. She could not remember being in his club yesterday.

'Making breakfast, to be precise.' He stretched and looked up at her. 'Nice outfit.'

'I'll be down in a second.' She forced herself to walk up the stairs and pretend that everything was alright. Her mind was racing to fit the missing puzzle pieces into the mess that was last night's memory.

The duvet was untouched apart from the side she had slept on. At least I didn't drink enough to invite him up here. Sandrine let out a sigh of relief. She took underwear, jeans and a dark sweater from her wardrobe. It would be good enough for the office.

She went down into the kitchen and found Léon at the table. A plate with an omelette was ready at her place and coffee dripped from the machine into a cup. Someone had peeled some fruits and arranged them on a plate. On the sofa she spotted a pile of blankets and a pillow. He slept here?

'I thought a solid breakfast would be best this morning.' He stood up to pour muesli and milk into a bowl.

When did I go shopping? Yesterday a mouse would have starved in her kitchen. There were very good reasons that Rosalie normally brought food when she visited.

'Where did all of this come from?'

'I borrowed it from your neighbour. A very nice woman. You don't seem to enjoy keeping supplies and the shops were already closed.'

'You went to Rosalie?' Her friend would not give her a quiet minute until she learned every detail about the guy. It would be hard to explain that all she knew was his first name, where he worked and where he trained. Even for her that was not much. She fell onto the chair and pushed the plate to the side. Looking at the food made her stomach somersault.

'She helped me carry you up the stairs. This morning she brought over everything for breakfast. A very nice landlady.' He was right about 'nice', and she did not have the energy to correct his assumption.

'Why did you bring me home?'

'I couldn't let you drive like that.'

'And where did we meet?' she asked quietly. It was embarrassing to have to admit that she remembered nothing.

'You turned up in the studio slightly drunk, insulted Lilou and then got into the ring with her.'

'Wow. The tall one.' She touched the bruise on her cheek. So, this was a present from her.

'Yup. That one.' A grin stretched the corners of his mouth. Léon rose and got the coffee from the machine. 'This should help. The fridge is empty, but your coffee stack is big enough to last for another year. Maybe you should work on your priorities.'

The memories were trickling back into her brain. The woman had laughed at her. Yesterday, that had clearly been more than Sandrine could bear. She looked down at herself. Lilou took part in the Brittany Championships. Of course she had had no chance against her, and would have expected more bruises.

'All in the right place. I wasn't that bad then.'

'Well, considering you had a lot of alcohol in your blood you were quite aggressive. No idea what it was that you had to get out of your system, but you gave your all.'

'Is she still alive?'

Léon laughed. 'I think she is doing better than you. We had

to drag you out of the ring, three strong men. I had no idea what curse words you knew. Might have learned a few.' He searched inside his jacket pocket and produced her car keys. 'The Citroën is parked in front of the gym. I think you might get a fine for false parking, but I am sure you can talk to your colleagues should that happen.'

'I'll get it later.'

'Take enough time to get the alcohol out of your blood. If they check you that wouldn't look too good.'

'Since when are we so familiar with each other?' she asked. Was there more that she should know?

'Since I got your drunk behind out of the ring, saved you from a beating by doing that, drove you home and put a bowl in front of your bed. I think that's enough to connect people.'

'Okay, all good. What else did I do?'

He pushed the plate with the omelette back in front of her. 'I think that was it. No idea how life is in Paris, but here in the provinces this is normally enough to fill one evening.'

She lifted the coffee to her lips and savoured it. Hot and bitter, the way she liked it best.

'I made the omelette after the recipe from the Mère Poulard in Saint-Michel. That way it gets especially thick and airy.'

'Thanks for all the work, but I don't feel like it.'

Sandrine stood up, placed the empty coffee cup back under the machine and took two aspirin from a box on the counter. She didn't think she had put them there. The man thinks of everything.

'You don't normally drink, do you?'

'Seldom. Why do you think that?' She took the two pills with a big gulp of water.

'You can't hold your liquor and the aspirin is about to expire.'

She looked at the packaging. He was right. 'You should work for the police.'

'I would prefer not to. Would have to deal with rotten people all day.'

'It's not that bad.' She returned with the coffee. 'Aren't you one of the rotten people as the owner of a club?'

'Not at all,' he answered with a smirk. 'Who is this Prosecutor de Chezac and what has he done to you that makes you go for the bottle?'

She rested her chin on both hands and let her eyes wander to the window. The corpse of Daniel Morvan reappeared in her memory. He had known something that no one was supposed to find out. If she had kept him under arrest and had checked the answering machine, he might still be alive. She had let him go though. And now he was dead, and she had no idea what he had wanted to tell her.

'It's connected to the case,' she said and took a sip of coffee.

A car drove down the gravelled street and parked in front of her apartment. It was Azarou's white Peugeot. She shook her head as if that would help banish the thoughts about the dead man from her brain. 'Thank you for bringing me home, but I have to go. Have to take care of rotten people.'

'Then until the next time.'

'There won't be a next time,' she replied. 'I already fulfilled my alcohol quota for this year.'

'I meant at the gym or the club.'

'We'll see.'

The doorbell chimed. He put the empty bowl in the sink while Sandrine opened the door for Adel.

Léon said goodbye and climbed into a Jeep which was also parked in front of her house.

The brigadier looked after him until he had turned the first corner.

'A friend?'

'An acquaintance.'

He waited at the door for her to get her jacket.

'You don't look too good today,' he noted.
'I had a shit night.'
'Same here. The boy's death was hard on me.'
'Then let's start looking for his murderer. That's all we can do.'

Chapter 6

The Morvan Family

Inès Boni had gathered the team and reserved the meeting room for Sandrine. The whiteboard was still standing where they had left it, though someone had cleaned it in the meantime. From the car Sandrine had listened to her answering machine through her phone. Last night she had been in too much turmoil and had not wanted to listen to it in front of Léon. The call had been made at 1pm and was from Daniel, as she had feared. His voice had been shaking.

'I have to talk to you. It's about Charles. Please.'

That was all he had said. If I had listened to the damned answering machine, he might still be alive. She stopped for a breath before entering the meeting room. No, he would still have been murdered.

'The second murder in just a few days. I didn't think this possible here.' These were the words with which Commissaire Matisse greeted her. He looked like he had not slept much and had already spent several hours in the office.

'Is the case ours again?'

'Of course. The two guys of Thierry's have the best alibis one could wish for. They are in prison and watched by de

Chezac. That means his theory is ready for the bin. The case of Daniel Morvan is definitely ours.'

'And Prosecutor Lagarde?'

'He will not annoy us. After he got himself celebrated by the media without having anything he will now lie low for a while, or at least be quiet until we can find proof.' He threw a look at the empty whiteboard. 'The case of Isabelle Deschamps still belongs to de Chezac, but only administratively. I assume, though, that he will not interfere if we keep investigating.'

'He will be happy to be rid of the case. So far, he has performed rather lousily, and that's bad for his career.'

'You are convinced that it's the same perpetrator?'

'I am quite certain, but that doesn't mean we can ignore other evidence.'

Capitaine Jenaud, Luc Poutin and Renard Dubois sat at the table. Each of them had a cup of coffee in front of them. Poutin smelled as if he had spent the night smoking one cigarette after the other. Inès, Azarou and Jean Claude Mazet entered through the door and found their seats. With that all were present.

Sandrine fixed once again the picture of Isabelle Deschamps on the whiteboard, and next to it one of Daniel Morvan.

'Two deaths in three days. The method points at one and the same perpetrator though we don't want to be too sure of that.'

'Who else would it have been if not the same person?' Poutin threw in.

'It could be possible that it was another man of Thierry's gang who wanted to give an alibi to his colleagues. Maybe Lago and Gradel were looking for something in the mobile home but couldn't find it. We don't know what they were searching for. It seems to be important enough though to justify a murder. That's why I find it plausible that there might be a third member of Kouame's gang involved.' Sandrine paused. 'But I agree with you, Poutin, chances are high that it's the same person.' She circled the pictures with a marker. 'What do we know at the moment?'

'Both victims died from a single shot into the chest,' said Azarou.

Inès spoke up. 'Doctor Hervé confirmed the cause of death and gave a timeframe between 3pm and 4pm. The results of the autopsy arrive tomorrow.'

Daniel had left the message on her answering machine two hours earlier. He had already been dead when she had arrived home. She would not have been able to save him. Why didn't he call here in the office where he would have been able to find me? He must have panicked or had suspicions against someone in the office. Sandrine noted the time of death on the board. 'I need a complete Tox screen,' she told Inès. 'With a comparison to the pills we found with Isabelle Deschamps. If the perpetrator numbed him before murdering him, it would tell us a lot about their relationship.'

'The bullet is from the same weapon.'

'Really? That was surprisingly fast.'

Jean Claude Mazet waved a sheet of paper. 'We got the bullet from Doctor Hervé last night and compared it with the projectile which murdered Isabelle Deschamps. The grooves are identical.'

'That makes the theory of it being the same murderer more plausible,' Poutin said.

'Any other news from forensics?' she asked Jean Claude Mazet.

'The motorbike boots which the victim was wearing fit to the prints on the crime scene. A crack runs over the right shoe, so it's without a doubt that he was close to the corpse on the night of her murder.'

'Poutin, did you find out where Daniel bought his new boots on Monday morning?'

'No, we were told it wasn't important anymore. Now that

he's dead it wouldn't help us either.' The man shrugged his shoulders. Sandrine's opinion of him sank with every word that fell from his mouth.

'Start searching again. I don't just want to know where and when he bought them but also who paid for them and if he was alone. If a third person was involved, he or she must have been very keen to keep him out of all of this. The question is why.'

'There are only two shops that are possible,' Dubois said. Poutin threw an annoyed look at his colleague.

'Let's sum up. The victims were shot with the same weapon. We know that Daniel was at the path around the time of the crime.'

'Why should he have murdered her? I don't see a motive.' Azarou played with a loose thread on his cashmere sweater.

'We know for definite that he was at the crime scene. We have no indication that it was him who murdered her,' she clarified.

'What else would he have been doing at that time in the area?' Poutin looked to Brigadier Dubois for support. 'In the middle of the night.'

The man was really getting on her nerves now. 'They were meeting in the alley. He wanted to leave Cancale with her. That seems a plausible cause for me.'

'He was there but didn't tell us about it. He even denied being there. All of this makes him look very suspicious.' Poutin wasn't letting the topic go. It was like he wanted to make Daniel the murderer.

'The corpse was moved,' Adel Azarou threw into the discussion. 'From the findings we can conclude that she fell backwards down the cliff and bled to death. It's for certain.' He looked at Jean Claude Mazet who nodded his agreement. 'Daniel was in the alley to pick her up. Maybe he lied to us and went looking for her after she broke his heart. This way he might have found her, pulled her out of the bushes and leaned her against the wall. It's a position with more dignity than lying on the ground. Wouldn't you do the same thing for a person you are close to?'

'Sounds plausible to me.' She supported her assistant's theory. 'He didn't inform the police. He was either scared of the real murderer, or he was scared to become one of the suspects. Maybe he recognised the murderer and wanted to protect him.'

'And who do you think it could be?' Commissaire Matisse straightened and looked at her with curiosity.

'The circle of suspects is tightening. Thierry Kouame is still part of it. It is possible that he is the third person who wants to finish the hunt for the mystery book. That he suddenly appeared is definitely not a coincidence. Apart from that all our clues lead to the Hotel La Baie or to the campsite on which the victims lived. We should have a thorough look around these places.'

'The Gendarmerie of Cancale has informed Daniel's family,' Capitaine Jenaud told them.

'We will meet them this morning.' She wanted to find out why Madame Morvan had lied to her when she had claimed that she did not know Isabelle Deschamps.

'Monsieur Mazet, please keep working on restoring the memory card and put the lab in Rennes under pressure. Maybe something from the phone can be saved. Inès, I need all the connection data of Isabelle, the Morvans, Kouame and the Trevilles.'

'I already sent out the requests. Lagarde has presented them to the judge. I don't think that there will be any problems, but it might take a few days.'

'We will exert some pressure,' said Commissaire Matisse. 'I am certain that the mayors of Cancale and Saint-Malo are on Lagarde's heels. Two murders in one week bring our little area into the focus of the media. Very bad for tourism.

'Inès, did you find out anything about the pictures in the newspaper?'

'Not yet. They still do their best to not let out any information. Hopefully the second murder will make them think.'

'Keep on it.'

Sandrine scanned through the assembled group. 'Questions?' No one said anything. 'Then let's get to work.' The members of the group rose and left the meeting room, which had from now on become the centre of the investigation. In the end only Brigadier Azarou and Sandrine were left.

'Where do we start?'

'First in the La Baie,' she decided. 'We should let the family know the specifics of his death. They will also have to answer some uncomfortable questions.'

'Madame Morvan won't like that.' Azarou was clearly not looking forward to the talk.

'No one has to like my questions.'

They left the carpark of the office in Azarou's car.

'You have no fault in what happened to Daniel Morvan,' he suddenly said.

'Why should I think that?'

'Until now I haven't seen you touch a drop of alcohol. This morning you had an evil hangover though.' He looked at her. 'And you looked like you had run against a wall.'

'That's not hard to see.'

She fell silent and let her gaze drift out of the window. He had hit the mark. She was feeling guilty.

'He might still be alive if I had ordered him to stay in the commissariat during the night,' she said.

'You acted according to the rules.'

'De Chezac took the investigation from me, and I didn't even open my mouth, didn't fight. That was a big mistake.'

'The Prosecutors Office handed over the case. Not us.'

'It was obvious that Lagarde was accusing the wrong people,

and I didn't even try to convince him otherwise or stop the process.'

As she spoke, it dawned on her that the prosecutor would have been more than happy to hand over the case. Whatever she would have done, no one would have really listened to her. The man had smelled a raise and promotion in helping his boss. Maybe even a move into the capital.

'What happened between you and de Chezac?'

Sandrine stayed quiet. It was a long story with heights, but many lows.

'Excuse me, it's none of my business.'

'No, it's your business too. We are partners in this case, and you have a right to know all relevant information.' She thought a moment about where best to start.

'For years young girls were vanishing in Paris. A few days would always pass between their disappearance and the appearances of their corpses. We were working around the clock, but we couldn't find anything. The perpetrator was working very methodically and carefully. To our luck one of the victims managed to escape. Her description of the perpetrator was good enough to justify a suspicion which I had had for a while. The man was part of the political elite. He was rich and influential. I got too close to him, and he flexed his muscles. I was taken off the case and assigned to another one. A case so easy that every beginner could have solved it.'

'Who took the case from you? Was it de Chezac?'

Sandrine nodded. 'Back then I didn't let him intimidate me, and I stayed on the guy. He mocked me and continued as if nothing had happened. He sent me the necklace of his last victim. He knew he was safe and that I couldn't reach him.'

He looked over at her for a moment while driving the car along the empty country road.

'Then I made a fatal mistake.'

'What?'

'I entered his manor to look for evidence.' She laughed bitterly. 'The police caught me. He had been waiting for me.'

'And they didn't directly fire you?'

'That was too easy for him. He wanted to see me thrash in his net so that he could gloat over my defeat. He didn't file charges. De Chezac was presenting everything to the Prosecutors Office. They wanted a direct degradation and suspension, which is what happened in the end.'

'That's why our files still said Capitaine Perrot.'

'That's over. My notice is written and on Matisse's desk.'

'You're giving up?'

'I was naïve and thought the police were there to find criminals and bring them to justice. Then I learned about the politics, and the lines between good and bad blurred together. Once you aren't able to clearly distinguish the two it's time to leave.'

'You don't seem the type to just give up.'

'Thank you, but I fear I have to disappoint. This will be my last case. Afterwards I am out of the game.'

The rest of the drive was silent until they reached the port of Cancale.

They crossed the street and entered the restaurant of the La Baie. The last hotel guests were just finishing their breakfast and leaving the room. A waiter was tidying up the plates and wiping the tables.

Madame Morvan stood behind the bar. Her hair was fastened up high on the back of her head, and she wore a simple black dress. It made her look even more strict, and her eyes were cold and piercing. She did not try to hide her displeasure towards the police.

'I am sorry for your loss, Madame Morvan,' said Sandrine while approaching the woman.

'You again? Do you not have enough work to do with the

investigation or do you have another ridiculous accusation that you want to hang on Daniel?'

'There were no accusations towards your son. He wasn't one of the suspects, only a witness. We let him know that.' She did not entertain the idea of them having falsely accused him. The woman was grieving her child. That she was bitter and searching for a scapegoat was normal.

'Sarah,' she called in the direction of the kitchen. Her daughter appeared shortly after. She too wore black under her apron. Her limp was more pronounced than the first time they had met. The young woman wiped the back of her hand over her red and swollen eyes. It looked like she had been crying only seconds ago.

'Lieutenant Perrot, Brigadier Azarou,' she greeted them and joined her mother behind the bar.

'Can you tell us who murdered him and why?' Florence Morvan started her own cross-examination. Sandrine knew exactly where this was supposed to go – she wanted to make the police look useless and incapable.

'We can't do that yet, but we are convinced that his death is connected to the murder of Isabelle Deschamps.'

Sarah pulled a tissue from her pocket and wiped tears from the corners of her eyes. Her mother braced herself with two hands flat on the counter and said, 'I've never heard that name. Who is that supposed to be?'

'In Cancale she went under the name Charlotte Corday.'

'Ah, that one,' she replied without any emotion. She clearly did not care in the slightest for Isabelle's death.

'Why did you not tell us that you knew the woman?'

'She was a ...' she paused as if to find the right words. 'She was an acquaintance of my son. Nothing more. We do not have any business with this type of person.'

'They were a bit closer than just acquaintances,' Brigadier Azarou noted.

'The slut was just out for his inheritance. She was pure poison, and he was like wax in her hands.'

'The hotel and the restaurant are doing very well. How come your son didn't work in the family business, but on Monsieur Treville's campsite?'

'Madame Treville's campsite,' she corrected the brigadier. 'The man is not worth anything. If he could sit in cafes all day and spend money he would.'

'Was there a problem between him and Daniel?' Sandrine asked.

'Not that I know of. Why would there be? He worked for a minimum wage.'

'He is ... he was very sensitive. Our father's death was very hard for him. He needed some time for himself. He would have returned to the hotel very soon,' Sarah explained. Her mother threw a derogatory look her way. She had either lost hope or thought her son had been useless.

'Your husband died last year?'

'Yes, at the end of March to be precise.'

'May I ask what the cause of death was?'

'I can't see why that would be interesting to you.' Her fingertips drummed on the polished wooden counter.

'He suffered from a weak heart. The stress of leading an establishment like the La Baie did not help his health,' Sarah explained. The bluntness of her mother seemed to embarrass her.

'What did you do after you left the commissariat with your brother?'

'Not much. We drove to the campsite where he stayed. Afterwards I went to the restaurant. The kitchen doesn't run itself.'

'Did he mention that he was scared of anything or anyone, or that he received threats?'

'Apart from the police?' Madame Morvan hissed.

'Maman.' Sarah admonished her mother before she could make another biting comment. 'No, he didn't mention anything like that. He came here in the afternoon to get a few things and some food, and after that I didn't see him again.'

'Can you imagine what would make him leave the campsite and go to that house?'

'Most likely he was looking for some calm and quiet. The death of the woman,' she looked at her mother as if to ask for permission, but Madame Morvan just pressed her lips into a tight line, 'shook him quite a bit. First his father and now this. I know you're only doing your job, but when he was suspected by the police it only made him more nervous.'

'I understand that.' Sandrine kept it to herself that Daniel had been near the crime scene. Maybe she would be able to use this information at a later moment.

'He definitely did not break in,' Madame Morvan said. 'I do not want to see anything like that in the newspapers. No member of our family is a criminal.'

'What else would you call it?' asked the brigadier.

The woman looked at him as if she was planning a murder. 'The house belongs to one of our guests. We send one of our maids to clean the house when he comes over for a weekend or has visitors.'

'Where are the keys kept?' Sandrine asked.

'In the box behind reception.' Sarah pointed at a metal box on the wall.

'So, he would have been able to take it anytime?'

'As I said, it wasn't a break-in,' Madame Morvan repeated. 'We are allowed to enter the house.'

A waitress began to arrange cutlery and prepare the tables for lunch.

'The restaurant is open?' Sandrine asked with genuine surprise.

'We have guests and reservations.' Madame Morvan looked

past her through the tall windows. The tide had pulled back the water and the fishermen's boats were resting on the wet sand. 'The La Baie is part of the harbour. As long as the harbour exists, we will be open.'

'Maman.'

She ignored her daughter and turned to Sandrine. 'The women of Cancale have learned to live with the cruel hand of destiny. La Houle was not just a harbour for crab and oyster fishers. The tall three-master ships, the Terre-Neuviers of the Newfoundland-ships spent the winter here. Since the end of the 16th century the men of Cancale left for the Grande Pêche in spring. The season to catch cod was until late summer. Many did not return from the arduous trip through foggy and dangerous seas. It was women who ran the farms, made money, raised children and buried them. They took care that there was food on the table.'

Sandrine had no problems imagining Madame Morvan in this role. She would clearly overcome every obstacle to care for her family, or the hotel. She was not so sure which of the two was closer to the woman's heart.

'I hope that was it. We have to prepare the restaurant and clean the rooms before the new guests arrive.'

'We will not take up more of your time. At least not today,' Sandrine said as a goodbye. She felt like the icy gaze of the woman was following her out of the hotel.

In the car, Sandrine called Inès.

'Could you find out who wrote the death certificate for Monsieur Morvan? I think it was Doctor Marais, the family's GP, but I'm not sure. It should be from March last year.'

She listened to the office manager before hanging up.

'We have a clue as to who sent the pictures of the crime scene,' she told Azarou. 'Inès is working on it.'

'What are we doing now?'

'You drive me to Saint-Malo, and I get my car.'

A grin spread over his face.

'Yes, you were right. I did have a bit too much to drink yesterday.'

'At least you had someone who was clever enough to take the keys from you and drive you home.' He started the motor and watched her. 'Your boyfriend. Admit it.'

'Not at all. He's really just an acquaintance from the gym.'

'Ah, I see,' he said, not sounding very convinced. 'And he stays overnight, of course.'

Half an hour later they stopped in the parking lot of the gym.

'Kickboxing and martial arts.' He looked at her with suspicion. 'Do I have to be scared?'

'Not at all. Last night I got a proper beating. So my skills can't be that good.'

'I thought you go running in your free time?'

'My parents always believed that it was more important for a girl to defend herself than to run away fast. That might have been because of their friends, too.'

'The same people who taught you how to break a lock?'

'No, that was Uncle Thomas.' What she knew about breaking in she had learned from him, and she was very thankful for the lesson. More than once this knowledge had helped her to solve a case. In the end it had also led to her suspension though. Everything had its light and dark sides.

'That's my car.'

'The little Citroën?' Now real surprise was written all over his face.

'Yes.'

'You want to drive around for the police in that?'

'Sure. We both fit in there.' And fifty kilos of potatoes and a barrel of wine, she remembered with a smile.

He turned towards her. 'I won't get in that thing. No chance. If you want to take that, why not use a horse cart?' He shook his head as if he had bitten into a lemon.

'Don't be so vain. It's a real French classic.'

'It can be a classic without me. I have a reputation to uphold.'

Most likely he was thinking about the jokes his colleagues would make if they saw him together with his boss in the little Citroën.

'We meet in two hours in the office. I've got something I need to take care of.'

She got out of his car, and Azarou raced off before she could even make it to her car.

She found Rosalie behind her laptop in the library.

'How's Commissaire Hugo Delacroix?'

'He's hunting a monster. Two, maybe three chapters, and he'll have him.' She closed the computer. 'What about your case?'

'I wish I could claim that it will be over in three chapters, but at the moment we are searching in the dark.'

'How?'

'It's like it always is, everyone lies. From Florence Morvan to César Treville, everyone has something to hide.'

'Isn't that the exciting thing about your work?' She beamed at Sandrine. Rosalie had a very rosy view of the life of every policeman or woman.

'More like the curse of my job.'

'Don't lie to yourself, you are loving this. You love to find out what people are hiding, from the smallest to the biggest dirty secret.'

'This is the real world, not a novel. But maybe you can help me to uncover some of the family secrets?'

'Happy to.' Rosalie snatched a madeleine from a bowl and took a bite.

'I can't figure out what is going on with Florence Morvan and how she plays into all of this. I feel like she is deeply involved in this case. However, we couldn't find anything to hold against her or even a motive that would explain anything. I am 100% certain that she knows more than we have been able to get out of her so far.'

'If someone was able to plan and execute the perfect homicide it would be her. She is as cold as ice. Ask her daughter if you don't believe me.' The rest of the madeleine vanished into her mouth, and she wiped her fingers on a tissue. 'This is what happens to you when fate is not kind.'

'The death of her husband?' Sandrine asked.

'There was nothing bad in Sebastian. No idea what he saw in Florence. I don't think that it was just the hotel and the money. He was a sentimental dreamer and a failed artist. I am not surprised that they think he had a drug problem.'

'What are people saying?'

'Cancale is such a small town. People are way too interested in what their neighbours are doing.'

'He died in March, didn't he?' Charles Carnas had vanished at the same time. 'She renovated the hotel after her husband's death?'

'Yes, but there was also her daughter's accident.'

'Sarah? I noticed she was walking with a slight limp.'

'It was a motorbike accident. She was driving with her brother, and a tractor didn't give way. The girl was in hospital for some time, and her knee never recovered entirely.'

'That must be very hard for her.'

'For Daniel too. First the accident with his sister, for which he blamed himself of course, and then his father's sudden death.

He left the hotel afterwards and moved to the campsite. No idea if he had any contact with his mother.'

'Where did the money for the renovation come from? The restaurant looks very elegant, and I am sure the rooms are also high class.'

'True. I assume they got a loan from the bank. The family has a very good reputation, and the hotel is in an excellent location with the view of the harbour and Mont-Saint-Michel. They also have a house between Cancale and Saint-Malo. That's quite a lot of money in property. Sarah is what you would call a good catch.'

'Does she have a boyfriend?'

'Not that I know of. She lives for her kitchen. I fear that she will turn out like her mother one day.'

'Can you tell me anything about the Trevilles?'

'No, sorry, I don't know anything about them. The wife seems to wear the pants in both the business and the relationship. He is one of those guys who lives well and fast. They say he runs after every skirt.' Rosalie lifted her hands. 'All just gossip from the neighbours. Most likely none of this is true.'

'Most likely.' She thought about the man in his rubber boots and overall. He did not seem like a womanizer. But then, what image people had of themselves did not have to equal reality.

'Let's get to the interesting stuff.' Rosalie leaned forward and established eye contact. 'Who was the handsome man who carried this drunk woman here last night?'

'Ah, that one.' She wanted to keep this topic as brief as possible. 'He's just someone I met at the gym.'

'That's one of those excuses that Commissaire Delacroix would slap in your face.'

'Those are just stories.'

'I write about life! And I know about life. A man who sleeps in the living room because he doesn't want to leave you alone during the night deserves to be more than just a quick adventure.'

'Adventure? There was no adventure. The guy is a barkeeper in a dodgy club and trains in the same studio as me. That's it.'

'If you say so,' she said with theatrical disappointment. 'If you aren't ready to admit it to yourself, I will give you some time.'

Sandrine sighed. She would have to come up with some story to calm her friend down.

'Why did you go on a drinking spree? That's not your style.'

'I had a really bad day and made lots of mistakes.'

The ringing of the telephone saved her from the embarrassment of having to give Rosalie every detail of her evening. It was Inès. Doctor Marais was waiting for her.

It was barely ten minutes from her house to the GP's clinic. The receptionist led her directly into one of the examination rooms.

Doctor Marais rose when she entered. The man was small and gaunt. He must have lost his hair years ago, and huge glasses balanced precariously on his nose. 'Your secretary informed me that you would like to speak to me. I can't imagine what I can help the police with.'

Sandrine showed him her badge and opened her jacket before sitting down. The man's eyes were glued to her gun. It was exactly what she wanted. She had to throw him off balance a bit, or he would just close up like one of Cancale's famous oysters. It had worked on Treville.

'It's about the death certificate of Monsieur Morvan.' She came straight to the point.

He sank into his chair and looked at her with raised eyebrows.

'I had nothing to do with Daniel Morvan's corpse. Shouldn't he be in the forensics department in Saint-Malo?'

'I am talking about Sebastian Morvan.'

The doctor froze. The blood drained from his face and gave him a waxen appearance.

'It has been over a year since I wrote the death certificate.'

'You gave heart failure as the cause of death, didn't you?' Her voice grew fast and hard.

'I ... I think so. As far as I can remember that is.'

'That's what's written on the certificate.'

'Then it will be correct.'

'Sebastian Morvan was an addict, wasn't he?' She pretty much shot the sentence at the doctor.

Doctor Marais wiped his forehead with a tissue.

'Why do you think that?'

'Is it true or not?' She did not give him a chance to wiggle out of the question.

'He had problems with his back. Maybe from time to time he took a painkiller more than he should have. Who doesn't do that? Is that a crime?'

'It is punishable to prescribe unneeded painkillers and falsify the death certificate once it goes wrong.'

'What do you think you are saying?' The man jumped up and audibly gasped for air. 'This conversation is finished.'

'As you wish.' Sandrine stood up and turned in a way that gave him another good look at her weapon. If possible, he turned even paler. She took her phone out of her pocket and held it towards him. 'I will now call Prosecutor Lagarde and request an exhumation. Forensics will know very quickly how his heart was.' A nerve under Doctor Marais' eye began to twitch wildly. 'I will give you one last chance to save your reputation and your license. You tell me why Sebastian Morvan really died, and I don't have to call the Prosecutor's Office. To dig up a corpse is always a nasty business, especially for the family.'

He stared at her like a mouse petrified by a snake. The little nerve kept twitching. *He only needs a little bit more.*

'Okay, if you refuse. It's your decision.'

She turned and headed for the door. Reaching for the handle, she called back, 'Sit down.'

He collapsed into his chair and Sandrine returned to the desk. She looked down at the man. 'I don't have time for chitchat so out with it.' *She had to keep up the pressure.*

'He was taking strong painkillers. I assume too many and too many times, but he didn't get them from me. I swear.'

'From whom did he get them?'

'I don't know. He would have bought them illegally. There's a market for everything.' Doctor Marais' voice was shaking. 'Poor Florence. She tried to not let it get to her but his addiction nearly led the hotel to its ruin. For the family it was probably a blessing when he expired, maybe for Sebastian too.'

'What was he taking?'

'Opioids. Next to his bed was an empty packet of Oxycodone. I assumed that he took an overdose on purpose. He couldn't live with the shame of having brought the hotel to its ruin. At least that was what was written in his goodbye letter.'

'You read it?'

'Sarah found the letter on his desk and read it. The poor girl had just been discharged from the hospital. It was she who found her father's body when she went to bring him breakfast. One can really pity the girl. It's a miracle how she works through everything that has happened to her.'

'Where's the letter now?'

'Florence burned it. She would never have admitted that someone from her family took their life.'

'Thank you, Doctor Marais.' She left the room. She had finally learned what she had wanted to know. 'Get your boss a strong coffee. He needs it,' she told the receptionist while leaving the clinic. *The drugs might be the connection to Charles*

Carnas. Her gut feeling told her that that was where she had to continue searching. This time she would listen.

'We have something interesting,' Azarou greeted her. 'Jean Claude's people saved some pictures from the memory card of the phone.' He handed her some copies. The woman whom she had only met as a lifeless shell was smiling at her, full of life. Clearly in high spirits, she was pointing at the naked man next to her in bed.

'They aren't very clear,' said the brigadier with a raised eyebrow, 'but it's easy to recognise César Treville. The two of them seemed to have been a lot closer than he told us.'

'Then we should go and talk to the unfaithful husband,' Sandrine decided. 'I am curious to hear what he has to tell us.' She took her car keys from her pocket.

'Don't even think about that,' he protested.

'About what?'

'We take my car. I have a reputation to uphold.'

'I would even let you drive. I'm sure you never had a car with a gearbox like this,' Sandrine offered.

'I pass.'

'Well, then we take your car.' She turned away and grinned. She did not mind having a chauffeur today. That way she would be able to think about the case without getting distracted by traffic. She felt like there was a little thing, some tiny detail, of which she had not fully grasped the significance yet. Something gnawed at her subconscious, but the more she thought about it the further it seemed to slip through her fingers. I will remember it, she hoped.

Azarou knocked at the reception's door. It was locked and the curtains drawn. Sandrine held her ear close to the glass. There was nothing but silence inside. The brigadier walked around the building. It looked like all the other mobile homes on the campsite.

'No one here,' he called. 'There's no car in the parking lot or behind the house.'

'You think he anticipated us visiting him again?'

'How could he know that?'

Sandrine stepped back and looked down the path to the mobile home which had been occupied by Isabelle Deschamps. The terrace had been framed with a white and red tape which read, 'Police Nationale' and a police seal was glued onto the door. Only when forensics gave the okay, would the house be open again.

The neighbours seemed to be unfazed by the development. Grey smoke rose from a barbeque and a man was turning sausages on a grill. His children were running after a ball, while his wife laid out the table. Perfect weather for a barbecue, Sandrine thought. She leaned her hip against the barrier. The brigadier called the number of the campsite. They could hear the phone ring inside reception. After the sixth or seventh ring the phone fell silent. The call must have been transferred to a mobile phone.

'Madame Treville,' she heard him say. He had found the owner. She repeated César Treville's story in her head once more. Everything he had said made sense, but still there was the feeling that she had missed something crucial.

'His wife has no idea where he might be. He's been gone since last night. She's coming here.' The brigadier leaned next to her. 'Do you think we have a third victim?'

'It's possible, but I think it's more likely that he left for a few days to get the police off his back.'

'Or his wife,' Azarou laughed. 'Maybe she has seen the pictures of her husband.'

'How stupid am I?!' Sandrine suddenly shouted and slapped her hand against her forehead.

The brigadier stared at her. 'You don't expect an answer, right?'

'Do you remember what César said? The two men surprised him at reception and dragged him along so that he could unlock the house.'

'True. There they kept beating him and searched the apartment. He said something about a book.'

'But he made a mistake, because he didn't want to tell us about the book. That's why I think it's true, that the two men were looking for it. The rest was a lie.'

'And you conclude that from which observations?'

'What Daniel told us didn't leave my head. Something didn't sound right, and now I know what it was.'

'Both sounded quite believable.'

'He returned with Isabelle from a trip to Cape Fréhel. From here they,' Sandrine held up her pointer and middle finger, 'saw two men heading in the direction of her mobile home. He didn't mention César Treville, only two of Kouame's men and that Isabelle panicked.'

'Treville must have been with them. His blood was on the kitchen bench in Isabelle's mobile home. We know that from forensics.'

'I believe Daniel. He had no reason to lie.'

'Why would César Treville lie to us about this?'

'Because that makes him suspicious. I am sure that he was already in the mobile home when the men arrived. The door was open, so he didn't have to unlock it for them.'

'What reason did he have to be there? Was he waiting for Isabelle?'

'On the contrary. He knew she was out with Daniel and was using the time to look around. He was searching for something.'

'Her phone? I can imagine that, as a "faithful" husband, he wasn't too pleased when she took pictures.'

'Don't be so cynical.'

'I'm sorry, but I can't stand men like that. Most likely she threatened to show the pictures to his wife if he wouldn't send her some money.'

'What do we know of Isabelle? She was the lover of Charles Carnas, a prostitute and a drug dealer. According to Kouame the two of them used to blackmail Isabelle's customers with pictures. Why would they break with an old habit?' She remembered Léon's statement. She had received money from time to time and had directly spent it on clothes, alcohol and drugs. On that evening she had thought that de Chezac had sponsored her in hiding, but she might have been wrong. It might have also been Treville. 'You are right. We can assume that she blackmailed him,' she said.

'So, he was looking for the phone or an USB?'

'The man didn't seem to be the brightest lamp, but even he should have known that the pictures would be saved on a cloud. It wouldn't have helped much to delete them from the phone. Moreover, who leaves their phone at home when going on a trip?'

'Maybe he learned by coincidence that she had signed in under a false name and wanted to see if he could find anything to blackmail her,' the brigadier guessed.

'She might have let something slip,' Sandrine agreed. 'It's possible that he knew about the book's existence from her first and not from Kouame's men. It would be valuable for him in two ways – he would have gotten rid of the person trying to blackmail him and would most likely have gotten a nice sum from Kouame. And then the two guys crossed his path and ruined his plans.'

'He's just an employee of his wife. She owns the campsite. I don't think he had a lot of money lying at his fingertips to pay for

Isabelle's silence,' Azarou thought out loud. 'You think it's possible that they met the night of her death for more money, but that she received something entirely different? That would explain why she didn't want Daniel there.'

'It's possible, but seems unlikely to me,' Sandrine replied. 'No one would have noticed if he gave her the money on the campsite. Why should she agree to a nightly meeting on the Brittany Coast Path? If someone invited me to that all alarm bells would ring.'

'She saw Thierry Kouame's men and didn't dare to enter the campsite again. She wanted to leave with Daniel that very night. Who would get the idea to look for her on a hiking path?'

'Sounds reasonable. It could have been like that.'

'There's Madame Treville.'

A slim woman with a flowery dress and her hair in a complicated updo walked out between two of the small houses. She had a mobile phone in her hand.

Sandrine introduced the brigadier and herself to the woman.

'We have a few more questions for your husband. Can you tell us where he can be found?'

'I tried to reach him, but his phone is turned off. What has he done? Is it about the slut in 335 again? She turned the heads of all the men with those short little dresses of hers. If you ask me ...' She did not finish the sentence, but it did not need much fantasy to guess at what she wanted to express. If she were to learn of her husband's affair with that woman, it would not end well for him. Understandable that he was hiding from her.

'We are investigating the two deaths.'

'I'm really sorry about Daniel. He was a nice guy who wouldn't hurt a fly. What a shame.' Lines drew over her face. 'I'm sure that woman has something to do with his death.'

'We don't have any indications for that,' Azarou tried to reassure her.

'Rubbish. I know an evil person when I see one.'

'Do you have any idea where your husband could be?'

'Why? It's not the first time that he's done something stupid and disappeared for a few days. Sooner or later, he will come crawling, but this time I will tell him something that he won't forget so fast.'

Sandrine had no trouble imagining that.

'How often does this happen?' the brigadier asked.

'Not a lot in the last few years. Happened most when he was after some woman.'

'When did you last see him?'

'Yesterday evening. Earlier that day, when I was in town, I heard what happened to Daniel. In the evening César and I talked about it briefly while watching TV, when suddenly he gets up and leaves. Then I hear the car start and he's gone.'

'Should your husband contact you, please let him know we are looking for him.'

'I will, but first I will tell him something else. If you want to send him to prison for a few days, you have my blessing.'

'We don't think that will be necessary.' Sandrine did not want the woman to warn her husband.

As soon as they were back in the car, Sandrine called the office.

'Inès, can you write out César Treville for a search?' She gave her a short description and the numberplate of the car. 'Is there any news?'

'Not really. Commissaire Matisse put some pressure on the newspaper, but Deborah Binet, the journalist who wrote the article, still refuses to give out the name of the person who sent the pictures.'

'I'm sure she paid a fair sum for them.' Azarou rubbed his thumb against his pointer finger as if he was counting money. 'But I cannot imagine that it was one of us.'

'Give me the woman's address. We'll visit her.'

'What's your plan?' Inès asked. 'She won't tell you the source either.'

'I can be incredibly friendly,' Sandrine said. 'I'm sure I can convince the journalist to be a tad more helpful.'

'If you want to, sure. I will arrange an interview with Deborah,' Inès suggested. 'She will be open to listening to me. We know each other from school.'

'The world is small,' mumbled Sandrine.

'Especially in Brittany,' replied the young woman.

'Please do that and call us as soon as you have a time and date. We are on the way to Saint-Malo.'

Inès called when they turned into the street of the commissariat. There was now a search for César Treville underway, and an appointment with the journalist had been made.

'To the old town,' Sandrine guided the brigadier. 'Madame Binet and I will meet for a coffee.'

They parked at the Quai Saint Vincent between the yacht harbour and the Grande Porte, the main gate of the medieval city wall.

Azarou unfastened his seatbelt.

'It's better if you stay here.'

'What's your plan? To hold the pistol straight up to her face?'

'Of course not. I will talk to the journalist woman to woman and that's it. If you come too, we will be two against one, and she will be even more on her guard.'

'And I just wait here?'

'Not at all. Inès sent us a list of bloggers who wrote about Isabelle's death. You can go through the articles and maybe find pictures resembling the ones from the newspaper. If Madame Binet keeps quiet, maybe we can find a lead that way.'

'Alright.' He leaned forward and grabbed the sleeve of her

jacket. 'You didn't lure the woman from her flat to go and rummage around without being noticed, did you?'

'I thought about it, but it won't be necessary. She will tell us who the pictures are from.'

'You think so?'

'One hundred per cent.' She got out of the car and marched in the direction of the city gate. Tourists were already milling in front of it, making it nearly impossible to get into the city without being in someone's pictures. Two round towers were guarding the entrance to the old town, barely leaving enough space to allow a mid-size car to pass. The crêperie in which they had decided to meet was situated in one of the typical five-story stone houses opposite the Best Western Hotel and the Grand Rue. A woman fitting the description she had received sat at one of the tables and watched the entrance. Sandrine went straight towards her.

'Lieutenant Perrot,' she introduced herself with her police ID. 'I assume you are Deborah Binet.'

'Correct.' The woman stood up and shook her hand before both sat down. The journalist could not be older than her mid-twenties. The case dress, the shining wedding band on her finger and her combed-back hair made her look more mature, which was probably exactly the intention of the outfit. At her age she was still at the beginning of her career. Sandrine assumed that the murder on the Brittany Coast Path was her first big story. She wondered why she had been assigned with it. Maybe the addition of the pictures had helped.

'Lieutenant Perrot, I'm very happy that you want to talk to me, but I have to say, if it's about naming my source for the pictures, you came a long way for nothing.'

'How are the sandwiches?' She avoided the topic.

'Not too bad. They are exactly how you would expect them to be in a tourist trap like Saint-Malo.'

Sandrine ordered a baguette with cheese and another one with grilled turkey, tomato, pepper and a salad for takeaway.

'Madame Binet, we are talking about murder.'

'I'm aware of that. Don't forget that I am reporting the whole affair.'

'The pictures you published might have been taken by the perpetrator.'

She wanted to answer but reconsidered. 'I can assure you that this is not the case.'

'You know the photographer?'

'That's a trick question I cannot answer.' The woman smiled. She seemed very pleased that she had recognized the trap and evaded it.

Or maybe she is congratulating herself for knowing more than the police. She must assume we think it was a man.

'I am sorry.' Sandrine pulled out her phone. 'In my job there are no real breaks. One message and I'll turn it off.'

'It's the same for me. Do your work.'

She typed a message and pressed send. Afterwards she let the journalist see that she'd switched off the phone.

'Now we get a quarter of an hour,' she said and pushed her phone into her jacket pocket.

'What can you tell me about Daniel Morvan? Are the deaths connected? He was one of the suspects in the investigation, wasn't he? Did he take his own life because he couldn't live with the guilt?'

Deborah Binet was pulling out the cliché of the repentant murderer. It spoke of her lacking experience with reporting criminal cases. People who had murdered pretty much never took their own lives. Normally they handed themselves in to the police or made a stupid mistake which led to them being discovered.

'There will be a press conference with Commissaire Matisse tomorrow. There they will give you all the news.'

'Don't forget, you asked for this meeting. It would be nice if you make a step towards me. My readers are waiting for updates. Or do you want me to use gossip and speculations?'

'I will make a suggestion.' She looked around as if she was making sure that no one was listening to them. The journalist leaned forward. She was expecting whispered secrets.

'What do I get in return?' Sandrine asked, dropping her voice.

'I won't give you the name of my source.'

'I understand. We are more interested in the perpetrator than the photographer. However, the pictures might help us in our investigation. They were taken before the corpse was discovered. Maybe our criminal technicians can find clues which the rain washed away later.'

'That seems possible to me. Maybe even likely. It was a very strong thunderstorm that night.' The journalist tried to make her wares more attractive, and Sandrine joined the game.

'My offer.' She looked around again. 'You send me the pictures. Of course, you don't have to include the name of the photographer. I, in return, will inform you as soon as we apprehend the murderer.'

Deborah Binet leaned back and stirred her coffee. She took a moment to think about the offer. Sandrine was sure that she would take the bait. To be the first one to report the arrest of a murderer would catapult her career forward. Instead of writing about the yearly meeting of the pigeon-breeders or the opening of a kindergarten, exciting stories would land on her desk. It was tempting. She could see in the woman's greedy eyes that she had swallowed bait and hook.

'Only the pictures. No sources.'

'Of course,' Sandrine reassured her. 'I assume that you already changed or deleted the meta-data which makes tracking impossible.'

The woman nodded and Sandrine switched on her phone. 'I will wait one hour. Afterwards the deal is null. I vouch for my word. You will be the first one who will learn of the murderer's arrest.'

'I will think about it.'

'One hour,' she repeated for the journalist. She stood up and went to the counter. The waiter handed her two paper bags containing her sandwiches and salad. From the corner of her eye, she watched the woman stirring her coffee. Without another look, she left the crêperie.

Sandrine joined Azarou in the car.

'Did you get bored?' she asked with sympathy.

He lifted his smartphone and rolled his eyes. 'I haven't seen that much rubbish in quite a while.'

Her phone rang. It was the person she had sent a message to in the crêperie – Inès.

'Thank you. That will help.'

She finished the call and unwrapped one of the baguettes. The other one she gave to the brigadier.

'One with cheese. I hope that's okay.'

'Definitely better than one with ham,' he said with a smile. 'How did you manage with the journalist?'

'We'll find out soon. First, show me the blogs written about our case.'

'Most don't report anything. It's bad for the general vibe. Only one was interesting because it posted lots of pictures from Cancale and the Pointe du Grouin. There weren't many typos either.' He showed her the smartphone. 'I will try to identify her.'

'"Facts and Trends from the Emerald Coast. Emely P.",' she read. '"News, Gossip and Viral Makeup."'

'I don't think that Emely P. will help us.'

'She's my plan B.'

Her phone vibrated. It was the photos of the crime scene from Deborah Binet.

'Plan A worked.' She turned to Azarou and smiled. 'Your charming colleague has bewitched the journalist.'

'She gave you the name? I would be very impressed if you managed that.'

'First, we have to talk to the residents again.'

'We will be hard pressed to learn anything new there.'

'Depends for what you are casting your rod. It's crucial to use the right bait for the right fish.' She placed the baguette on the dashboard of the car. 'First, I'll get us a coffee. There's a stand there.'

'No chance. You already paid for the sandwiches, so the coffee is on me.'

They walked through the front garden of the Tanguy family home. She had no intention of ringing the doorbell and stood on the flagstones between the flowerbeds. Madame Tanguy stepped up to the window and Sandrine gestured for her to come to the door. Shortly afterwards, she opened the front door and came outside. Her bathrobe was covered in stains and wet on the left shoulder. Most likely she had just fed the baby and it had not quite gone to plan. Her hair was hanging to her shoulders in greasy strands, and her feet were spilling out of well-worn slippers. Under her bathrobe one could see wide jogging trousers. With the baby monitor still in hand, she sank down on the stairs.

'Did you catch the murderer?' It sounded more like she was trying to make polite conversation than actual interest.

'The baby didn't sleep through last night?' Azarou asked.

'Nothing to be done about that. He wakes up from the smallest noises and it takes hours until he goes back to sleep.'

'That must be exhausting. One starts to fear that they never learn to fall asleep, but so far, every child has.' The brigadier sounded as if he knew what he was talking about. He had never mentioned a wife or a family. And I didn't ask. I barely know anything about him.

'I will lie down on the couch later. Nicolas will take care of the little one in the afternoon, and for that he gets a free evening with his pals. Unless he falls asleep next to me that is.'

'Did you remember anything that you didn't tell us yet? Sometimes memories only resurface after a while.'

'Sorry.' She straightened her bathrobe and wiped over the wet patch on her shoulder. 'Normally I'm very vain about how I look. A year ago, I would have never dared to come to the door looking like this, but now ...' She yawned and stretched her arms. 'I am only exhausted. Saturday night I slept deep though. Only the idiot on the motorbike woke me up.' She covered her mouth with her hand. 'Maybe I shouldn't say things like this. There's talk that he was murdered too.'

'He didn't act very considerately.' If something like this had happened to her, she would have probably insulted him more. Residents of Paris were definitely less friendly than the people of Brittany.

'Then we shall leave you to rest. I hope you have a quiet night.' Sandrine had not expected to learn anything new, but it had been worth a try.

'Thank you.'

Behind one of the top floor windows of the neighbouring house stood Carine Fortier who was watching what transpired. Sandrine waved at her. From the corner of her eye, she saw Madame Tanguy frown. She did not seem to like her neighbour much. Maybe she could recognise her older self in the woman and wished her life back.

'You should talk to her. Often I see light in her home office until the middle of the night.'

'Do you know what Carine Fortier is working on?'

'We don't talk a lot. As far as I know she studied something with journalism. It doesn't look like she has a normal day job though. Nicolas said she was writing blogs. I always wondered if that pays enough to live from. At least she inherited the house and doesn't have to pay rent.'

'Not my field of expertise either,' said Sandrine. She looked at her watch. 'We'll get going.'

'Make sure you catch the criminal soon. Then we can all sleep better.'

'We do our best,' Sandrine assured her.

They crossed the street and entered the garden in front of Carine Fortier's house. She opened the door for them before they had to ring. Again, they were not invited to enter. She was protecting her privacy.

'I am sorry that you had to come all this way for nothing,' she excused herself, as she had no new details for them either.

'It wasn't very likely that you would remember anything monumental, but it's part of our routine. Most people imagine an investigation like this as exciting because they watch too much TV.'

'I help whenever I can,' said Carine Fortier.

Sandrine supressed a sarcastic comment which normally would have slipped easily from her lips.

'There is a small thing that you could really help me with.'

'Yes?'

'When I left a crêperie in Saint-Malo this morning someone bumped into me, and my phone fell on the cobble stones. The camera lens broke into a thousand pieces.'

Carine Fortier expressed her sympathy.

'I need pictures from here in the direction of the Brittany Coast Path. Would you be so kind as to quickly take some for me on your smartphone and send them to me? Then we don't have to come over again.'

'As I said, I help wherever I can.' Carine Fortier produced a white iPhone from her pocket and took several pictures. Sandrine handed her a card with her number on it. It only took seconds for the pictures to appear on her screen.

'Thank you. You saved my day,' she said as a goodbye and they returned to the car.

'Do I need to know what that theatre was all about?' Azarou asked as they drove off.

'I am sure that Carine Fortier was the one who took the pictures of the crime scene.'

'Enlighten me, please.'

'The journalist is one of Inès' schoolfriends.'

'Everyone in the area is an acquaintance of hers.'

'The woman wore a wedding band. Have a guess what her maiden name was?'

'Fortier?'

'Quite a coincidence, isn't it?'

'To prove she took the pictures will be difficult.'

'It's as good as done. Carine Fortier and Deborah Binet have each sent me pictures on my phone. Every camera has pixel errors if you look closely enough. It will be an easy game for Jean Claude Mazet to find out if the pictures were taken with the same phone. If that's the case, we've got her. The woman must have withheld a few things.'

He looked over at her. 'Is there anyone who can keep a secret from you?'

'Unfortunately, yes. I barely know anything about you. How do you know things about babies? For someone who has children himself you work too much overtime.'

'I have three older, married sisters,' he said with a grin. 'We are a big family.'

'That explains many things. So, you are the baby of the family.'

'What's your plan?' He changed the topic. 'You want to bring the two of them to the commissariat because of obstruction of investigation?'

'I have the feeling that we can find out more if we are patient and dig a little deeper.'

'And how do we do that?'

'Organize Carine Fortier to be monitored.'

'For how long?'

'With all that I noticed a few hours should be enough. From late afternoon to midnight is enough.'

Azarou looked at her with suspicion. 'Did I miss something again?'

'You will think of it by yourself, I am sure.'

'Well, I will be surprised. Dubois will happily take on the monitoring as long as he can sleep all morning. He's quite the night owl.'

'No problem.' She had no trouble working with Renard Dubois. Had he suggested Luc Poutin she would have objected. The man was getting on her nerves. 'Any news concerning César Treville?' she asked.

'Not yet.'

'There's something you need to know.' She told him about Thierry Kouame's visit to her house.

'Do you believe him?'

'Like all good liars he hides his lies in a neat package of truths and half-truths. It's hard to look through them without knowing where to start. However, that his men didn't kill Isabelle makes sense to me. That she tried to blackmail him is also a possibility, even though I think it's suicide to make enemies with a man like that.'

'He could have shot her.'

'At the time of death he was in Paris. Our colleagues confirmed that.'

'What led him to Cancale at exactly that moment?'

'He claimed that his men had roughed up Isabelle's house to scare her. The longer I think about it the more certain I am that it is a lie. Of course, Isabelle might have tried to blackmail him with testifying against him, but in reality, it's all about this book he wants. Whatever is in it must be more threatening than Isabelle in court.'

'Maybe he's here to search for it himself.'

'That sounds plausible.'

'And the real estate business he talked about, all just decoy?'

'Maybe Inès can find out who the estate agent is he works with and what properties he's interested in. Most likely it has nothing to do with the case, but it can't hurt to find out as much as possible.'

'And what do we do?'

'We drive to my place, order pizza and then I leave the couch to you for a nap. My gut tells me we have a long night ahead of us and should sleep when we can.'

'We have to go.' Sandrine woke up Azarou who had done his best to make the couch as comfortable of a bed as possible even though he was too long for it. She had been too tense to sleep and had spent the waiting time with a big latte macchiato and Rosalie's newest book.

He sat up and yawned. 'What happened?'

'It's an hour until midnight. Dubois just called.' She put two cups of espresso on the table dividing the living room from the kitchen. 'Nicolas Tanguy left a while ago. Dubois is waiting in a side street and watching the house of Carine Fortier.'

'His wife told us. It's his free evening which he spends with his friends. What do you hope to achieve with the surveillance?'

He folded the woollen blanket he had slept under and laid it on the end of the sofa.

'Maybe it's a waste of time, but my gut tells me it could be an enlightening night. Before you start fluffing the pillows, you'd better have a coffee.'

The brigadier let his eyes wander through the living room. 'It's quite cosy in here.' He fluffed up his pillow and leaned it against the sofa's side rest. 'Why didn't Dubois follow Tanguy?'

'It's much more interesting to see where Carine Fortier will drive.'

'If she leaves the house at all. It's possible that Dubois will spend his night there for nothing.' He stood up to join her at the table.

'Thank you,' he said and took one of the cups. He looked at the kitchen. She assumed that he was looking for saucers. Azarou was the dream of every mother-in-law, as well as an efficient police officer. She could have been far worse off with her assistant. It was a shame that they would only work together for such a short time.

'It's just a feeling really. Should I be wrong Dubois' next Pastis goes on my bill.'

'He would be quite happy about that.' He drank his coffee and left the cup in the sink. 'Then we should get going and take over.'

The Rue du Port Mer, in which Carine Fortier lived, was a dead end. Azarou parked in a small side street above the house. They watched Renard Dubois as he drove off.

'You would prefer to handle this differently?' Sandrine asked the brigadier.

'I don't have your experience.' He evaded the question.

'What would you do? Tell me.'

'We have a few people on our list which are much fishier than Fortier.'

'Treville?'

'Exactly. He wanted to get rid of his affair.'

'It's one possibility. Maybe he found the weapon in Isabelle's home,' Sandrine mused.

'Or his wife lied to us and knew of her husband fooling around. I would trust her to go to lengths like this.'

'I trust her to play out a huge scene and maybe even start a fistfight with another woman, but I don't think she would get a weapon, lure her to an abandoned place and shoot her.'

'Or this Kouame might have had another man follow Isabelle. We can track the weapon back to his gang,' Azarou suggested.

'Only to Charles Carnas. We are missing the connection to Kouame. Maybe Carnas gave the weapon to Isabelle. She was his girlfriend after all. She was scared and took the gun along to the meeting. The perpetrator took it from her and shot her.'

'Florence Morvan. I feel like she's deeply involved in all of this.'

'Yes, but we can't reach her with vague suspicions and accusations. As long as we don't have anything precise, we will bounce off her like water on a Teflon pan.'

'What motive could Fortier have?' Azarou asked.

'I don't assume that she has committed the murder, but she's hiding something, and I can't stand that. Tonight, we will find out what this is all about. We will see if it helps us at all, and until then the Gendarmerie will search for César Treville.'

'She's leaving.'

A motion sensor switched on a lamp in front of the entrance door. It was easy to recognise Carine Fortier in the bright light. She locked the door and went to her Peugeot 206. Sandrine crouched down low when she drove past them. As soon as she turned onto the country road, Azarou started the car and followed her.

'Don't lose her.'

'I'll keep my distance so she doesn't notice us. There isn't much traffic at this hour.'

Carine Fortier did not drive as if she suspected she was being followed. She did not make any unexpected turns, stopped at red lights, and waited her time at the roundabouts. After ten minutes she parked in front of a country inn.

'Looks like she's meeting someone.'

'And I know whom.' Sandrine pointed at the car of Nicolas Tanguy.

'The good father.' Azarou whistled quietly. 'I didn't think that of him.'

'That's how you can be wrong.'

'The two are having an affair and meet in secret in a hotel. I don't like saying it, but it's nothing unusual. Not even here in the countryside.'

'Let me have my fun.'

'What's your plan? To look through the window?'

'Maybe a little bit more,' she chuckled. 'I have a hidden trump in my hand.'

'But you won't tell me what it is, right?'

'I don't want to ruin your surprise.' A light was switched on on the top floor. Shadows were moving behind the curtains. 'We give them a quarter of an hour and then we act. You can call two police cars, but without sirens or blue light.'

'Can I see your ID?'

Sandrine pulled out her card and showed it to the receptionist.

'What room did Monsieur Tanguy rent?'

'The married couple Tanguy is in room 123. Shall I let them

know that you are coming?' He reached for the phone, but Sandrine waved his offer away.

'That won't be necessary, but please give us a key in case he doesn't want to open the door. I don't want any furniture to get scratched.'

'Do you have a judicial approval?'

'If there's imminent danger, I don't need one.' That was true, but she was relieved that the man did not ask what danger she was talking about.

He wrote several numbers on a piece of paper and handed it to her.

'You can get inside with the code. I would prefer it if you didn't make too much noise. We don't want to inconvenience any other guests.'

'I will do my best.' She paused. 'There might be problems with the bill later.'

'Don't worry about that. With couples arriving separately we insist that they leave their credit card details for the mini bar.'

'Very clever.'

The man beamed at her. Either he enjoyed her praise, or he was just thankful to get his boring routine mixed up a bit.

Sandrine put her ear against the door of the room. 'I think we came at the right time.'

She knocked at the door. 'Please open up, Monsieur Tanguy. This is the police.'

'We have the code,' Azarou said and handed her the paper from the receptionist.

'That one is only for emergencies. I am not a voyeur and the man is too much of a coward to flee through the window. He will open,' said Sandrine.

'Is there a problem?' Nicolas Tanguy called from inside.

'Please open the door.'

A bed creaked and they could hear feet patting quickly over the floor. She knocked again. The man opened the door a crack, the security chain still secured. He wore trousers and a t-shirt, but no socks and his hair looked dishevelled.

'You?' His eyes widened. 'Can't you leave me alone? I told you everything I know.'

'We have a few questions.'

'Can't they wait until tomorrow?'

'Yes, they could. You are right. We were just in the area and saw your car in front of the hotel.' She turned towards the brigadier. 'I told you we should have driven to Madame Tanguy first.'

'True, but since we are already here ...'

'What do you want from my wife?' The pitch of his voice shot up in panic.

'Just a couple of inconsistencies, but if you don't have time, we will check with her.' She patted her colleague's shoulder. 'Let's go. I told you we would be coming at the wrong time.' Sandrine walked two steps down the hallway before turning around again.

'Shall we give your greetings to your wife?'

'This is police harassment,' hissed Nicolas Tanguy.

Sandrine kept walking and the brigadier followed along.

'Come in,' he called after them.

'You're asking us to enter the room?' Sandrine made sure.

'Yes, damn it. Before you wake up my wife and the baby for no reason in the middle of the night.' He unlocked the door. The chain rattled and he let them inside.

'You were already sleeping?' The duvet was ruffled, and one pillow was lying on the floor, covering half of a pink sock. She and Brigadier Azarou sat down on the two chairs next to a table in the corner of the room.

'Do you have anything to add or correct to what you said about the night Isabelle Deschamps was murdered?'

'No, I told you everything.'

'Are you sure?'

'What's this all about? Of course, I am sure.'

'And Madame Fortier?' Azarou asked.

'How should I know what my neighbour told you?'

'Then we should ask her.' The brigadier stood up, went towards the bathroom, and knocked against the door. 'Please come out, Madame Fortier. We know that you are hiding from us.'

Slowly the door opened, and an angry Carine Fortier glared at him.

'What gives you the right to barge in here and disturb our privacy?'

'Monsieur Tanguy asked us to come inside.' He looked at the man who was looking rather pale. 'Isn't that so?'

'Idiot,' the woman snapped at the man.

'What should I have done? Otherwise, they would have gone straight to Leonie.'

She sat down on the bed and pulled the missing sock onto her foot. 'You are a wimp.' Nicolas Tanguy gasped as if she had slapped him and looked at Azarou as if he was searching for help. Azarou only shrugged his shoulders. Sandrine had to quietly agree with Carine Fortier.

'Please, tell us the truth about all that happened during that night, Madame Fortier.'

'I have nothing else to say.'

'Are you serious?' Azarou asked, doubt lacing his voice.

The young woman stayed silent and pressed her lips together. Sandrine stepped to the window and looked outside. The two police cars she had requested were waiting. She waved at one of the policemen who was watching the window.

'Then we will take you into custody. There's lots of time to straighten one's thought in a cell.'

'You can't do that!' Now it was Carine Fortier who hissed.

'I can detain you without charge for the next 24 hours, after which we will transfer the case to the DA's office.'

'I didn't kill that stupid wench.' She jumped up, looking for help from her companion, but he just stared back at her.

'We don't assume that you did. But you made a false statement, hindered police work, destroyed crime scene evidence, and tried to screw me. Do you think we will let you get away with it?' snapped Sandrine.

'You can't prove anything.'

'Do you know the journalist who wrote the article for the Ouest-France?'

'Maybe.'

'She wears this wedding band, very flashy but without much taste. I wondered what her maiden name was.'

'Yes, we know each other.'

'I would think so. She is your older sister.'

'That doesn't prove anything.'

'You are both from a very friendly and attentive family. Deborah was nice enough to send me the original pictures from the crime scene which she received from an unidentified source.'

'Stupid cow.' Her head drooped.

'And look what we found; the pictures have pixel errors that are identical with the ones from your phone. You remember that you took some pictures for me this afternoon. It was an easy game for our forensic technician.' Now let's see if she calls me a stupid cow too.

Sandrine took the smartphone from the nightstand and dropped it into the plastic bag which Azarou offered to her. 'Who knows what other pictures we will find on there or in the cloud?'

A knock sounded from the door, and Sandrine opened to the policemen who escorted Carine Fortier and Nicolas Tanguy outside.

'The questioning can wait until tomorrow. Let the two of them sit a bit,' Sandrine decided.

'Who knows what stories they will come up with.'

'I bet they can't wait to tell us a lot more about what happened the night of Isabelle Deschamps' death, after some time at the police station. They both know more than they admit.'

Chapter 7

Dinan

Sandrine had rewarded herself with a long breakfast. The cell's new occupants should be ready by now. If they were adamant about staying quiet, she would have to keep them a couple more hours in custody, but she did not think that would be necessary. The question now was, who would spill the truth first?

'Good morning,' she greeted Inès who was handing out the mail.

'The phone records have arrived.'

'Quick work. Thank you.'

She pulled the fat envelope towards her.

'We have to go,' Azarou called. 'They found Treville.'

'Where?'

'In the hospital in Dinan.'

'How did he get there?' She put the gun in her holster and shrugged into her jacket. 'Did someone try to murder him?'

'A car accident. The local Gendarmerie didn't want to give me any more information.'

'Inès, please call Capitaine Jenaud. It would help if he let them know we are coming. Let them have a policeman wait at the door. I don't want to lose another suspect.'

'What about Mademoiselle Fortier and Monsieur Tanguy?'

'They will have to wait,' she called back.

Without waiting for an answer, she followed Azarou down the stairs.

'How long does it take to get to Dinan?'

'Half an hour, if we hurry.'

'Then let's go.'

He did not underestimate the time. A few eventual speeding tickets later they stopped on the parking lot of the Centre Hospitalier in Dinan.

Azarou locked the car and scanned the area. 'I hope Jenaud reached the Gendarmerie's boss. Otherwise, we made the journey for nothing. We are not the most popular here.'

She nodded. His fears were not without justification. Dinan was too small to have an office from the Police Nationale. With that it was part of the countryside, and the Gendarmerie took care of all crimes. The relationship between the two law enforcement offices was anything but harmonious. It was not that long ago that the Gendarmerie Nationale reported only to the Ministry of Defence, and the Police Nationale to the Ministry of the Interior. Two different and independent police forces that existed side by side.

'There's our reception,' Azarou said, looking towards a uniformed man waiting at the entrance.

'Lieutenant Sores,' he introduced himself. 'Capitaine Jenaud informed me about the reason for your visit.'

'It's very urgent. We need to talk to César Treville.' Sandrine did not beat around the bush.

'There's a search running on his name? May I ask why? So far, I've never had to sit one of my men in front of a hospital room.'

'He's a suspect in a murder case in Cancale and evaded questioning by fleeing,' Brigadier Azarou answered.

'The dead woman found on the Brittany Coast Path?'

'Exactly.'

'I read about it in the newspaper. Hard to believe that this man could be a cold-blooded killer.'

'A suspect. Whether we ultimately accuse him of the crime and charge him depends heavily on today's questioning,' Sandrine corrected him. 'How is he anyway?'

'He was damn lucky. A broken bone and a couple of bad bruises, that's all he got.'

'What kind of accident was it?'

'He went off the road on a straight stretch and crashed head-on into a tree. He wasn't wearing a seat belt and was thrown through the windshield, right into the bale of straw with the Tourist Board advert on it. That must have saved his life. Besides, he wasn't going very fast.'

'He had an accident on a straight line?'

'We are still waiting on the results of the alcohol test. It's unusual to drive into a tree without some alcohol being involved.'

'External influence?' she asked.

'Not that we know of.' Surprise was written on his face. 'Do you think someone had a hand in the accident?'

'We have to be prepared for everything. This case has already cost the lives of two people.'

'And I thought here things like this wouldn't happen. Please, come with me.'

He marched ahead of them and into the hospital. The policeman slumped on the chair in front of the room rose when he saw his boss.

'Any incidents?'

'Apart from a doctor and some nurses no one has entered the room.'

They had given César Treville a single room. His left arm was wrapped in gypsum and rested on the duvet. His face was covered in cuts, patched up with bandages and band aids and it was hard to recognise him. He looked bad, but considering he'd been thrown through a windshield there were minor injuries. He must have been very lucky.

He stayed quiet, but his eyes showed that he had recognized them the instant they had entered the room and that he was not too pleased by their appearance. Sandrine pulled a chair next to his bed and sat down with her underarms resting on the back of the chair. The two men drifted to the window and left the talking to her.

'You again?' He greeted her icily. This seemed to have become a standard greeting the last few days, but she could not really blame him. He was trapped without a way out.

'As you tried your best to get away from us, we made the way to Dinan.'

'I've got nothing else to tell you. All I saw you know.'

'What happened that brought you here?' She changed the topic.

'I must've fallen asleep and then there was a crash. They call it a momentary lapse.'

'Just like that?'

'Yes.'

'You had an affair with the woman who called herself Charlotte Corday.'

'I didn't!' he snapped at her. 'Who said something like that?'

'Your wife,' she lied.

'Did the slut ...' He tried to sit up but fell back into his pillows and grunted from the pain. 'The bitch lies the second she opens her mouth.'

'Does she?' Sandrine took out the photograph of Isabelle and César in bed and threw it on his duvet.

'Shit,' was all he said.

'Do you still want to deny the affair?'

'That wasn't an affair. We fucked from time to time. That's it.'

'Charlotte and you? I wouldn't have guessed you were her type.'

'Yes.' He lifted his head and attempted a smug grin, which he failed at. 'What can I say? Women like me.'

'And take secret pictures of the meetings.'

'A reminder of the best sex she ever had.'

'Or to blackmail you with the pictures.'

'How did you get such a crazy idea?' His eyes darted from Sandrine to Azarou. The brigadier was still leaning against the window and watched without emotion.

'You were already in her house when the two men arrived. They then beat you and turned the place upside down.'

'No, I wasn't.'

'We have a witness who gave us the report.'

'Ridiculous.'

'You were the one who searched the house first. What were you looking for?'

'I didn't, and you can't prove anything.'

'I imagine it like this: Charlotte Corday, whose real name was Isabelle Deschamps, threatened to send the pictures to your wife. She owns the campsite and is not the type of wife who just goes along with her husband having an affair. When Isabelle was out with Daniel you used the time to have a little look around. You just didn't anticipate the two guys who caught you.'

'I won't say anything more.'

'Isabelle spotted the men and knew she had to leave. For that she needed money. Did she hold the pistol to your chest? How much did she want? It must have been more than you had.'

'Stupid.'

'If not only one's marriage but also economic existence is at stake, one's nerves can snap quickly. Isabelle was no longer allowed to be seen at the campsite. Did you suggest the Brittany Coast Path as a meeting point? It's only a short walk away. I believe you didn't mean to kill her, but you didn't have the money. It got out of hand, and she ended up dead.'

'I didn't kill that bitch. You can't prove anything.'

'You have a motive and no alibi. We can already prove some things; the rest is just a matter of diligence. Make it easier on yourself and come out with what happened that night.'

'You need a murderer and want to blame me.'

'We aren't accusing anyone for no reason.'

'I won't say anything without a lawyer.'

'I am sure your wife will get the best lawyer in town.' Sandrine could not supress the little jab.

'Has Marie seen the pictures?' His voice was shaking, and he suddenly looked drained and tired. His run had come to an end, and he was realizing it.

'Ask her yourself.' Sandrine stood up. She left the room followed by the two men. They would not get another word out of César Treville. The drive to Dinan had not been worth it.

'Can you send him to the Centre Hospitalier in Saint-Malo as soon as he can be transported without problems?'

'I will talk to the doctors and see what I can do. Capitaine Jenaud will keep you updated.'

'I want to see the spot where the accident took place.'

'What do you hope to find?' Lieutenant Sores asked.

'The story about falling asleep feels too simple for me. We made it here in half an hour. César Treville was trying to get away from the police. I doubt that he was feeling sleepy.'

'I can get you there. Just drive behind me.'

The bark of the plane tree was shredded where César Treville's car had hit it. Broken glass and the remains of bandages lay scattered on the grass. In front of them rose the round bale of straw, about two metres high, that had saved the man's life. Colourful flags were stuck on the top and fluttered in the rising wind. The advertising for the tourism association had been torn off on one side and was hanging limp.

Sandrine walked down the street in the direction César must have come from. After about a hundred metres she bent down and picked up something off the ground, which she examined more closely.

'Found what you were looking for?' Azarou stepped behind her. 'Looks like a shard of glass from a headlight.'

'Could be.'

His phone rang and he went back to the car.

'Then you are correct, and someone crashed into his car. We'll check his car for any telling paint damage.' Lieutenant Sores kneeled next to Sandrine and picked up another shard. 'I will send my men to check the area.'

'We need to drive back to the hospital,' the brigadier chimed in after finishing his phone call.

'News?'

'The flat in which Daniel Morvan was murdered is covered in César Treville's fingerprints. Jean Claude explained that it looks like he was searching for something.'

'Like in Isabelle's mobile home.'

'Exactly.'

'Why does the guy not wear gloves?' Sandrine wondered.

'Maybe he didn't have any on him or was panicking. Ask him.'

'Shall I come along?' The lieutenant looked at them.

'That won't be necessary. The clues on the road are more important.'

'We would have checked closer if we had known that the man was involved in a murder. As no one else was injured and he admitted his fault we didn't investigate.' Sores excused himself and his colleagues.

'Understandable. But now we need any clue we can get,' Azarou reminded him.

Sandrine stormed into the hospital room. The door banged against the doorstopper. César jumped in his bed and his eyes widened in fear. Next to him sat a man in a cheap-looking dark suit, most likely his lawyer.

'What is ...?' César started.

'Be quiet,' she snapped at him. 'I'm done with your stories.' She stood at the end of the bed with her hands on the chrome metal frame. 'I'm arresting you for the murders of Isabelle Deschamps and Daniel Morvan.'

'You can't do that! Do something!' he shouted at his lawyer.

'I just did. As soon as you can be transported you will be taken to Saint-Malo into pre-trial detention.'

'Shall we call your wife, or would you like to do that yourself?' the brigadier asked the man, who just stared with wide eyes. Treville's jaw dropped open, but no words escaped. It was obvious that he wanted to avoid his wife finding out about his infidelity.

'You are in shock. That's understandable. You will stop at the campsite on your way back and inform your wife of your imprisonment. Of course, she'll need to know the details.'

'I didn't do anything and definitely didn't murder anyone. I'm the victim here,' he stuttered.

'Your last chance to tell us the truth. One more lie, and we meet you in court. For a double murder you should serve a long time,' Sandrine snapped.

'I told you everything. You have to believe me, I didn't do anything to anyone.' He sighed deeply and his head rested back on the pillow. 'I couldn't do anything like this. I'm not strong enough.'

With that he's probably right, she thought.

'Isabelle blackmailed you with the pictures?'

'I had no idea that she had taken any, that bitch. She was always short on cash and wanted money from me, but how would I've been able to take any money without my wife noticing? She didn't care about that.'

'You were in her home. What did you search for? Her mobile phone?'

He lifted his head back up. 'I'm not stupid. As if she would leave the house without that thing! The pictures were already somewhere on the internet. She showed that to me once. Just to make fun of me.'

'Then I don't understand what you were looking for.'

'Do you think I was the only one who had to bleed for this gold-digging slut?' He shook his head. 'She was constantly babbling that she had a pretty big fish ready for the catch. I was only a side dish.' His lawyer handed him a glass of water and he took a big gulp. 'She must've hidden this book that she used to blackmail the other guy with. She was too careful to carry it around with her. It could have been taken from her easily. So she hid it.'

'The two men surprised you.'

'They scared me shitless when they suddenly appeared at the door. Before I could say anything the first one had already struck me.'

'And then?'

'I told them that I was into women's underwear and wanted to look around my neighbour's drawers. They only laughed. When they started to turn the place upside down, I realized what they must be searching for. The woman must've been crazy to blackmail people like that.'

'What were they searching for?'

'I told you already. One said something about a book, but that's all I know. Didn't want to ask. After a while they gave up, said goodbye to me with a few extra punches and left with the key.'

'Then you were lucky that's all that happened to you.'

'The newspaper wrote that you caught them.' He stopped and looked at the ceiling as if lost in thought. 'When I heard that the men had found Isabelle and murdered her, I nearly went crazy from fear. If they had assumed that I had found something I would've been the next one to push up the daisies. They didn't look like they cared if it was one or two corpses.'

'That's probably the case,' she said. Most people who had met with Thierry le Sauvage's men had regretted it. 'Did you see them again?'

He nodded and took another sip of water. 'I think so. At least one of them. On the evening Daniel was killed. In front of his hiding place. One of those pimp-cars that you only see in American films parked in front of it. I hid until it drove off. Then I went inside to see how he was doing.' His voice broke and tears welled in his eyes. 'He was a good guy. He didn't deserve that.' He pulled up the duvet with his right hand and dried his eyes. 'They murdered him. They just shot him like a dog.'

'You recognized the man?' She waited for an answer. The evening of Daniel Morvan's death, Gradel and Lago had been in prison. It was impossible that they had been in Cancale.

'No, but who else would have driven a car like this? I know every car in Cancale, and that one wasn't from here.' He shook his head. 'No, I didn't recognize the driver. It was too dark for that. Couldn't see more than a shadow. It was only one man though.'

'What did you do?'

'I panicked and searched through the flat.'

'What for?'

'Isabelle must've had something that was important enough

to murder people for. There was nothing in her mobile home, I was sure of that because I know every angle in the houses. I found a bag with pills, but that was it. Who would she have given something valuable to if not Daniel? The boy was crazy about her, and she had wrapped him around her little finger. The men would've certainly come back for me, and I had nothing to give them. Believe me, I was afraid for my life and so I left.'

'Why didn't you inform the police?'

'As if they would have protected me. No, I didn't want to take that risk.'

'They found you?'

'A white midsize car. I thought they wanted to overtake, but they crashed into my car. The last thing I saw was some shit tree I was hurtling towards.'

'That should be enough,' the lawyer interrupted. 'My client didn't commit the murders. For everything else he will show himself responsible in court.'

'That's without any question,' Sandrine said. 'As long as he stays in the hospital the police will sit in front of his door. If it comes to a hearing in court the Prosecutor's Office in Saint-Malo will decide.'

'But ... my wife!' he shouted. Sandrine turned around again and left the room.

They parked at the port of the Rance. The river ran between Dinard and Saint-Malo and finally joined the sea. Motorboats were fastened to the walls, and Azarou waved at one of the hobby-captains who relaxed on the deck of his boat in the sun.

'Stress seems to be an unknown word here. We could use a bit of calm and quiet,' Sandrine said.

'I would be happy with lunch.' The brigadier looked in the direction of the beautifully decorated restaurants surrounding the port.

'Sure. Would you mind if we walk a bit before? The street up from the river and to the city is supposed to be medieval and very picturesque. Should help us think, too.'

'Not at all. It's very pretty here, maybe too many tourists but it's survivable. I remember I came here a few times with my school.'

'You grew up in Brittany?' she asked.

'Yes. Are you surprised?'

'I normally have a good ear for accents. You don't really have a Brittonic accent like Inès though. To be honest I thought you sound more like you are from the south, maybe Hérault.'

He nodded. 'I was born in Beziers. During my childhood we moved to Saint-Malo. That you can still hear from my voice. I am impressed.'

'Only slightly.' So far both had not talked much about their private lives, and Sandrine did not mind it at all to keep their relationship purely professional. It would make her inevitable goodbye easier.

The stones of the Rue du Petit Fort were old, crooked and smooth from many footsteps. They led up the steep hill, and Sandrine mused that she would not have made an elegant picture trying to get up here with pumps. When working Sandrine only wore shoes in which she could walk, run and if necessary, kick. She had always preferred to hit her opponent in painful spots to take them out before she had to resort to the gun.

'Quite steep.' She turned and looked back. 'I don't envy anyone who has to carry their things up from the port.'

'To row from the sea up the Rance was by far less dangerous than to take the road. The port made Dinan rich.'

'You can see that from the houses.'

Stone houses and timbered houses lined the street. Most were small shops selling art to tourists. She assumed that it would get very crowded in the summer months.

'That's a cosy looking crêperie. It's warm enough that we can sit out on the terrace,' she suggested.

The brigadier agreed and they sat down at a table. The house had a little modern conservatory in which the other guests sat. They preferred to stay out in the fresh air. It was sunny and no one was sitting close by who could listen to their conversation. They both ordered a galette with mushrooms, cheese and egg, and cider and mineral water.

'Do you think Treville finally told us the truth?'

Sandrine considered his question for a moment. 'He confirmed a few things that he couldn't deny, and we also learned some new things. All in all, yes. I especially believe him when he says that Isabelle had someone else who was ready to pay more for a silence than he ever could.'

'The car in front of Daniel's hiding place. Maybe César Treville saw the murderer on that evening who took what she had been blackmailing him with.'

'You assume that he saw Thierry Kouame leave the crime scene?' Sandrine asked. She had entertained the same thought. The only problem was that it did not seem to fit. She could not picture the man she had met in his elegant outfit driving a pretentious car like that.

'He's the first one that comes to mind. His men roughed up the mobile home in search for something. After they didn't find that something, and went into cells, he came personally to finish the job.'

The waiter brought their drinks. Azarou stayed with Perrier. She poured herself a glass of cider and toasted towards him.

'Something doesn't fit,' the brigadier started. 'How could Isabelle have anything that could potentially be dangerous to Kouame? She was a little fish. What could she have known of his business?'

'That's the question. If we find that out, we will get a lot closer to the solution of this whole thing.' Sandrine took another sip of her cider. It was wonderfully cool and refreshingly tart. A good choice.

'I think investigations in this direction will lead us into a dead end. I think Treville is trying to occupy us with something and invented the blackmail of an unknown party to introduce a new suspect to the case. The man was looking for the pictures or the smartphone in the mobile home and in Daniel's place. He was wetting his pants thinking about his wife learning of his affair,' Azarou said after a moment of consideration.

'Do you think the man has the guts for a double murder because of an affair? To plan and do this ... I think he is too much of a coward and too simple-minded.'

'He was trapped. A trapped man is capable of anything.'

'But to shoot her? If Isabelle had been struck dead with a spade or a hammer then yes.' She crossed her hands behind her neck and stretched her legs. 'The weapon doesn't fit. We can draw a connection to Charles Carnas. From him it could have gotten to Isabelle, but how to Treville?'

'He searched the mobile home. Maybe he found the gun and took his chance.'

'Why did he murder Daniel? It seemed as if he really liked him.'

'Doubtless Daniel was on the Brittany Coast Path. Maybe he saw Treville close to the corpse or even witnessed the murder. If he didn't want to go to jail for a long time, he had to get rid of that witness. Friendship doesn't count for much in such cases.'

'It's possible. If Daniel surprised him at the crime scene, why wouldn't he tell us? It was his girlfriend that was killed.' Sandrine could just not imagine Treville to be a murderer.

'No idea. Friendship and false loyalty?' He shrugged his shoulders.

'And the accident. How does that fit the picture?'

'Maybe it was really just a normal accident. Sometimes a cigar is just a cigar,' said Azarou, hinting at a quote from Freud.

'Well, it was a small white car instead of a pretentious pimp-car. It might very well be that you are correct. Our perpetrator would have probably ended the whole thing and simply shot Treville. He hadn't been very hesitant so far.' Some of the puzzle pieces fitted together, but there was no clear picture. At least not yet. 'Let the campsite be searched again, especially the mobile home in which Daniel lived. If Isabelle was hiding something there aren't too many places she could have chosen.'

'Jean Claude will be elated.'

The waiter placed two plates in front of them.

'No word about the case during lunch. I want to enjoy this,' Sandrine warned him. She took a fork and pierced the egg yolk. The yellow centre spilled over the galette.

'No problem,' he agreed with her. 'I hope it tastes as good as it looks.'

On the way back Azarou stayed under the speed limit for most of the time. They returned to the commissariat in the early afternoon.

'The two of them have waited long enough. We should question them,' she suggested when entering the office. 'Please ask Poutin to have a look at the phone records of all suspects in our case. I want to know was in contact with whom during the last few months.' It was an advantage to have a team, even if it was just to delegate unwanted tasks. Brigadier Poutin would like the job. He could stay in the office, drink litres of coffee and take all the smoking breaks he wanted while cross-referencing the records. Sandrine was sure that he would not finish the work fast, but at least very thoroughly.

'I put the files on his desk this morning,' he answered. 'Why the last few months? Isabelle Deschamps had only lived on the campsite for the last two weeks.'

'Maybe some of the suspects were already in contact with each other before she left Paris. I am most interested in the calls that we can trace to Charles Carnas.'

'The man was last seen in Calais. It's quite far away from here. The prosecutor assumes that he was clever enough to take the money and run to the UK.'

'His gun made it to Cancale. Why not him too? If we find the way the gun went, we will also find the perpetrator.'

'I will let Poutin know.'

'Who shall we talk to first?'

'Tanguy – he will sing in seconds.'

Sandrine agreed. The man must be under a lot of pressure. How was he to explain to his wife that he had spent a night in prison without admitting to the affair with Carine Fortier? She would not want to be in his skin. Tanguy and Treville. Two adulterers in one investigation was not a record, but it was still interesting.

'I want two separate rooms for them. I agree with you. We will start with him.'

Nicolas Tanguy sat at the table but jumped up as soon as they entered the room. He looked pale. A night behind bars had clearly done nothing for his nervous constitution. She assumed that he did not get any more sleep here than he would have gotten at home with the screaming baby. Sandrine and Azarou sat down opposite him.

'This is outrageous how you are treating me. You can't keep me in custody, I haven't done anything illegal,' he started complaining.

Unimpressed by his outburst she switched on the tape recorder, gave her name, place and time, and the questioning started.

'What are you accusing me of?'

'False testimony and obstruction of a police investigation.' She looked at the brigadier. 'Anything else?'

'Blackmail and sexual coercion might be added depending on what Carine Fortier will tell us. Or do you think we believe that a young attractive woman like her went to bed with you of her own accord?'

'She wanted it. It was her idea.' His eyes darted from one to the other as if he was not sure which of them would be the easiest to convince. Red blotches appeared on his cheeks.

'Sit down,' she commanded.

'But ...' He sat down reluctantly.

'You voluntarily refuse the presence of a lawyer?'

'I have done nothing wrong. Why should I need one?'

'We know that Carine Fortier was at the crime scene. The photographs in the newspaper were made with her phone. We can prove that she lied to us. The question is why you covered for the woman. You were watching her, weren't you?'

He wiped his forehead with his sleeve. He looked like he was just starting to regret his decision to not ask for a lawyer.

'I have nothing to do with anything that happened on the Brittany Coast Path.'

'This is your last chance to correct your statement. What did you see?'

'As I stated before, the baby woke up around midnight which is unfortunately nothing unusual. I went with him into the living room to not wake my wife. She's barely slept the last few months.'

'What woke the child?'

'I only woke up from the screaming. I thought it might have been the gunshot. The window in the nursery faces the path.'

'And then?'

'Through the window in the living room I saw that there was still light in the top floor of the neighbouring house. Carine normally works until late in the night. Shortly afterwards she left the house with a flashlight in her hand and went in the direction of the hiking trail. I was wondering why she was walking that carefully. She kept stopping and looking around, but I didn't think anything of it.'

'She climbed down the stairs out of view? What happened afterwards?'

'The guy with the motorbike parked at the end of the road. He waited for a while, ran up and down a bit and then followed Carine.'

'Did he wait long?'

'Not really. As long as it took me to change a nappy. Not more than five minutes.'

'You weren't worried about your neighbour? She steals out of the house and down a dark path in the middle of the night. Shortly after a stranger appears and follows her. Isn't that suspicious?'

'What should I have done? Run after them with the baby and played the hero?' He raised his hands in defence. 'And I knew him. It was Daniel Morvan. We went to school together. He was a few grades below me.'

'You didn't tell us that before.'

'The guy was totally harmless. Why would I bring him into all of this? He could never have killed anyone.'

'How did it continue?'

'Daniel was gone for ten, maybe fifteen minutes. When he reappeared, he jumped on his motorbike and raced off. That's when I went outside to check if Carine was okay.'

'Bit late, wasn't it?' the brigadier interrupted.

'She came up the end of the trail before I reached the garden door.'

'Did she have an explanation for her nightly excursion?'

'She claimed that she heard noises behind her house and went to check.'

'You believed her?'

'Since her parents died, she's lived in the house. Why would she lie to me?' For a long moment he stared at the tabletop in front of him. Sandrine poured a glass of water and pushed it towards him. 'Only when the police appeared the next morning did I think about her behaviour. I stood at the fence and watched what was happening. She noticed me and came over.'

'Did she give you another explanation for her behaviour?'

'No, but she asked me to be quiet as she had nothing to do with anything that happened.'

'You agreed?'

'First no, as it is my duty as a citizen to tell the police.'

'What changed your opinion?'

'I was sorry for her. She's a nice person, and I was sure that she wouldn't hurt anyone.'

'And on top of that she is sexy and made a promise to you,' Azarou said.

'She offered to meet me for dinner,' Tanguy admitted.

'And you happily took the opportunity?' the brigadier added. Sandrine remembered Leonie Tanguy sitting in the kitchen without enough energy to brush her hair. She could imagine that there had not been any fun in the bedroom for a while.

'I was happy to finally talk about something that was not baby-related.'

'So, she was the one who started it?' Sandrine asked.

'Definitely. The suggestion came from her.'

'And you willingly accepted it?'

He nodded. It was enough for her, and she switched off the recorder. They would not be able to get anything else out of him. It was time to haul in the bigger fish.

Carine Fortier was much more aware of her situation and had a lawyer by her side. The attractive woman wore a grey suit and had fastened her blond hair into a ponytail. She threw a hard look at Azarou.

'Lianne Roche,' she introduced herself. 'I am here to speak on behalf of Madame Fortier.'

'Your client is up to her neck in shit. You will have your hands full to keep her out of prison. Even with your questionable methods.' Azarou looked at the lawyer as if he personally wanted to poison her.

Sandrine switched on the recorder and went through the routine.

Madame Roche directly went for it. 'My client did not do anything to justify your actions.'

'That isn't necessary. It's our job to accuse her of a crime and that's what we are doing,' Sandrine replied. 'Let's start with obstruction of police investigation and coordinated false statement with Monsieur Tanguy. Moreover, we have the justified suspicion of a homicide and intentional destruction of evidence. All this depends on how cooperative your client is.'

'Madame Fortier is innocent in all points and will not make a statement.' She checked her watch. 'After 24 hours you have to release her.'

'Or apply for an arrest warrant,' added the brigadier.

'You have nothing to justify the accusation.'

'We can prove many things,' Sandrine clarified. 'Your client was at the crime scene at the time of the murder and moved the corpse.'

'I didn't,' snapped Carine.

'On your phone, which we took yesterday, we found pictures of Isabelle Deschamps leaning against the wall. We also found some in which she was lying between the bushes at the cliff. Every judge will agree that the corpse must have been moved. It isn't a long shot to realize that it was moved by you to receive more money for better photos. Nicely placed victims look a lot better on the frontpage.'

'I didn't touch the corpse,' she stated defiantly.

'With that you admit finding the corpse.'

'Don't say anything else,' the lawyer cautioned her. It was not necessary, judging from how Carine pressed her lips together.

'The most plausible solution is normally the correct one. In this case, it is that you shot the woman. Afterwards you begged your neighbour, Monsieur Tanguy, to lie to the police for you to give you a false alibi. That is what he told us.'

'I didn't do that. Why would he claim something like this?'

'You knew how susceptible your neighbour would be to sexual favours.'

'This has nothing to do with the case.'

'An attractive woman like you and someone like the slightly dull Nicolas Tanguy, it's hard to believe.'

'But that's how it was.'

'Since when have you been having the affair?'

'Only since recently.'

'Where do you normally meet?'

'In hotels or at my place.'

'Please give us a list with hotels and dates each,' Azarou asked.

'I don't remember.'

'Stop with the theatre. We have his statement, and every judge will believe it. You were at the crime scene, left traces on the corpse and bribed a witness with sexual favours. That's enough for an accusation.' She made a sign to the brigadier. 'Have her taken away and apply for an arrest warrant.'

'You can't do that! I have nothing to do with the murder,' she shouted.

Sandrine had begun to stand up and now fell back in her chair.

'Then please tell us what really happened.'

'It's okay.' She held back her lawyer who was just about to

protest. 'I was working on a blog article until the middle of the night. Around midnight I heard a loud bang, most likely the shot that killed the woman.'

'You went out to check what happened?'

'I studied journalism. Of course I wanted to go and check, or do you think I want to spend my life blogging about gossip and makeup?'

'What happened next?'

'There was light in the Tanguy's house and the baby was crying again. I hoped to get past unseen, but the man is like a nosy grandma. Nothing and no one can slip past him. For weeks he had been staring after me and undressing me with his eyes, disgusting man.'

'You found the corpse?'

'Yes, she was lying in the bushes close to the cliff.'

'Was there someone else?'

'I could see a figure leaving in the direction of Cancale. I didn't go after the person though. Wanted to keep my life. Who shoots one woman has no problem shooting a second.'

'Could you describe the person?'

'No. It was pitch-black. I couldn't even say if it was a man or a woman.'

'And afterwards?'

'I took a few quick pictures. Suddenly, I heard footsteps approaching. I thought my heart would stop, and I hid in the rhododendron bushes.'

'Daniel Morvan?'

'Exactly. I knew him from seeing him around. The guy started to bawl his eyes out and dragged the woman from the bushes. It wasn't that easy. He sat her up against the wall and wiped the dirt from her face. I thought he didn't want to leave, but finally he stood up and ran away. I heard how he raced off on his motorbike. I took a few more pictures and returned to my house.'

'Where you met Nicolas Tanguy?'

'Yes. He stood at the door and stared at me. Obviously, I went over to him and flirted a bit so that he would stay quiet. Why shouldn't I? I had nothing to do with the murder.'

'And when the police turned up the next day you got nervous and offered him sex for his silence,' the brigadier continued.

'Never. Do you think I am a slut?' Outraged she looked at Sandrine. 'He came to me and blackmailed me. What choice did I have?'

'He gave us a different report.'

'Then the pervert is lying.'

'Do you have anything to add?'

'No, that was it.'

Sandrine switched off the recorder. 'You have to wait here until the report has been typed. Afterwards you can go. The Prosecutor's Office will contact you.' She rose. Azarou opened the door for her.

'I want you to arrest the guy,' Carine called after them.

'Why?' Sandrine asked curiously.

'Rape.' It burst from her lips.

'Brigadier Dubois will hand you the report to sign and can take your complaint and legal report. I am sure that your lawyer will help you with the paperwork. Au revoir, Mesdames,' she said as a goodbye.

Capitaine Jenaud entered the office. Commissaire Matisse had called all members of the case for a meeting.

'Thank you for your support,' Sandrine said to Jenaud. 'The boss of the office in Dinan was very helpful.'

'Of course. Without you we might have never known that it was an attempted murder. The tracks from the accident site have now been recorded and are on their way to the laboratory.'

'I am curious about the results.' She looked in the direction of the briefing room. 'The others are already here, let's get started.' The man led the way and sat down. All eyes turned to Sandrine.

On the table was a thermos with coffee, milk, water, and a bowl of croissants, triangles aux amandes, and chaussons aux pommes. Commissaire Matisse had reached into his own pocket to cheer up his crew, for only one of two reasons: he was dissatisfied with the way the investigation had gone so far, or the politicians were showing their displeasure.

Sandrine summed up the results from the questionings of Carine Fortier and Nicolas Tanguy.

'Then we can cross them from the list of suspects.'

Poutin wiped sugar from his chin. Somehow, she felt like he was gloating. The man had clearly still not made his peace with her leading the investigation.

She sat down on a chair and looked at her assistant. 'Brigadier General Azarou what are your thoughts on César Treville?' She used his full title to remind Dubois and Poutin that he was above them in rank and would still lead them when she was gone.

He fixed a photograph of the man next to the one of Isabelle Deschamps.

'Treville is in our circle of suspects. The first victim blackmailed him with photographs. His wife owns the business, so he wasn't able to pay the money himself without her learning about his escapades. With Isabelle's death his problems would vanish. He couldn't stay on the campsite because he feared Kouame's men, so the meeting place on the Brittany Coast Path is not outlandish.'

'That's motive and opportunity, but we are missing the means,' Poutin interrupted. 'The weapon could be tracked to Paris. How could someone like Treville get his hands on a weapon like this?'

'The last owner was Charles Carnas, Isabelle Deschamp's boyfriend. He could have given her the gun to keep, or she stole it from him to protect herself. Treville has admitted to searching the mobile home. The man has been servicing and fixing these things for years. He knows every crack and corner and every hiding place. If she had the gun and hid it in the vacation home, he would have found it.'

'And the two men from Paris took the weapon from him and shot the woman like their boss asked,' retorted Poutin.

'That's one possibility that we have to consider,' Azarou admitted.

'And Daniel Morvan? What reason should there have been to commit the second murder?' Poutin did not stop. Treville seemed to be no believable suspect for him. Strangers from Paris seemed much more likely to commit atrocities.

'We have two possible motives. Treville might have assumed that Daniel was in possession of the photographs, and he wanted to take them from him. The other possibility is that he knew, and we know that he knew because he told us so himself, that Isabelle had a much more interesting, bigger fish on the line. Somewhere she must have been hiding the material to blackmail the big fish, and why shouldn't he switch roles and become the blackmailer? Daniel refused to give him anything and his nerves couldn't handle it.'

'Speculation,' said Poutin. 'I am not convinced of any of this.'

'So far he's only a suspect, not a defendant,' Sandrine noted. 'We follow all clues.' She turned to Poutin. 'Is there anything in the phone records?'

'Between Isabelle and César there were tons of text messages. Saturday evening around 10:00pm she sent the last one. Nothing afterwards. Treville still tried to contact her until Sunday morning. That would speak against him killing her. Why would he send messages if he knew she was dead?'

'The man is not the brightest lamp but not totally stupid. How would it look if he stopped contacting her directly after her death?' Azarou said.

'Who else did she have contact with?' Sandrine finished the banter between the two colleagues.

Poutin leafed through his mountain of papers. 'She called a number in Paris a few times. It's registered on a laundry facility in the 18th Arrondissement, close to the Porte de La Chapelle. That brings Kouame's gang back into the game. They like to use little shops like these as hiding places to wash money from drug dealing. I assume that she called, blackmailed him and he sent his men over. They got rid of Isabelle but got caught by us. Finally, the boss comes over and finishes up the rest. Et voilà, we have our murderers.' He seemed very pleased with himself and looked around the room as if awaiting praise.

'That Kouame might be the big fish is possible,' she agreed with him. 'It would be fitting for the woman to seek the protection of the Prosecutor's Office while torpedoing the investigation with a lucrative blackmail scheme. If she was even serious about testifying against him.'

'Most likely the victim only used de Chezac for her own gains. He was so greedy to have success that he didn't question her intentions,' said Dubois who had been quiet so far. 'Who knows if she ever gave him any useful information?'

'When he realized that he got rid of her before his bosses could learn about the failure,' mumbled Matisse just loud enough to be understood.

'Monsieur le Commissaire!' Lagarde protested.

'All good, it was just a joke,' Matisse waved his comment away.

Remembering how de Chezac had left them searching in the dark and tricked them in the end, Sandrine could understand Matisse's sarcasm.

'Where is Thierry Kouame staying right now?' she asked to change the topic.

'As posh as possible, in the Oceania. With a few of his so-called business associates,' Lagarde said. She assumed that it was his job to have the man watched. She would learn the details later from Matisse.

'Apart from a few clues and wild speculations we don't have much.' She gave a sign to Poutin to continue.

'A lot of contact with Daniel, but also with his mother.'

'With Madame Morvan who found the corpse?' Matisse raised his eyebrows in surprise. He seemed to know the woman or at least the hotel. Sandrine was not surprised. The excellent reputation of the La Baie was known throughout Saint-Malo.

'Her name definitely shows up in many places during this investigation. Azarou and I will visit her later.'

'Yes, a few messages. Isabelle Deschamps wrote her a few times during Saturday. She received an answer around 8:00pm.'

'What business could Florence Morvan have with someone like Isabelle?' Sandrine thought out loud.

'She was the girlfriend of her son after all,' Azarou noted.

'Whom she couldn't stand and whom she had never met.'

'She lied to us during the questioning and claimed that she didn't know the woman in the picture. Who knows what else she is lying about.'

'We have to find out more about the family. Inès, could you compile a file with information about the family?'

'No problem.'

'Those are all the suspects we have, Treville, Kouame and maybe Florence Morvan?' Commissaire Matisse asked to clarify.

Brigadier Azarou nodded. 'So far, yes.'

Sandrine hesitated. She had a crazy idea, but she could not get it out of her head even though it looked unlikely at first glance.

'There is one more,' she added quietly.

'Who should that be?' Matisse wanted to know.

'Charles Carnas.' She looked into the round. She had everyone's full attention. Some shook their heads in disbelief, others looked surprised. Poutin drew a face as if a lemon had been shoved into his mouth.

'How do you get to him?' Prosecutor Lagarde asked after a moment of silence. 'The last time we saw him was over a year ago in Calais. Since then, he has been on the run. There is no clue that he was ever in Brittany, or Cancale. You'll waste your time if you follow up on this.'

'Most likely you are right. It's a pretty far-fetched idea. However, my gut tells me there might be more to it.'

Azarou wrote the name on the whiteboard and nodded slowly. He clearly also thought her idea was a bit crazy.

'He's the only one we know that owned the gun. We can only guess at how the weapon might have made its way to any of the other suspects.'

Matisse nodded slowly.

'He left Paris because he is said to have betrayed Kouame's gang and taken the loot from the robbery of the money transporter. It was nearly one million euro,' she explained. 'Instead of Isabelle, who was nothing but a little pawn, he had quite a bit of influence in, and knowledge of, the gang. Maybe he took some files as a form of life insurance in case someone was going to start a vendetta against him.'

'Something like this mysterious book that Thierry's men were after?' Matisse seemed to be less adverse to the idea.

'Gradel and Zaha mentioned the book when they turned the mobile home upside down,' said Sandrine. 'And Treville claims that Isabelle bragged that she had a bigger fish and more blackmail.'

'That could have been anyone,' Dubois shrugged his shoulders, 'or she lied.'

'I don't think so. Kouame mentioned during his visit that she had indicated she would withdraw her testimony if he paid her to do so. I believe she tried to blackmail him, but not with a shaky testimony in court that his attorneys would have ripped apart in five minutes. I bet it was about those papers she must have gotten from Charles Carnas.'

'What information could be contained in them?' The commissaire was getting curious.

'No idea, but I assume that Prosecutor Lagarde will be able to help us with that.'

'Why do you think that?' His voice shot up in timbre.

'What did de Chezac promise you?'

'I would also like to know that. Spit it out,' Matisse added. The kind, friendly man was gone. Lagarde shied away from Matisse's harsh command. 'I am sure that you are supporting our investigations, or am I mistaken?' the commissaire snapped.

'Of course. I just doubt that the contents of that notebook, if it exists at all, would help the case.'

'Leave that to us,' Sandrine clarified. 'What's written in the book and who owns it?'

'Alright.' He took a deep breath. 'Isabelle claimed that Charles stole files from Kouame.' He looked at her. 'As you said earlier, like a form of life insurance. Before he disappeared, he showed her the book and she said she knew where it was.'

'What's in it?'

'No one has seen it yet. She talked about names and appointments. Bought police officers, bribes to customs officials, friendly politicians and so on. Explosives which could put many people in jail.'

'I can imagine.' It would also have guaranteed de Chezac the post of chief prosecutor. Especially if he could have made certain names disappear.

'People would murder for that,' she heard Dubois say.

'The Prosecutors Office has enough safe hiding places for

witnesses in Paris. It must have been Isabelle's suggestion to come here. It couldn't have been the nightlife that brought her to Cancale. She wanted to come here to search for the notebook.'

She looked around the room. 'And that means that Charles Carnas has hidden it somewhere close. He must have been in the area and maybe still is.'

'Why would he shoot his own girlfriend?' Lagarde raised his hands in question. His entire world was different from the one of fight and survival that Isabelle had lived in.

'It wasn't a romantic movie-relationship,' Sandrine said. 'She was prostituting herself for him and sold drugs. The book was a life insurance. If she stole it from him, he would do everything, and I mean everything, to get it back. It would have been his life or hers. He must have seen the corpses of people who tried to steal from Thierry. Not a nice sight to behold. I can assure you of that.' Images flashed behind her eyes which she had hoped to wipe from her memory forever. 'When one of his dealers took a few extra grams, he wrapped a bicycle tube filled with kerosine around the dealer's neck and set it on fire.' A bitter taste crept into her mouth. Back then she had thrown up until nothing had been left in her stomach. Even Poutin put his almond pastry away.

'If he didn't find the notebook with Isabelle it would make sense to search Daniel next. If she really was crazy enough to blackmail Thierry, Charles must have really snapped. The Ivorians now knew that the book was in Isabelle's hands. If they suspected he was still alive, they would search for him. Without the book, his life insurance policy was blown. In his world, that alone was reason enough to kill her. And Daniel too, because he won't share his girlfriend if he doesn't get paid for it.'

'Then we keep Charles Carnas on the board.' Matisse looked at Lagarde. 'Can you get us the bastard's file?'

'Of course.' He had abandoned his resistance. Most likely he was beginning to understand how Isabelle had played de Chezac. It could not look very attractive to count on de Chezac to help his own career along. De Chezac would probably prefer to forget the whole affair, and everyone involved. Only the solving of the case might grant him a transfer to Paris. It was not too hard to understand what made Lagarde's brain tick. For criminals with a certain amount of wit it would be a feast to subdue Lagarde in court.

'Anyone else who should go up on the board?' Not that she was expecting anything, but she still waited one moment before finishing the meeting.

'We will pay a visit to Florence Morvan. She has a few things to explain,' she said to Azarou.

Before the big tourist season during July and August, it was not hard to find a parking space at the port of Cancale. Sandrine approached the quay wall. A fresh wind was tousling her hair and swept the smell of salt and seaweed to her nose. She pulled the zipper of her jacket up to her chin. Dark clouds were covering the horizon. Mont-Saint-Michel had already been hidden by the rain. She would ask Azarou to drive her home after the questioning. It would not be long until the rain pouring down on the other side of the bay reached them. Now it was time to step back and think. That was easier on the couch in her living room than in the noisy office. There should not be any big news today which would warrant her being there anyway. The forensic technicians in Rennes were still working on Isabelle's phone. So far, they'd had no success, and the owner of the Cloud sat in another country and refused to give them access on the saved files and pictures. She also doubted that Lagarde had enough rhetoric skills to charm his way to the file of Charles Carnas. De Chezac would not let go of anything that might be useful against Kouame. She had only suggested it to keep him busy. As long as he had something to do, he would not randomly appear at the commissariat and stretch her already strained nerves. That was far more important than the file of a criminal who might or might not have gone incognito in the area.

'Lieutenant Perrot and Brigadier Azarou,' someone addressed them from behind her. She turned around in surprise. It was Léon. He wore high wellingtons and an olive-coloured rain parker that reached nearly down to his knees. His hair was wet and stuck to his head, but he still smiled at them happily.

'I would ask you two if you would like to come for a coffee with me, but you look like you are still working. And I,' he looked down at his outfit, 'am not really dressed properly. The water is sloshing in my boots, and I stink of fish.'

'Then we don't want to keep you.' She sounded a bit harsher than she had intended. She was here for an investigation and the man had nothing to do with work.

'I understand. You still have to catch a murderer.' He laughed, not like he was looking down on them, but like their job was nothing but fun and games which he would have liked to join. At least he did not get too friendly with her in front of her colleague.

'Once the persecutor is behind bars, we will have more time to come visit the Équinoxe,' said Azarou.

'I hope just for a drink,' he replied. A SUV parked at the side of the road and the driver honked. He turned towards it and waved. 'I have to go.' He kicked against the filled water bucket at his feet. 'The catch is supposed to go on the grill tonight.'

'Enjoy,' she said.

'We'll see each other in the studio?'

'Most likely.'

'Then we can continue our little chat on the mat.' He shook her hand and also said goodbye to Azarou. 'You better be careful, Brigadier. Your colleague is dangerous.'

Azarou looked after him until he stowed his catch in a box

in the boot of the car and got in. Sandrine observed how the female driver kissed his cheek. She was quite attractive. Maybe a few years younger than him with long blond hair and a face that seemed made for photographs.

'His girlfriend?' the brigadier asked.

'How should I know that?'

'I thought because ...'

'There's nothing to think about. He drove me home and slept on the very couch on which you also slept. That's it.'

'I didn't mean to pry.'

Then stop. They were on duty and her private life was not a topic she liked to discuss.

'Let's go,' she said, finishing his speculations about her love-life.

Like the last time, they found Florence Morvan behind the restaurant's bar, between the espresso machine and the cash register. In front of her lay an open book listing all the reservations. A shadow fell over her face as soon as she saw Sandrine and the brigadier.

'What do you want now?'

'I hope we aren't interrupting.' Lunch was over and the tables were already prepared for dinner. It might get crowded around 8:00pm, though it felt unlikely that on a Thursday evening before the season the restaurant would be full. Tourists staying for a short time normally frequented the restaurant during the weekend or for lunch. In the evening it was most likely only the hotel guests.

'At least you have the decency to not show up when it is full.'

'We do our best to interrupt daily life as little as possible.'

'Then hurry up and ask your questions, and then go back to hunting my son's murderer.'

'And his girlfriend's,' Sandrine added.

'That girl was not his girlfriend. She was only using him. When it came to women, he was a very naïve boy.'

'Don't say that, maman.' Sarah Morvan had left the kitchen and joined her mother behind the bar.

'Why would I lie to the police?'

'Because at the moment it might look like you are happy about the death of the woman.' Sarah looked at Sandrine. 'My mother didn't always agree with Daniel's taste in women, but he had his own life. Neither of us told him what he should or shouldn't do.'

Florence huffed in disdain. She obviously thought she would not have had any trouble straightening her son's head and clarifying what was proper for a member of her family.

'When was the last time you saw Isabelle Deschamps?' Sandrine asked.

'I never saw that person. People like that do not frequent my hotel,' replied Florence.

'Daniel didn't bring her here a single time?'

'He knew she was a slut.'

'Maman!'

'What? It's true.' She closed the reservation book and pushed it aside. 'Word goes around that she also had César in her bed. That tells me everything I need to know.' She was clearly not putting her family on the same level as the Trevilles.

'And you, Sarah, did you know Isabelle?'

'Not really. Only from seeing her around. Maybe we spoke two sentences. She didn't care about what we do. What should we talk about?' She had no doubt that the chef was referring to the restaurant and the hotel. She was as involved in the family business as her mother and her grandfather. Daniel had been the black sheep of the Morvan family. Sandrine wondered what had happened to him to make such a deep cut between his family and himself.

A man in wellingtons and green overalls opened the door by pressing his shoulder against the handle. In his hands he carried a box full of salad and vegetables.

'How many times have I asked you to use the back door?' Florence Morvan eyed the boots and the polished wooden floor. 'Now I have to clean again.'

'Someone's parked in the entrance. I can't get past with the truck. Is it better if I leave everything out on the sidewalk?'

'Just bring it in the kitchen, Alain,' Sarah told him. She seemed a little embarrassed by the way her mother talked to the supplier in front of strangers. In this way, the two women were polar opposites. Sandrine had trouble imagining how the young cook managed her days under her mother's strict regime.

'You buy from the local farmers?' she asked.

'Everything has to be fresh. That's important,' Sarah answered. 'How can vegetables taste good if a truck has driven them through the country for hours?'

'Alain rents the farm of our grandparents. Why should we buy products from anywhere else?' said Florence Morvan.

'I am sure the commissaire is not here to talk about our cooking,' the daughter reminded.

'Lieutenant.'

'Should the case not be with someone of a higher rank?' Florence Morvan asked pointedly. She clearly had not been able to resist that jab.

'Commissaire Matisse is the head of the operation.'

'Why has he not been here yet? My son is one of the victims.'

'He will make his appearance soon, but at the moment we are in the stages of gathering evidence.'

'That means you still have nothing?' It was like the woman was shooting the words at them. Sandrine pitied anyone working here.

'We are checking up on some new evidence.'

'Anything else? There is work waiting for me.'

'You claim that you never met or talked to Isabelle Deschamps. Is that correct?'

'That is what I said. Several times, as far as I remember.'

'How come then that she sent you messages from her phone?'

'Messages? Messages from that little slut?' She shook her head as if Sandrine had been telling lies about her. 'Never.'

'We have the phone records from Isabelle Deschamps. It can be seen clearly.'

'Then it must be a mistake. That happens all the time with all of this computer stuff nowadays. I normally only use the landline. Those phones are so small, they are never there when you need one.'

'Then you surely don't mind handing over your phone so we can make sure that there was no contact between you and the victim.'

Florence looked under the bar and then on the shelves.

'Ah, there it is.' She pulled it out from behind some glasses and held it in her hand.

'She doesn't have to do that,' Sarah interjected. 'It's not okay to corner my mother like this and take her phone away.'

'I have nothing to hide,' said Florence.

'If they cannot show us a judicial decision I wouldn't give it away.' Sarah stayed with her opinion. 'Who knows what they'll do with the phone?'

'To get a judicial decision is no problem.' Azarou's voice sounded harsh. Sandrine sighed inwardly. Florence did not like the man. That would only increase her distaste.

'Then we will do that,' decided Madame Morvan. 'If you actually find an examining magistrate who believes me capable of going around the Brittany Coast Path on a pitch-dark night to shoot a woman I do not know, come back with a letter like that. Until then, I keep the phone here.' She crossed her arms over her chest and looked at Azarou, waiting for him to start a fight. Sandrine did not even try to persuade the woman. It would be pointless.

'As you wish. We will come back tomorrow,' she said.

'Do that.'

'One last question.'

'If you finally leave after that, go on.'

'Do you know a Charles Carnas?'

For a moment, Madame Morvan lost control of her features and stared at Sandrine. Anger flashed briefly in her eyes, but she quickly regained her mask.

'Never heard of him. Maybe someone by that name stayed at the hotel at some point, but I really cannot remember all the guests.'

'Was just an idea,' Sandrine said. 'Why would you know your husband's dealer?'

'What makes you think that?' Sarah called out. 'My father never did drugs. Why do you want to smear his reputation?'

'It's okay.' Florence turned away, took a glass from the shelf and poured herself a cognac. She downed it. 'This lieutenant cannot catch your brother's murderer, but she is clearly good at digging in the mud.'

'What is that supposed to mean?' Sarah asked her mother.

'The police went to Doctor Marais.' She put the empty glass in the sink. 'He is an old friend. Of course, he informed me of the visit.'

'From whom did he get his drugs?'

'He did not take any drugs. Only painkillers because of his back. Sometimes he took sleeping pills and maybe more than he should have. There is nothing illegal about this.' That was nearly the exact same phrasing which the doctor had used.

Sandrine stayed quiet. Old drug offenses were at the bottom of her list unless she could use them as a lever for information. 'Doctor Marais wrote some prescriptions for him, but there were other doctors in the area too. Sebastian was excellent at finding doctors who were not too difficult to convince.'

'That must have been quite expensive after a while.'

'We are not a poor family. The hotel and the restaurant run exceptionally well.'

'Especially since you renovated last year.' Sandrine looked around. 'The furniture is very classy and tasteful. You must have invested quite a sum.'

'We have a perfect reputation in the area. Why would any bank hesitate to give us a loan? We always paid back our debts.'

'I am just asking out of curiosity.'

'Our finances seem unlikely to be important for this investigation.'

'Not at all,' Sandrine said and made a mental note to find out more about that loan. 'We will return tomorrow with the necessary papers. Be careful that the phone doesn't get lost somewhere.'

'You will find it here tomorrow.' Florence Morvan opened the cash register and put the phone inside. With a strong push she closed the drawer.

'Alain,' Sandrine called after the man who was just closing the back of his dark-green truck. He turned and looked at her with curiosity.

'I am sorry, but I overheard your name in the restaurant.'

'Alain Thibaud,' he introduced himself and shook her hand. 'You look like you take care of your nutrition. We also deliver to private households.'

'That does sound very tempting, but I don't have much time

to cook with my job. Is it possible that I saw your car in front of my neighbour's house, Rosalie Simonas?'

A smile spread over his face. 'Yes, sure. She orders from me quite a lot. She's a very pleasant woman.'

'And an excellent cook. Then I must have had the pleasure of your vegetables many times.'

'Happy to hear that.' He checked his watch. 'How can I help you?'

'Do I understand it correctly that you rent the Morvan's farm?'

'I have my own farm,' he explained with pride in his voice. 'I rent some extra land, some of it is from the Morvan's.'

'Are there any buildings on the land that you don't use anymore?'

'There's an old house which is rented out to the Nogents. They also renovated the old stables into holiday homes.'

'Thank you very much. That helps me a lot.' That was a lie but at least sounded polite. 'Then I don't want to keep you from work.'

'You aren't keeping me. That was my last delivery of the day. Today is our monthly barbecue evening. A few friends will be over, and we're going to grill fresh fish.' As if to underline his point he swiped his tongue across his upper lip. 'And grilled vegetables straight from the garden.'

'Then I hope you have a nice evening.' Apparently, all of Cancale had decided to start barbecue season. Maybe she should buy herself a small gas grill. On the weekend she could drive to Leclerc or one of the hardware stores and check if they had anything on offer.

Azarou had already gone down the street and waited next to the white Peugeot with his phone in hand.

'One more thing,' the farmer said.

'Yes?'

'Another building.'

'Which is?'

'There's an old barn which hasn't been used for anything in ages. I've never been inside. Most likely it's just filled with old rubbish.' He rubbed his cheek in thought. 'And the roof must be leaking too.'

'And the barn is part of your rental agreement?'

'It's part of the land and fields. As I said, I don't need it. All the machines I need are in the yard. If you want to you can have a look inside.'

'Where is the barn?'

It turned out to be on the other side of the street from his house, and only a few kilometres away from her house.

Alain Thibaud climbed into his truck and she said goodbye, deciding to pay a visit to the barn in the next few days. At the moment, there were more pressing matters to attend to.

In the car Sandrine called Inès and asked her to apply to the Public Prosecutor's office for a permit to confiscate the mobile phone and to inspect the bank documents. It should not be too difficult for Lagarde to convince the coroner.

'It's about to get dark. Time to finish work,' she suggested. 'Tomorrow we will take a closer look at the Morvans.'

'Do you think that will be useful?'

'As soon as we have insight into the phone data and can read the messages, we will have made one step forward. At the moment we only know that the two women had contact. We don't know what they were writing about. Isabelle's phone is dead, but maybe Madame Morvan's will offer the motive for the murder.'

'Until then all the data will be deleted. She isn't stupid enough to give us clues just like that.'

'What worries me more is that we haven't found anything about Charles Carnas.'

'The man might only be a ghost.'

'Did you see Florence Morvan's face when I mentioned his

name? That was the only moment when she lost control. I bet she knows him and not just from sight.'

'Couldn't be missed. Same with Daniel. Only César Treville didn't react to the name, and the guy is a terrible actor.'

'Something must have happened between the Morvans and Charles Carnas. As soon as we find out what it is all about, we will be closer to the solution.'

'Shall I drop you at your house?'

'No, I'll go to the gym. To punch something helps me think.'

'Well, everyone has their own method.' Adel grinned and started the car.

Sandrine threw her bag with the sweaty sports clothes on the passenger seat of the Citroën. The lockers of the gym did not feel safe enough to her, and she had left the SIG Sauer in her desk at work before coming here for her training. It was not very likely that she'd need the gun at home, and she wasn't going to drive the extra kilometres to collect it.

She started the car and rolled through the quiet evening ambience of Saint-Malo. The thought of treating herself with a drink at the Équinoxe was tempting, but she decided against it. She felt drained and eight hours of sleep would definitely be better for her than alcohol. She also remembered that the club was closed on Thursdays.

It was around 11:00pm and barely a car shared the street with her. The rainclouds had blown away, and a full moon shone softly from the dark velvet sky. A farm appeared in her headlights. In front of it was parked the truck she had seen in front of the La Baie. That has to be Alain Thibaud's farm. Hardly any frost in winter, no prolonged periods of heat and yet plenty of sun made the wide strip along the coast of northern Brittany a perfect vegetable garden, Rosalie had recently lectured. Sandrine looked across fields of cauliflowers and artichokes to a clump of trees surrounding a barn. Without thinking twice about it, she pressed the brakes and steered the car energetically onto a dirt road. *While I'm here, there's no harm in taking a look.*

The Citroën rumbled over the rutted and bumpy path. Mud sprayed sideways and slapped the underbody. She clung to the steering wheel as the car bounced from puddle to puddle. Next time, a little slower, she decided. At the end of the path, she stopped and got out. Her car would definitely need a wash tomorrow.

The barn was not very high, maybe three or four metres. Trees lined the two long sides, their branches reaching over the moss-covered roof. The sun and the salty wind off the sea had bleached the wood of the building. In the light of the flashlight, there was hardly anything of the former colour to be seen. She stepped closer and tried to peer through gaps between the boards, but to no avail. Inside was deep darkness. Sandrine rattled the gate, but it did not budge. An iron bar was in place and secured with a massive padlock. The metal of the bolt was covered with rust, but the lock shone like new. *What could be in the barn that requires protection like this?* Her curiosity had been woken. She went back to the car and took the lockpicks she had thrown into her bag before leaving.

Good that Adel isn't here. He wouldn't like any of this. The lock was a bit more of a challenge than the door of the mobile home had been, but after a few tries it clicked open.

She put the padlock into her jacket pocket, undid the latch and opened the gate a crack. At that moment her phone rang. It was the brigadier. *Had the man placed a transmitter in her car?*

'What is it?' She listened for a moment. 'He tried to escape? In a wheelchair?' She shook her head. César Treville had only gotten to the hospital's exit before the police had caught him. The man must be desperate. She was not sure who he was more scared of, his wife or the police. Most likely the former.

'Give me the details tomorrow in the office. Where am I? I am just about to check the Morvan's barn ... No, I don't have a search warrant. No, I am not breaking in. The tenant has allowed me to enter.' She pulled the wing of the door, and it moved with a complaining creak. 'It's open ... no, I don't always have a pair of lockpicks in my pocket.' Sandrine sighed. The brigadier was very careful to follow the rules. Maybe even a bit too careful. He should relax a bit more.

'That's not necessary ... definitely not ... okay. I will wait for you before I go inside. You'll make the long drive for nothing though. Most likely there will be only straw and old bric-a-brac ... Yes ... See you soon.'

She slipped the phone back inside her pocket. He had not been dissuaded from coming. The man was intelligent and athletic, in his early thirties and handsome, so one would expect him to have better things to do in the evenings than tramp through a dusty and dilapidated barn with his boss.

Sandrine turned on the flashlight and stepped through the gate. The thought of actually waiting for the brigadier struck her as utterly nonsensical. This was an abandoned barn in the backwoods of Brittany, not a club full of violent mobsters in Paris.

Wind blew in from the sea, kicking up dust that flashed like shooting stars in the cone of light. As expected, hay bales, old barrels, crates, scythes and rakes were stacked along the right wall. Several wooden sheds divided the opposite side. Horse boxes, Sandrine guessed. A trailer on flat tires sat at the far end. At first glance it did not look like anyone had been here in recent years. Except for the tire tracks on the dirt floor. Sandrine knelt and shone her light on the easily recognizable tire tread. It was too small to have come from a tractor. The prints led to one of the wooden shacks. To get to the door, she pushed aside two bales of hay. She pulled on the door and the hinges squeaked metallically.

What do we have here?

Behind the cover was a parked car. Not just an ordinary one, but a black Firebird Trans Am with bright red stripes on the sides. You could hardly drive around much more conspicuously. This was certainly César Treville's idea of a pimp car.

Sandrine did not doubt for a second that she had found Charles Carnas' car. She held her breath and listened in the darkness. She almost thought she heard a sound, but now it was quiet enough to hear her own heart beating. 'Keep calm, there's no one here,' she murmured to ease her tension.

If Carnas had hidden his car here, he was somewhere nearby. Should he see the light of her lamp, he would come and find out who was around. She cursed softly. Now she would have liked to have her gun with her. Sandrine aimed the beam of the flashlight at the ground and walked slowly around the car. It looked as if it had only recently been parked here – the key was even in the ignition. The killer drove it to Daniel's hideout.

On the passenger seat lay several boxes and bags.

Oxycodone, she read. Strong opium-based pain relievers only available on prescription. Next to it were pain patches containing fentanyl, but also pills pressed in the shape of skulls. The same variety they'd found with Isabelle Deschamps. Ecstasy. So, Charles had continued to supply his girlfriend with drugs.

Let's see what else we can find. Most likely more surprises. With luck, the money from the robbery.

She aimed the flashlight at the boot and pressed the latch. It clicked, and the lid popped open. Her expectant grin broke, and she turned away from the sickening sight. Sandrine ran to the wall and leaned forward. Her stomach jerked in spasms. With her hands firmly on her thighs, she breathed in and out deeply to keep from throwing up.

She had found Charles Carnas, but not in the way she had imagined. He could not possibly have killed Isabelle. Decaying corpses only walked around in films.

The squeak of the gate made her jump. Sandrine turned around. Her hands groped for her service weapon. Damn. It was in her desk.

Against the moonlight all she could make out was a dark shape in the doorway. Something shimmered metallically, and she jumped to the side. The sound of a gunshot filled the barn, and a searing pain shot through her upper left arm. With a desperate leap, she made it behind a stack of hay bales. Two more shots rang through the air. The impact rammed the bale into her back. If the shooter came in, she would be helpless without a weapon of her own. She looked around, trying not to panic. There was no escape. The attacker blocked the only exit. I can't get past him. Her breathing was shallow, and her heart was pounding wildly against her ribs.

She dragged a fallen pitchfork towards her with her feet. She gripped the handle and pulled her legs up. Should the shooter venture near her, she might surprise him. But the odds were miserable. She listened for footsteps, but there had been silence since the last two shots. She dared a peek from her cover. The figure was gone. What is he planning? At that moment, the gate's wing slammed shut. The sound of the bolt being fastened made her stay still.

He wants to lock me in. Sandrine jumped up. Holding the pitchfork in both hands, she ran to the gate and kicked it. It was locked tight. A bright laugh reached her.

She stepped aside. If he's stupid enough to shoot through the closed door, he won't get me here. She pressed an ear to the wooden wall and listened. Nothing could be heard outside. He must have left. Maybe it's enough for him to know that I can't track him. Suddenly footsteps approached again. Is he coming back to finish his work? Her eyes darted around the barn, but there was no way out except for a window that would have been too narrow for even a toddler. It's pointless too; in the open field he would shoot me like a rabbit. The moonlight was enough for even a mediocre marksman to hit a target.

She lifted the pitchfork and aimed at the crack between the two wings of the door. Should the stranger open it she might be able to get him before he could shoot. She breathed with her mouth wide open to be as quiet as possible. Her last chance lay in surprise.

Water splashed against the wooden wall, and the laughter started again.

A red haze shimmered through the wooden boards. Gasoline, shot through Sandrine's head. He went back to fetch gasoline to burn down the barn with me inside. Smoke swelled through the cracks, and the wood caught fire. She coughed and drew back from the wall.

Something shattered and she jumped back. The glass of the tiny window had shattered and cascaded down like crystal raindrops. A burning bottle followed. The bottle burst upon impact with the earth and flames shot up. The hay caught fire in seconds. Thick smoke began to cloud her vision. Someone honked outside, then she heard a motor roar and a car drive off.

Sandrine threw herself against the door but bounced back like a tennis ball. A searing pain shot through her upper arm. She touched the place from which the pain radiated, and her hand came away wet. Blood. More haybales caught fire. The heat and the smoke made her breath catch in her throat. Thoughts were racing through her head. Suddenly she froze. The car. Sandrine pulled her T-shirt over her mouth and nose and ran through the burning barn. When she found the car, she jumped behind the Trans Am's steering wheel. She turned the key. The car stuttered. 'Come on!' she shouted and kicked the gas-pedal down several times. With a loud howl the motor finally responded. Seatbelt, she told herself. The seatbelt clicked, and she rammed the back gear in. The sportscar shot out of the horsebox with full speed. She turned the steering wheel, braked hard and the Trans Am slid over the dirt floor until it came to a halt. Sandrine aimed for the middle of the door, put it in first gear, and pressed the gas until it hit the car's floor. The eight-cylinder engine made the tires spin before the car jumped forward like a rocket.

'Shit!' she shouted. With a deafening boom the bumper crashed into the door. She was thrown forwards, but the seat belt caught her and yanked her back again. Wooden shards rained through the air, striking the car like a hailstorm, while she raced out of the barn and straight towards her Citroën. She cursed and tore the steering wheel to the side. She missed her car by a hair but hit a bump in the ground which gave wings to the Firebird. She shot up high and flew several metres through the sky before coming down and crashing into the wet vegetable field. The drugs from the passenger seat flew through the car like tiny bullets, and the boot flipped open with a crack. The rest of Charles Carnas rained onto the cauliflower. The car stopped. Sandrine fell back against the backrest. That was close. She had survived.

Sandrine looked back. Flames were reaching out of the roof and licked up the barn's side into the night sky. The leaves of close-by trees did not take long to burn like lanterns. Her wheezing breath dampened all other sounds, the loud crackling of the flames and the voices of the two men running towards her over the field. This will cause trouble; she thought while getting out. Her knees were shaking, and she sat on the car's hood. She was scared of fainting and supported herself with one hand on the roof. The car was scrap metal. She looked at the field in front of her. Exactly like the rest of Charles Carnas.

'Is it you?' She heard a familiar voice.

'Léon? What are you doing here?' The man seemed to pop up whenever she did not expect him.

'I was at Alain's. We grilled fish behind the house.' He stepped closer to the barn. 'Is the brigadier still inside?'

'No, I was alone.'

'Lucky for him. Not so much for you.'

'Could you call the fire brigade?'

'Useless,' Alain called and appeared out of the dark. 'There's nothing to save and they will just squash everything on the field.'

Léon sat next to Sandrine on the car's hood.

'My first impression of you was that you were a dangerous woman. I had no idea how right I was.'

'Nonsense. Someone locked me in there and set the barn on fire. They're the dangerous one, not me.'

'You're bleeding.' He reached for her dripping sleeve.

'Yes, he or she tried to shoot me.'

'We heard it, but thought it was a car backfiring. Who assumes that there is a shooting in a cabbage field?'

'What is all of this stuff lying around here?' Alain called and leaned over one of the dark lumps.

'Please, leave the corpse alone,' Sandrine advised him.

He jumped back in shock. 'What?' Without waiting for an answer, he ran behind the Citroën. She heard him retch. The corpse of Charles Carnas had been a dreadful sight before, but now the view would rattle even the most experienced investigator.

'Take off the jacket.'

'What? No chance.'

'You're bleeding and we have to bandage the arm.' He looked at Alain who was still throwing up. 'To search for a first aid kit in this car is probably pointless.'

'Definitely. The car is evidence.' On top of that the decomposing bits of a man had been in the boot. 'The Citroën is open. There's a first aid kit inside.'

She watched him go, then slipped out of her jacket and carefully touched the hole in her sleeve. Blood was soaking through. Léon was right. The wound would not be dangerous but had to be bandaged before she lost too much blood. I will not sit here in front of him in my underwear. It's way too cold for that. She stuck her finger in the hole and pulled with a strong tug. With a tear the fabric ripped, and a flesh wound appeared. Her adrenaline was slowly draining, and the pain came to the forefront. Her left shoulder and chest would be a huge bruise tomorrow and hurt like hell. She would have said that the Trans Am was from the 70s. At least Charles had built in a seatbelt. Without it the impact would have finished the marksman's work.

'That works too,' mumbled Léon and ripped the tear further open. He fashioned a bandage, and Sandrine bit her teeth together to stop from groaning from the pain.

A car with a blue light was approaching. It had to be Azarou, who must have seen the fire kilometres away.

'Your colleague?'

'Most likely.'

'Why did he let you come here alone? Shouldn't you take care of each other?'

She watched the car roll towards them and park next to the Citroën. The brigadier jumped out and ran towards her.

'All okay?'

'The barn's on fire and there's a corpse littered all over the field. Apart from that all is good.'

'She's been shot,' said Léon and tied the bandage.

'Badly?' Adel asked.

'It's nothing compared to the lecture Jean Claude Mazet will give me once he has to clean up this mess,' Sandrine replied.

'Well, he hates it when a corpse gets moved.'

They looked at each other and then burst out laughing.

'There's the fire brigade. I bet; the Gendarmerie will be here soon too.' Alain Thibaud came up to them and leaned against the damaged fender.

'Are you all right?' Sandrine handed him a cloth from the first aid kit. He wiped over his mouth and chin, took a step back and looked at the car which had sunk up to the axles in the mud. The boot lid jerked in the wind.

'You've been shot, the barn is basically gone, and there's a shredded corpse in the field. What happened?' Léon asked her.

'Normal police work.'

'Maybe where you come from, but here definitely not. Who shot you?'

'If I knew that the case would be solved.' She turned towards the brigadier. 'Would you be so kind and wait here until forensics turns up? I would like to drive home, shower and lie down before I faint.'

'No chance,' he retorted. He pointed towards the approaching cars with their blue lights. 'The Gendarmerie is here. The clean-up of the mess you made is their job, and of course Jean Claude's.'

'And what's your plan?'

'I put you in my car, and we drive to the ER in Saint-Malo where they will give you a proper treatment.'

'It's been done.' She pointed at Léon.

'And he will also write the letter for the Prosecutor's Office. That wasn't a sport injury. We have to follow rules here or a clever lawyer will get us with this later.'

Her knees were still shaking, and she felt drained. All she wanted was to crawl in her bed even though she knew that the brigadier was right.

'Okay, then let's go to the hospital.' She made her way towards her Citroën with unsteady legs and found the key in her pocket.

'Don't even think about it.' Her assistant's voice showed that he was not in the mood for jokes.

'I can't just leave my car here.'

'That's not a car anymore, it's evidence.'

'Nonsense, what does my Citroën prove?'

'Not the car itself, but there's some bits on it that I am sure Jean Claude wants to collect.'

She heard Alain Thibaud retch again.

'Alright.' She was defeated. If she did not agree the man would arrest her and drive her in chains to the ER. At least he had not noticed the padlock in her jacket. He would know that she had picked it, and she really did not want a lecture.

Chapter 8
Arrest

Azarou had driven her home after she had been discharged from the hospital and picked her up the following morning. At first she had refused, saying she wanted to use the motorbike but agreed quickly that the wound on her arm would hurt too much to steer the heavy machine.

Inès met them at the entrance to the commissariat. She must have seen their arrival from her window. Or the security guard at the door had informed her. Thinking about the office manager's astounding connections, she was leaning more towards the latter option.

'How is it? We were terribly worried,' she greeted Sandrine and gave her a hug.

'Nothing really happened to me, but now my bodyguard dotes on me like a mother,' she replied and twisted free from the embrace.

'And that's good. Who knows if the shooter will try again?' She gave the brigadier a cheerful knock on his upper arm. 'Take care of her.'

Sandrine rolled her eyes. If there was one thing she could not stand it was being mothered. It seemed like her team was very susceptible to worrying too much. At least Azarou and Inès.

'The boss wants to speak with you. He said as soon as you enter the building.'

'How angry is he?'

'For someone who nearly lost his leading investigator in a nightly shoot-out he is holding up pretty well.' Inès stepped closer to Sandrine. 'One can't claim that of Jean Claude though. He spent the rest of the night trying to secure evidence with his team which you ... how did he say?' She thought for a second. 'Forgot to destroy. Then followed a comparison with Godzilla.'

'I wasn't the one who set the barn on fire. If I hadn't used the car to break open the door all evidence would have been destroyed.'

'The cleverest thing to do would have been for us to both drive there with our guns and check the place.' The brigadier was on the side of the forensic technician. She took it as a sign of him being worried about her life. The view of the burning barn must have shocked him quite a bit. Otherwise, he would have never driven his clean car into the field.

'The shooter might have been there to get rid of the Firebird. Then we wouldn't have found anything useful.'

She knocked at her boss' door.

'Come in,' he called. A chair creaked and Jean Matisse came to the door before she could even open it fully.

'How are you both?'

'All good.'

'Apart from Lieutenant Perrot being shot,' Azarou interjected.

'Just a graze at the upper arm. Nothing to worry about. Even the doctor in the ER wasn't very impressed.'

'On the inside of the left arm. A finger away from the heart.'

The brigadier seemed determined to make things look a lot more dramatic than they were.

'Sit down.' The commissaire led them to the table and placed a chair for her. The only thing that was missing was a cushion. Clearly he was also part of the people who would mother her now.

'Thank you.'

The boss took a file from his desk and then sat down with them.

'I would understand if you wanted to take a few days off after everything that's happened the last few days.' It was not really a question, but he looked at her like he was expecting an answer.

'I can serve without any restrictions. Once the investigation is finished, I will enjoy a weekend in a spa.'

'Do you think we came close to the perpetrator? As far as I understood from the report, which Brigadier Azarou finished last night, you weren't able to see the shooter. He escaped and so far, we have no sign of him.'

'I had time to think, and I am sure now that it was a woman who tried to barbecue me. The voice was quite high when they laughed while locking me in the barn and setting it on fire.'

'She must have arrived with a car and taken the gasoline from an extra canister. It couldn't have been a car with diesel fuel. That wouldn't burn well enough,' Adel added.

'How did you even get the idea to check the place during the night?'

'The data we got from the phone all pointed at Florence Morvan. She had contact with Isabelle Deschamps and Isabelle's last message was to her. Only two hours after the murder. There might also exist a connection to Charles Carnas. Sebastian Morvan bought opiates from Carnas. There was Oxycodone and Fentanyl patches in the car. There were also the Ecstasy pills which Isabelle was dealing.'

'And you thought Carnas might be hiding in the Morvan's barn? A strange hiding place for someone who has over a million Euro.'

'I didn't think that he personally would be in the barn. I hoped more for a drug depot or other evidence which might help us find the right way.'

'You think that the corpse is Charles Carnas?'

'I do.'

'The Firebird Trans Am,' Azarou threw an angry look her way, 'with which Lieutenant Perrot drove through the door was owned by the man. The corpse is with forensics. I fear we won't be able to get any fingerprints from a corpse as decomposed as this one. However, Paris has data on his teeth and DNA samples. We should be able to identify him soon.'

'Your intuition seems to have proven correct. Now we need to wait to see if we can use any of the evidence. You went in the building without a search warrant. Some judges might throw all we found out of the window because of that.'

Sandrine could imagine what was happening in Matisse's head. He knew the story of her being suspended, and now he was asking himself if it had been the right decision to put her on the case. She could not really blame him.

'Nothing illegal has happened,' she clarified. 'The barn was rented by Alain Thibaud from Florence Morvan's father. That he doesn't use it doesn't matter. He said it was no problem if I have a look inside. Everything I found should be useable as evidence.'

Commissaire Matisse looked relieved. She did not plan on mentioning the padlock until she had found out if the farmer had put it there. She had placed it into one of the evidence bags the very night she had broken it open.

'How do you want to continue?'

'We have to take Florence Morvan into custody.'

'The old woman?' Matisse gasped. 'Do you think she would be able to murder two people?'

'Three. Don't forget the corpse in the barn.' They still had to wait for the results from forensics, but she was sure that the victim had been shot and with the same gun that had also been used for Isabelle and Daniel. Normally, people did not crawl into a car's boot to die there in peace.

'Don't forget the phone data of Isabelle Deschamps. Florence sent her a message two hours before her death,' Azarou reminded them.

'Do we know the content?'

'Not yet, but Lagarde sent us the decision to confiscate her phone.'

Commissaire Matisse leaned back. His chair creaked with every movement. 'Get the woman in for questioning. It will be easier here than in her hotel. If necessary, we can keep her for twenty-four hours, but make sure that the evidence is 100% waterproof.' His fingers drummed on the back of his chair. The man was nervous. To accuse a successful businesswoman from one of Cancale's oldest families would cause a huge uproar. If the suspicion did not prove right, he would be under a lot of pressure.

'Then we need a warrant to search the hotel. The woman has to have hidden the weapon somewhere, and this is the place she knows best. The gun certainly wasn't in Carnas' car.'

'I'll take care of that,' Matisse decided. 'As soon as we have the paperwork, I'll let you know.' He went to his writing desk and picked up the phone. 'Capitaine Jenaud will send men to search the hotel. Cancale is part of the area which the Gendarmerie Nationale covers. The Police Nationale will just be a welcome helper.'

They said their goodbyes. Matisse was already talking to the prosecutor when they left the office.

· · ·

'Shall we go?' The brigadier searched his pockets for his car keys.

'I have to do something first. It might take a while until we get the warrant and Capitaine Jenaud's people are ready.'

Sandrine took the shoulder holster from her drawer and put it on. The weapon would not have helped her much last night. She had barely seen the figure at the door before the shots started. However, it would calm her colleague if she took it. As if Florence Morvan would try to shoot me in the hotel or the quiet Sarah attack me with a steak knife.

She made her way to forensics, knocked at the door and entered. In the open plan office, it looked like someone had set free a mad scientist. Machines, of which she had no idea what were used for, lined the walls and stood on tables. Jean Claude Mazet's colleagues looked up from their work when she entered, some nodded at her while others just focused back on whatever they were working on. Their boss sat on a comparably tidy desk in front of a window. Sandrine sat on the chair he offered her.

'I just wanted to apologize,' she said.

'Thank you. I appreciate it.' He poured some coffee in a clean cup and pushed it towards her. It must be his version of a peace pipe.

'The crime scene you left for us was a total disaster.' Sandrine opened her mouth to defend herself and explain how this had happened, but he waved her off. 'Of course, it wasn't fully your fault. If you hadn't driven the car through the gate there would have been nothing left, and we would have lost a great investigator.'

The boss of forensics did not seem like someone who wanted to suck up to her, so she appreciated the compliment.

'Only one request.'

'If it's in my power, sure,' she answered.

'Next time you ram a car through a closed barn door, chase it over an earth ramp and then try to plough up a vegetable field, please close the boot lid first. Especially when there's a dead body inside.'

'I must have been slightly distracted by the fire, but I will make it my priority to think of it the next time I find myself in a similar situation.'

'It was a really nice car,' Mazet murmured in thought. 'At least before it fell into your hands.'

'It's confiscated,' she said. 'The owner is dead, and I doubt that there is an heir. I assume it will be put on auction after the case. Knock out a few dents, a new radiator, a fresh floor covering in the boot, a little scented tree and it'll look like new again.'

'You think so?' A soft smile played around the corners of his mouth.

'I am sure of it. Would suit you very well, a Firebird.'

'Ah.' He waved her statement away and suddenly looked shy. 'If I was 20 years younger than maybe, but now?' He pulled a drawer open and took out Sandrine's car key. 'No muscle car but also a classic. And a French one on top.' He handed her the key.

'I am allowed to take my car back?'

'We took all the evidence we could find, and the intern went over it in the yard with the steam jet. The baby is completely at your disposal again.'

'I have one more small thing.' Sandrine took out the plastic bag with the padlock. 'Could you check it for any useable fingerprints?'

He nodded and took the bag.

'We have some good news for you.' He waved at a woman who looked young enough to have just left school. Most likely one of Inès' classmates. She wore a pair of red headphones over a coiffure of tightly braided plaits that reached to her shoulder blades and had brightly coloured wooden beads attached to them. A light-coloured T-shirt with African prints draped over jeans that looked like they'd had to fight through a pack of hungry wolves to get to work this morning.

'Hello.' She greeted Sandrine with a strong handshake. 'So, you are the wonder woman who had a stand-off in the middle of the night?'

'Marie!' Her boss clearly thought her greeting was too casual.

'I am sorry, but I can't compare to a superhero,' Sandrine replied. 'And the shooting only came from one side. I hid behind a bale of hay and prayed not to be hit.'

'If you say so.' She looked at the pistol in the shoulder holster.

'Marie is our megamind when it comes to bits and bytes. She was the one having another look at the memory card.'

'And?' Sandrine straightened in anticipation. Jean Claude would not have brought the woman in for no reason. Many bosses pinned the credits of their employees on their own lapels, but the head of forensic science evidently did not. He was competent enough himself to give his people their due credit.

'You want all the technical explanation?' Marie asked.

'The results are enough for me.'

She spread three pictures on the table.

'The quality is not the best, but I couldn't get more.'

'That's enough for me. Can you find out if she sent the pictures somewhere, and if she did to whom?'

'From the connection I can only see that files were attached and sent to the phone of Florence Morvan and the strange number in Paris. I cannot say though which pictures we are talking about.' She shrugged her shoulders.

Sandrine took the pictures and jumped up from her chair.

'Great work!' she said and marched from the room. The noose was tightening around Florence Morvan's neck.

. . .

They parked Azarou's car at an angle to the hotel and waited for Capitaine Jenaud to receive the search warrant. Sandrine handed him the pictures Marie had restored.

'That's the barn and this is the car.' He whistled in surprise.

'Now we know that Isabelle Deschamps was there. She must have recognized the Firebird.'

'You think she looked inside the boot?'

'I am sure the woman searched the car for drugs. Behind the seats lay empty cans which held Oxycodone,' Sandrine said.

'Why the pictures?'

'Remember what César Treville told us. She was waiting for a bigger fish with a lot more money.'

'But who could that be? Thierry Kouame?'

'That's one option. Where else would Carnas have hidden his life insurance if not in his car? She must have found the book Lagarde was talking about. After everything we learned about the woman, I think it's possible that she was stupid enough to blackmail Kouame.'

'Maybe she thought he was the murderer of her boyfriend and wanted revenge?' Azarou guessed.

'Then all she would have had to do was give the book to de Chezac. That would have sent him on a straight line to prison, and most likely many of his associates too.'

'If she tried blackmail then the stolen money could not have been in the car. Otherwise, she would not have taken the risk.'

'That's the question, where is the money? We are talking about nearly one million euro.'

'No idea. Maybe he hid it somewhere else? It's likely that his murderer took it after Carnas' body was shoved in the boot. A bag full of money is a solid motive to murder someone.'

'We have to find that out if we want to arrest her. I assume Daniel said more than he should have while being on drugs,' Sandrine said.

'Why would Madame Morvan tell her son that she shot a

criminal, stole his money, and hid his body in the boot of a car? Normal mothers don't do such a thing.'

'Yours maybe not, Azarou, but you also didn't help to remove a corpse like Daniel.'

Capitaine Jenaud waved at them.

'It's starting,' said Azarou. 'About time.'

They followed the men of the Gendarmerie who entered the building from the front through the reception and the restaurant.

'What's happening?' Madame Morvan complained loudly. The employees who were in the restaurant were led by police officers to a table where they were told to wait. Sarah looked out of the kitchen and rushed to support her mother, as if the harsh woman needed it.

Sandrine gave way to the senior Capitaine Jenaud. Cancale was his area of responsibility.

'What nonsense!' Florence Morvan crumpled up the search warrant and threw it over the counter. 'What do you think you will find here?'

'Clues linking you to the murder of Isabelle Deschamps.'

'I have never met that woman in my life, nor heard anything from her,' she insisted.

That was Sandrine's cue.

'The search warrant includes your cell phone.' She turned to her daughter standing by the cash register. 'Sarah, would you be so kind to pass it to me?'

She looked at her mother and only moved once she nodded.

'Let her have it. Whatever could they use it for anyway? I have nothing to do with this whole drama.'

Sarah opened the cash register and took out the phone. Azarou offered her an evidence bag, and she dropped it in.

'Thank you.' He pocketed the bag.

Sandrine and the brigadier sat down at a table. They would leave the search to Capitaine Jenaud's men. They were not needed for this.

They looked out of the wide panorama window onto the harbour. The sea had pulled back, and the flat fisher boats and a white catamaran lay on the sand. She could make out the form of Mont-Saint-Michel in the background.

'We found something interesting.' Capitaine Jenaud sat down and pushed a clear freezer bag with a watertight zipper over the table.

'A Glock 17. Calibre 9mm. Exactly the weapon we are looking for.'

'Where did you find it?'

'Where every gendarme who's worth money would look – in the toilet's cistern in Madame Morvan's apartment.'

Sandrine took the bag, opened it and carefully sniffed.

'The gun was used not too long ago.' She put the bag back. This thing had nearly murdered her last night. Previously it had taken Isabelle Deschamp's and Daniel Morvan's lives. She did not want to touch the weapon and pushed it as far away from her as she could.

The brigadier took it. 'I will hand the gun over to the lab.'

'Do that. Should we find more evidence I will have everything brought to Saint-Malo,' said Capitaine Jenaud.

'We are also interested in the finance documents of the last three to five years,' she reminded him.

'Already packed and ready to go for you.'

'Would you arrest Madame Morvan and bring her to the commissariat?' She noticed the surprised look of her assistant but did not care. She had no problem with giving the local police force the honour of making the arrest.

'Of course.'

'You and your men work very efficiently, Capitaine.'

'Thank you. It's a pleasure to work with you too. I hope we will be able to work together again in the future.'

'Not to dampen your spirits, but I would prefer if we didn't have to.'

'Ah.'

'A few break-ins and small criminals are enough for me. I don't wish for another homicide case.' Moreover, she would soon leave the police service, but that was not the man's business.

'I have no trouble imagining that. In one week, we've had more murders in the area than we've had in the last ten years.'

'Once the case is closed, we'll have a drink and toast to the next ten years being quiet ones again.'

'Count me in.'

They left Capitaine Jenaud and began their way back to the commissariat. She noticed how Sarah Morvan glared after them. The idea that her mother was a cold-blooded killer must be shocking. But it would not have been the first time that daughters did not know what their mothers were up to, and the other way round.

The brigadier dropped Sandrine off at her house. Her arm was hurting, and she wanted to change the bandage.

'Shall I pick you up later?'

'Not necessary. I'll call a taxi. Make sure that the evidence gets to forensics. I have to take care of a few things and will join you at the commissariat early afternoon. Stop Matisse from calling a press conference. We don't have a confession yet.'

'What about César Treville? Shall we cancel the arrest warrant?'

'I think so. Everything else we can drop under the table. It's too much work and he fears his wife more than us anyway.'

'True.' He honked and drove off.

The door to the main house opened, and Rosalie stepped out.

'Come in,' she called.

'I have to change the bandage first.'

'Nonsense, you need two hands for that, or it won't be done properly. I've got everything here that we need. You've also got some mail.'

Apart from a few bills and letters from the Paris Police Department she never received any mail. Only a few of her friends even knew that she was in Cancale.

A basket with a bottle of red wine and a selection of chocolates and truffles awaited her in the hallway. Better than flowers, she thought and pulled out the card.

I hope you get well soon, Léon.

'They're from the tall, handsome man who brought you home after you fell in the glass.'

'Yes, my personal guardian angel.'

'You could use one of those.'

Sandrine grabbed a box of artisan chocolates before Rosalie escorted her to the kitchen table. She pulled off her jacket and draped it over the back of the chair. With her right hand she touched her shirt. She could feel the bandage underneath. Small, red-brown dots were spotting the fabric at one place.

'Stay seated, I will be with you in a sec.' Rosalie opened the drawers of the old apothecary cabinet that took up almost the entire head end of the kitchen. The other furniture was also antique, not dainty Louis XV tables, but rustic furniture made to serve more than one generation. Most were a little crooked, the wood of the kitchen table warped in places, but everything exuded a charm that modern things lacked.

'There you go.' Rosalie came to the table and sat down next to her. She put bandages, wound ointment, a bottle of disinfectant and a pair of scissors in front of her.

'Can you handle it?'

'Hey, I write detective stories. I know about wounds.'

'Theoretically. It must be the first gunshot wound you have seen with your own eyes.'

'Yes,' she muttered. 'Now I can describe one much more vividly in the next novel.'

'For a glass of red wine, you can even touch it.'

'You are on duty, there's nothing to drink for you.' That did not stop her friend from pulling the open bottle of cider over to pour herself a glass. 'Unbutton your shirt.'

'Only if I can get a coffee first.' She pointed to the thermos on the table.

Rosalie poured a cup while Sandrine unbuttoned her shirt and manoeuvred her left arm out of the fabric. With her right hand she freed some chocolate from its wrapping and took a bite.

'Very good,' she said, and rolled a praline in Rosalie's direction. 'Try one.'

'So, the guy doesn't just have good taste in women.'

'Léon is a casual acquaintance, nothing more. He runs a club in Saint-Malo and happens to train at my gym.' She popped the rest of the chocolate into her mouth. 'His shop doesn't exactly have the best reputation. I will probably have to arrest him soon,' she mumbled.

'How exciting. With handcuffs and all?'

'The places your mind goes ...'

'I'm a writer. My readers are interested in things like that.' She pulled off the bandage carefully. 'Looks good,' she said and tapped a few drops of disinfection onto the wound. She was right. There was already a dark crust covering the cut. 'Was it worth it to get shot?'

Sandrine had nearly had to resort to force to make her friend go away last night. Rosalie had bombarded her with questions.

'You know that it's everyday work for investigators.'

'Only in my novels, but not in real life.' She took Sandrine's hand and gave it a squeeze. 'It could have gone wrong.'

'It didn't. I was very careful.'

'Obviously.' Rosalie tapped her finger against the wound.

'Hey!' Sandrine twitched. 'Don't be a sadist.'

'Only because you made me sick with worry.'

'I am sorry. How can I make it up to you?'

The moment she saw her friend's eyes glint, she knew she had made a colossal mistake.

'I want to know everything that you are allowed to tell me.'

'Then basically nothing.'

Rosalie retracted her pointer finger in a warning that if she did not spit it out, she would be poked again.

'Maybe you can give me some advice? The case is pretty much closed, and Matisse will give a press conference tomorrow at the latest. You have to promise me though that nothing of this will be written in the next Commissaire Delacroix.'

'Everything that makes it into the newspaper is public property.'

She laughed, told her about Florence Morvan, and Rosalie listened, enraptured.

'You think she is capable of murder?' Sandrine finally asked.

'One of the old wenches from Cancale? They are capable of anything. Their men left for half a year to catch cod around New Zealand, and they stayed back and took care of everything. It was their job to make sure the family survived until the men came back with their meagre salaries, if they came back, that is. They were formed and made strong by this. This place has been matriarchal for a long time, and you can still feel some of that today. Florence is one of them.'

'Capable of committing murder?'

'To kill a stranger dealing drugs, endangering her hotel and family and a woman blackmailing her? Any time.'

'Her own son?'

Rosalie took her glass and drank from the cider. For a while she watched a log of wood burning in the fireplace. The sizzle and crackle of the flames was the only sound in the silence. In the end, she shook her head.

'She was hard on Daniel, but in the end, she loved him. Maybe even more than Sarah who seems too weak to her. She doesn't show the strong will of the other female Morvans.'

'She loved him more than her hotel?'

'Nothing is as important to her as the La Baie, not even herself.' She put the empty glass down. 'Maybe she loves herself least of all. Florence is a complicated woman.'

'If it was Daniel or the La Baie, she would choose the hotel?'

'I'm not sure.' She shrugged. 'Try to get her off balance. It's possible that she will make a mistake. If someone can manage it, it's you.'

Sandrine ran her hand over the new bandage. It barely hurt anymore. Florence Morvan had a strong hold on her thoughts. There were only a few but very important puzzle pieces missing until the picture was complete. If luck was not on her side, it would be hard to prove that the woman had committed three murders. Most likely the Prosecutor's Office would win a trial based on circumstantial evidence, but she did not want to risk it. She needed a confession.

Adel Azarou sat at his desk, fighting through a pile of papers. Sandrine threw a quick glance at them while walking past, but it was nothing but number clusters, so most likely the finance reports of the hotel. Sandrine was thankful she could delegate these tasks to someone.

'Any findings from the tables?' she asked. He closed the file he was reading and threw it on the desk.

'I marked the most interesting places.'

He dug in the pile of paper and fished out an envelope.

'One of the coroners called.'

'That fast?'

'He couldn't tell us much. The time of death is around the date when he was last seen. Most likely he tried to throw us off by hanging around Calais and then came here.'

'Cause of death?'

'So far unknown. He was only able to rule out a gunshot.'

'So, he was murdered and then his killer took the weapon from him.'

'Looks like it. Unfortunately, there isn't one useable fingerprint on the gun. Everything was wiped very cleanly before it landed in the cistern.'

'Damn, a set of prints would have helped us.'

Sandrine sat down and looked through the files handed over by Azarou. When she reached the last sheet of paper, she sat up straight and clicked her tongue.

'That pins her down, doesn't it?' He grinned at her.

'It does indeed.' She puts her gun in the drawer and stood up. 'Let's see what excuses the woman has prepared for us.'

Florence Morvan waited for them in one of the interrogation rooms. She was not alone. Next to her sat Lianne Roche, the lawyer she had already met. Azarou saw her and cursed to himself. He seemed to hate the woman. Sandrine could not help but wonder what might have happened between the two. Once there was more time, she would have to have a little chat with Inès.

'Madame Morvan,' she greeted the suspect. 'An excellent idea to have a lawyer close by. In a situation such as yours it is a wise step to take.'

'Sarah has hired her. I doubt that it will be necessary as I have done nothing that is against the law, but one never knows what police will come up with to present someone as the culprit.'

'My client is a well-respected businesswoman. She has lived in the area her entire life. To escort her out of her own hotel in handcuffs is a disgrace. And all of that on the basis of some unconfirmed accusations.'

The lawyer started aggressively before Sandrine had even sat down. She had sat through too many investigations to be impressed by that. The brigadier, however, pulled up his shoulders, leaned forward and looked at the woman, frowning. Her method had worked on him. He looked tense. Humans ready to enter a fight normally switched off their brains. They had more in common with Neanderthals than one might believe. However, she did not need this during her investigation. If he did not pull himself out of it, she would have to give him some other tasks.

Without a reply she switched on the recorder and named the assembled.

'I want to know what my client is accused of,' Lianne Roche continued.

'I understood that.'

'Then answer me.'

Sandrine looked openly at her watch.

'We are heading towards the end of the day. Maybe we should postpone the questioning until tomorrow. We've had lots of overtime the last few days. What do you think, Brigadier General Azarou?'

'My family would be happy if I make it home on time.' He understood what she was playing at and joined in.

'You can't do that,' the blonde woman flared up. Instead of Sandrine she now glared at the brigadier. The antagonism seemed to run both ways.

'What paragraph are you referring to? I am not aware of being forbidden to finish work on time.'

'I ...' She banged the file which she had been holding in her hands onto the tabletop. 'You want to threaten and frighten my client. That won't work. After 24h you have to release her. The law holds you to it.'

'That's correct.' Sandrine put a lecturing tone in her voice. 'Prosecutor Lagarde is preparing an arrest warrant as we speak. This allows us to keep your client in remand as soon as the coroner signs it, which, in this case and with all the evidence, should not be a problem.'

Their eyes met. Lianne Roche held her gaze for a while, but then dropped her eyes. She knew that she had to admit defeat in this.

Florence Morvan sat at the table with a face set in stone, not betraying any emotion. The clash between Sandrine and her lawyer seemed to bounce off her without leaving any traces.

'Then let's start from the beginning.'

'What are you accusing Madame Morvan of?' The lawyer's voice was quieter but had not lost its biting edge.

Sandrine opened the file on the table and leafed through it.

'We accuse your client of the murder of Isabelle Deschamps.'

'How do you get to such nonsense?' Florence Morvan broke her silence and spoke directly to Sandrine. 'I never met the woman. I definitely did not murder her. What a ridiculous accusation.'

'We also suspect your involvement in Charles Carnas' death.'

'This is the second time I've heard that name from you. Who is that?'

'A drug dealer who committed a robbery in Paris last spring. He went undercover in the area. We think that he supplied your husband with opiates.'

'All the painkillers Sebastian took were prescribed to him. All legal. Or can you prove something else?'

'We had a look into your finances,' Azarou said. She let him take this part of the questioning. He had a better understanding of how everything was connected.

'Are they allowed to do that?' Madame Morvan asked her lawyer.

'Nothing we can do there,' she admitted. Sandrine thought she could hear her grind her teeth.

'And from those reports you think you found out that Sebastian took illegal drugs?' she asked the brigadier.

'Not only that. Three years ago, according to Doctor Marais, the time when the drug usage of your husband began, the private withdrawals from the company bank account increased noticeably. The hotel slowly began to struggle.'

Rosalie had also hinted at that. The woman knew God and the world in Brittany. She was the perfect source for inside information.

'We spent a bit more than we should have. That's not a crime.'

'No, it isn't, but we were wondering where the financial means came from that allowed you, just after your husband's death, to renovate the entire hotel and restaurant.'

'Our family and the La Baie have an exceptional reputation. Why should a bank hesitate to give us a loan?'

'You were making losses. That is reason enough.' He skipped through a few more pages. 'I can also see no mention of a loan anywhere. There is no payment of interest charges or transfers to a financial institution.'

'We keep savings.'

'I also can't find any invoices from the renovations.' He looked up from the numbers. 'Did they all work for free because you are such an esteemed member of the community?'

'Okay, you got me,' she admitted. 'The workers were paid in cash. No honest businesswoman can afford the taxes nowadays.

The government takes your money and spends it on God knows what.'

'Madame Morvan did evade taxes. Who doesn't?' her lawyer supported her. 'That's not a reason for the accusations you're throwing at her.'

'Brigadier.' Sandrine turned to her assistant. 'Did the lawyer just admit to betraying the tax office?'

'She claimed everyone was evading taxes. That would include her.' He grinned and Lianne Roche rolled her eyes.

'Stop the games,' she hissed at Sandrine. 'My client has no connection with a criminal like that. What motive would she have?'

'There would be the drug dependence of her husband threatening the hotel's existence.' She tried to make eye contact with the accused. Madame Morvan just looked back at her without flinching.

'On top of that comes the money from the robbery which the man had with him. Nearly one million euro. An amount of money like that can make a crime tempting. The things one could do with so much money ... like renovating a hotel or building a restaurant.'

'You cannot prove that.' Florence Morvan's voice was still devoid of emotions.

'The evidence speaks loudly. The money is the connection to Charles Carnas. The bills were paid in cash not because of the taxes but to veil where the sudden riches were actually coming from.'

'Those are speculations, nothing else.' The lawyer tried to wipe their arguments from the table.

'It will be enough for the prosecutor to open the proceedings and check accounting in detail. Should your client be unable to show what the source of the money was she will find herself in jail for a long time,' Sandrine clarified.

'There would also be the strange incident of how the corpse's weapon came to be in her apartment. The same weapon with which Isabelle Deschamps was murdered,' Azarou added. It was easy to see that he enjoyed having delivered a blow to Lianne Roche. He had to work on his poker face.

'It was planted to frame her.'

'Then someone went through a lot of trouble. If I was a judge, I wouldn't be convinced by that, but Madame Morvan trusts your skills or otherwise you wouldn't be here. Maybe you managed a sleight of hand that you are so practiced in. I will watch the process with interest.'

'And what wild speculations will you pull out of the hat for the murder of the woman from Paris?' The lawyer changed topic from Carnas to Deschamps.

'Are you still denying knowing the victim?' Sandrine asked Madame Morvan directly.

'I never met this slut. She was after my son's inheritance.'

'She sent you several messages which were answered from your phone.'

'That's a lie.' Florence Morvan pressed her hands on her thighs. It was the first sign that she feared the case might turn.

Sandrine placed the phone on the table.

'Is that your phone?'

'Looks like it.'

'The messages from Isabelle Deschamps were deleted. Not professionally though. Our technician had no problem retrieving them.' She pulled a sheet of paper from the file.

'At the beginning of last week, Isabelle wrote: "I know that you murdered Charles. You will pay for that, or I will go to the police."' She pushed two pictures of the barn over the table directly in front of Florence Morvan. 'You know the building?'

'Of course. It has been owned by my family for generations.'

'The next message included this picture.' She pulled the picture of the Firebird Trans Am from the file and arranged it next to the others. 'In this barn, in the boot of this car, we found the remains of Charles Carnas.'

'Who knows who put him in there? Were there any clues indicating my client? He was a criminal. Very likely that it was an act in the drug milieu.'

'The car is still being searched. No worries though, they always find something,' Azarou confirmed. Sandrine had her doubts on that. The woman seemed like someone who acted methodically and without panicking. She would have tried to not leave any evidence that could be traced back to her.

'When we found the corpse, I was shot at. The bullets were from the weapon Madame Morvan was hiding,' said Sandrine. 'But back to Isabelle. She knew exactly the amount of money your client had taken from Carnas, and she wanted it.'

'I do not know anything about this message,' assured Florence Morvan.

'They were on your phone,' the brigadier snapped at her.

'I don't care,' the older woman hissed back. 'The phone lies at reception for most of the day. I am not one of those people who carry the thing around all day.'

'As my client stated, anyone could have used it.'

'Madame Morvan answered the message.' Sandrine put a printed sheet in front of the lawyer. 'On Saturday evening the men who were searching for Isabelle found her on the campsite. She panicked and tried to get away from here. Isabelle Deschamps sent three messages on that day.' She leaned back and looked at the woman in silence for a long while. 'We wondered how they found her in Cancale. When we looked through the list of calls, we noticed the phone number of one of Kouame's lawyers. Through the blackmail you knew that Charlotte Corday was Isabelle Deschamps and hoped that with a call to Kouame he would get rid of this little problem for you. But she got away from his men.'

'That's nothing but speculation again,' Lianne Roche interjected.

'After Isabelle saw the men, she panicked and wanted to leave.' Sandrine tapped on the print on the table. 'Isabelle settled for half the amount, but it was to go through the same day.'

'Where would I have gotten that much money from?'

'The girl was too greedy to ask that question. That was her mistake. In the last message you asked her to come to the Brittany Coast Path under the Rue du Port Mer. Exactly where you, the next day, reported the finding of a corpse. The woman was shot with the weapon we found in your apartment. That isn't a coincidence.'

'I have nothing to do with that.'

'The evidence says something else. We can prove that Isabelle Deschamps tried to blackmail you and that you wanted to meet at the time and place of her murder,' said Sandrine.

'Every single one of these alleged pieces of evidence could have been planted on Madame Morvan,' the lawyer argued.

'Maybe one, but here we have too many. No judge would believe this conspiracy against your client.' Sandrine shook her head in disbelief.

'And Daniel?' Florence Morvan asked. 'You want to tell me that I murdered my own son? What mother could do such a thing?' Her voice shook albeit barely noticeably. Her stony façade was slowly cracking under the weight of the evidence.

'A mother who was about to lose everything she has worked for and already killed two other people,' Sandrine retorted.

'It was the same murder weapon, and Daniel opened the door of his own accord. It must have been someone he knew and trusted.' Adel did not have to say whom he was talking about. It was clear to everyone.

'Then it is no use to keep talking to you,' Florence Morvan decided.

'You refuse to testify?'

'Exactly.'

'As you wish. Your lawyer will advise you. I personally would recommend a confession.'

'I have nothing to confess.' Every bit of life had drained from Florence Morvan's voice. She could clearly see the fate in front of her and the impossibility of avoiding it. The evidence was crushing. Sandrine switched off the recorder.

'We will leave you and your lawyer. Ring once you are finished, and you will be led to your cell.'

Azarou and Sandrine left the interrogation room. Their talk would not be a pleasant one. She did not envy Lianne Roche's job of showing Madame Morvan the advantages of a confession.

'We nearly finished our first case together. To solve three murders in one week is something you can be proud of,' Sandrine said to her assistant.

'Even though it was only a few days, I've learned a lot from you, Lieutenant Perrot.'

'Don't forget, it's only two months and three weeks and then I am gone.'

'If that's the case I better take notes.' He smiled at her, and she could only smile back.

She offered her hand to the brigadier. 'It's time to go on a first name basis. I'm Sandrine.'

'Adel,' he said and took her hand.

'Let's hope that the next few weeks will be calm and quiet.'

'Saint-Malo is a peaceful place. You will get bored soon.' He looked back to the door of the interrogation room.

'What happened between you and Lianne Roche?'

'That's a long story.' He evaded the question.

'We have some time.'

'First we have to finish the paperwork.'

If he wanted to keep it private and it did not hurt the case, she would not keep pressing.

. . .

'Lieutenant Perrot,' someone called, and Sandrine turned. Sarah Morvan stood at reception and waved.

'Mademoiselle Morvan, how can I help you?'

'How is my mother?' She looked pale and her eyes were red. She had a few reasons for crying.

'She's talking with her lawyer at the moment. She's doing well given the circumstances.' She had nearly said that she was fine, but that would have been a lie. The woman was sitting in a cell with a charge for murder looming above her. No matter how tough she tried to appear, no one could ignore something like this.

'My mother can be a difficult woman who hates to show weakness, but what other choice did she have? She was the power that made the La Baie into what it is today.'

'You seem to be a big help to her.'

Sarah shook her head.

'I work only in the restaurant. Without her the hotel's existence is in danger.'

'How can we help you?'

She held up a folder with signatures. 'Maman is the boss and hates to delegate tasks. I need a few signatures to even out bills and transfer the salaries to the employees. It won't take long, but the people need their money.'

'Brigadier Azarou will bring you to your mother. Only for the business, and afterwards you have to leave.'

'Thank you.' Sarah grabbed Sandrine's sleeve before she could leave. 'Do you really think that she did all those horrible things? It feels impossible to me.'

'Not even to save the hotel?'

'She would never kill a human, least of all Daniel. She loved him despite everything.'

'I am sorry, but the evidence is clear. We will transfer her to the Prosecutor's Office. Afterwards, it's up to the judge to decide what will happen to her.' She carefully pulled the woman's shaking hand from her sleeve. 'I have to go back to work.'

Chapter 9

Farewell, La Baie

Sandrine jumped up in the early hours of the morning. An idea had woken her, but she could not fully grasp it now. It's starting again. She cursed. The case had fully engulfed her, and all her thoughts were circling around the investigation. Even during sleep, she could not fully relax.

'You have to stop,' she mumbled and threw back the duvet. Two months and three weeks and then she could start a normal life without any corpses involved. In only her panties and a long mono-coloured t-shirt, she took some woollen socks from the wardrobe and put them on. Just like her mother's, her feet got cold very fast. That was just one of many reasons why her parents had moved to the Cote d'Azur last year.

Wood burned in the oven, and a soft and comfortable warmth filled the living room. The flickering flames were enough light, and she did not switch on any lamps. She pushed the armchair and the fitting footstool to the terrace door, threw a blanket over the backrest and got a glass of Bordeaux from the kitchen. The wind ruffled through the trees and bent the grass flat on the ground. It was still too dark outside to let her glimpse the sea. It must have been like this when Isabelle met her murderer.

A shadow raced through the room, jumped on her lap, and rolled into a fluffy ball.

'Up that early, Pauline?' The cat purred while Sandrine petted her back. In the right hand she held the glass and took a sip from the red wine. She went through all the evidence in her thoughts. She came to the same solution over and over again. Florence Morvan had, to save the La Baie, murdered two strangers and her own son. It did not sound very believable, but everything pointed to it. Every judge would sentence her. That she did not doubt a second. And still, she was still searching for one last piece to seal the deal and finish the puzzle. Somewhere in the files it is hiding and laughing at me. I could always count on my instinct.

A gust of wind swept over the house and shook the door. The cat raised its head and looked at the old lock. Sandrine had planned on having it changed a while ago but had always pushed it to another day.

She straightened suddenly. That's it. She put the wine down and took her phone to type a number.

'Yeah,' a sleepy voice answered.

'Monsieur Mazet, it's Lieutenant Perrot.'

'Are you still celebrating the success of solving the case, or why else are you still up at this hour?'

'Not at all. I have a question and then you can sleep.'

'As if that would be so easy after you woke me up.'

She had a quick chat with the forensic technician, listened and thanked him. She had found the last puzzle piece. Tomorrow she would receive the confession. She was sure of that. Excitement rose up in her, and nothing could keep her in the chair. Pauline jumped to the floor and meowed her misery before curling up next to the oven.

Sandrine made herself a strong espresso and dressed in her running clothes. On her way out, she downed the coffee. If she still believed in her theory after the run, that would be it.

The door shut behind her. She put the headphones in her ears and switched on her headlamp. Shortly after she climbed down the stairs of the Brittany Coast Path and ran towards the Pointe du Grouin.

Sandrine parked the Citroën in front of the commissariat and ran up the stairs. She was too impatient to wait for the elevator.

'Inès?' She called for the office manager who was already at work and distributing files to each desk.

'Here that early? You caught the murderer, you should sleep for the first time in days.'

'You know everyone in Saint-Malo, right?'

'Well, some people, yes.'

'Something is stuck in my head,' she began.

'I know that problem.'

'You are exactly the woman I need.'

'If I can help, sure.'

'We better get a coffee from the vending machine first,' she suggested.

'Nonsense. I have a small but excellent coffee maker here in the office. Come with me.'

Sandrine followed the woman. Another shot of caffeine could do no harm.

After a conversation with Inès, Sandrine returned to her workplace. Her phone rang and she took the call. It was Azarou. She paid attention to what he was saying and nodded. It was time to get going.

She went to the interrogation room Florence Morvan was waiting in.

'Ready for a confession?' she asked the woman who looked at her as if she despised her.

'My lawyer has pressed me to do this to get a milder sentence. What could be mild in falsely confessing to the murder of one's own child?' Her hands wiped imaginary dust from her simple dress. 'It is not sad about the other two, a blackmailer and a drug dealer. I am more surprised that the police actually care that something happened to scum like that.'

The woman was bitter. Drugs had murdered her husband, and nearly destroyed her family and her source of income. If Charles Carnas had not shown up in Cancale, her husband and son might still be alive. Most likely no one was shedding a tear over Carnas' or Isabelle's bodies.

'Let's take a trip. I need a confession before I can finish the case with good conscience.'

'You will not receive one.'

'We will see,' she answered. She left the woman in the dark as to where she wanted to drive and why. The surprise was important for her plan to work.

Sandrine stopped on the parking place opposite the La Baie in the port of Cancale. They had decided against a police car as it would attract too much attention. No one cared much for the Citroën.

'What are we doing here?' Florence looked over at the restaurant. A delivery man in a screaming red jacket with a logo on the back had just left the hotel. Apart from that all was calm. Breakfast was finished and on one table sat two women: Sarah and Lianne Roche.

'Your daughter and your lawyer. What do you think the two are discussing?'

'Nothing unusual about that. There are many things that

need to be taken care of while I am being held. They will also prepare my defence.'

'I think so, too.'

'Why the waiting? Let us go inside if you want to talk to Sarah so desperately. It is beyond me why though. She cannot help you.'

'You don't think much of your daughter?'

Florence Morvan watched the restaurant in silence for a moment.

'She is good in the kitchen,' she finally said. 'But she is no real Morvan. Life is not as hard as it used to be, and one can see that in one's children. She is lacking strength and ambition, the main qualities which always lifted the women of the Morvans above everyone else.' She turned her attention from the restaurant to Sandrine. 'The will to go forwards in a straight line even if sacrifices have to be made is not in her. The La Baie does not need someone who can just bake perfect croissants. If you understand what I mean.'

'I do, even though I think that you two are more similar to each other than you realise.'

Florence blew air from her nose. She did not hide how little she liked her own daughter. Sandrine was surprised that the young woman had not packed her bags years ago and left.

The brigadier stepped next to their car and leaned down to the window.

'Dubois did not take his eyes from him. He's parking and will go inside soon.' Azarou turned. 'There he is.'

Sandrine noticed the man in his expensive coat cross the street and make his way towards the La Baie.

'Do you know him?' Sandrine asked.

'No. Never seen him. Someone like this is not part of my clientele.' The brigadier grimaced. The woman was not hiding her opinions on people with different skin colours.

'This is Thierry le Sauvage. Another person whom Isabelle Deschamps tried to blackmail.'

'Then you should arrest him and not me. He already looks like a criminal.'

Kouame knocked at the restaurant's closed door. Sarah opened it and locked it again after he had entered. Most likely she did not want to be interrupted. She led the visitor to the table Lianne Roche was sitting at.

'Now I am very curious to know what they are talking about. Let's head over, Madame Morvan.' Sandrine unfastened her seatbelt and got out of the car. Together they crossed the street and walked to the restaurant's entrance. She pulled a key from her pocket. They had taken it from Madame Morvan upon her arrest.

'May I?'

Without waiting for the answer, she unlocked the door and let the two go first.

'Maman!' Sarah shouted and jumped up. 'How did you get here? Did the police realise their mistake and let you go?'

'The police did no such thing. Your mother is still under our custody,' Sandrine replied. 'But we didn't want to hide from her how the hotel is running while she is gone. May we sit with you?'

Sarah looked at her with a mixture of surprise and curiosity.

'Of course,' she answered.

Thierry Kouame rose. 'Then I will leave you to your discussion and come back later. Maybe for dinner. It is supposed to be delicious.'

'You stay too,' said Sandrine and pulled her jacket to the side ever so slightly. She patted the gun in its shoulder holster. 'They are so uncomfortable, but after someone tried to shoot me it's better to have one handy.'

'Are you threatening me?'

'Not at all.' She waved and two armed policemen entered the restaurant. 'For that I brought my colleagues. They are much better at threatening than me.' The man sat back down.

Lianne Roche opened her briefcase and starting collecting the documents which had been spread on the table. With a quick step Sandrine made it to the table and placed her hand on the papers.

'Those are private. They don't concern you,' hissed the lawyer.

'I assume they are under legal protection as you are part of Madame Morvan's defence?'

'Exactly.'

Her hand still on the papers, she looked at Florence Morvan.

'May I take them? I think this could be interesting for both of us.'

The woman stepped closer and looked at the lawyer with narrowed eyes.

'You may not,' she answered to Sandrine's disappointment. Her plan was jeopardized. 'I will do that myself.'

She handed her the documents, but not without having a look at the front page. Now it all depended on how the woman would react. Her strategy could end up in a complete disaster.

Sarah stared at her mother with wide eyes while she read the paper. Her lips were pressed into a tight line, and all blood seemed to have drained from her face. Lianne Roche was nervously playing with her butter knife. Only Kouame looked relaxed.

Madame Morvan dropped the documents on the table. 'You wanted to sell the hotel behind my back?' Her voice was sharp enough to cut ice, and Sarah looked at her mother as if ready to fight. Sandrine had not expected that from the young woman. 'You do not have the right. I own the La Baie.'

'I wouldn't be so sure of that.' Madame Morvan's head jerked to look at Sandrine. 'You signed a lot of documents yesterday. All given to you by your lawyer. Did you read every single piece of paper?'

'What are you insinuating?' she asked sharply.

'Madame Roche and your daughter are very close.'

'That's a speculation.' The lawyer straightened and threw an angry look at Sandrine.

'At least close enough that Sarah spent last night at her place.'

'How do you ...?' Now it was Sarah who glared at her. All softness had left her face.

'I know it because Brigadier Azarou saw you leave her house this very morning. For how long has this been going on?'

'There's no law against it.'

'How long?' Sandrine's voice increased in volume.

'One year,' Sarah admitted.

'And when did you decide to get rid of your family to get the hotel for yourself?'

'You have a great imagination. Not even my own mother would think that I could dream of such a thing, let alone being capable of executing it.' She pushed her chair back, crossed her arms in front of her chest and looked at Sandrine challengingly. 'You can't prove anything. It was my mother who shot Daniel. She will go to prison for that like a murderer should.'

'And what was your plan during all of this? To sell the hotel? I thought you loved your job and were working towards your first Michelin star. Was I that wrong?'

Sarah Morvan looked around and her demeanour grew hard and cold. 'This hotel is like a vampire. It sucks you dry and doesn't give anything back. It already stole my childhood. Instead of playing with my friends I had to help make the beds. I was nothing but an unpaid servant.' She looked at her mother.

'You owe me something, and I will take it now if you like it or not.'

'Only over my dead body.' Florence Morvan's voice was cutting.

'Unfortunately, they got rid of the death penalty in this country. A shame if you ask me,' her daughter answered, in the same cold and sharp tone as her mother.

'And you, Monsieur Kouame. You entered the hotel world?'

'I have nothing to do with the murder and the crime. My only goal is to invest in a promising business. That's why I will take my leave now.'

Sandrine picked up the contract and searched for the price. She whistled.

'Your offer is far higher than I would have assumed the price for a hotel in the French province to be. So, you got blackmailed?'

'I am not being blackmailed in the slightest. What brings you to such a preposterous theory?'

Sandrine went to the bar and took the thin parcel the courier driver had left while they had waited in the parking lot.

'I assume this is yours, Monsieur Kouame?'

'How could it be?' He looked at Sarah.

'You are not allowed to open that parcel,' the young woman called.

'I think it still falls under yesterday's search warrant.'

Sandrine opened it, and a small notebook slipped out. Neat written lines of names and numbers filled the pages. Thierry Kouame looked around. All exits had been blocked. For a business meeting with two women, he would not have brought a weapon, but she was still glad about the presence of the policemen and the taskforce.

'Prosecutor de Chezac has had to wait quite a while for this notebook. He will be pleasantly surprised that we found it.

Three people had to die for it. And you, Mademoiselle Morvan, killed them.'

Sarah was silent, and Lianne Roche stammered, 'How could you know that?' Her arrogance had crumbled in on itself.

'Brigadier Azarou was keeping an eye on you after Sarah left this morning,' she said, turning to the lawyer. 'I was not sure if you worked for Florence or Sarah Morvan, but our office manager was able to report a few details about your private life. I could guess at the rest. Very clever. Most likely I would have thought of something similar if I had wanted to hide the subject of blackmail from the police. The courier picked it up from you this morning, and of course I was wondering why you would send a package by courier and not take it yourself as you had planned to meet here. It had to be something that would not cause a stir.' She turned to Kouame. 'The women thought you capable of taking it by force.'

'I have nothing to do with this notebook.' Thierry Kouame stood up. 'And I will leave the restaurant now unless you want to arrest me on account of your fantasy.'

'Monsieur Kouame, I will take you into custody. The police will refer you to the Prosecutor's Office in Paris.' She waved with the thin book. 'This should send you to prison for a couple of years.' She would keep it in Saint-Malo for a while until de Chezac came crawling and begged her for it. Why should she not enjoy this little sliver of revenge? She waved two policemen towards them who fastened handcuffs on the man. 'Please, take Madame Morvan as well. We don't need her here anymore.' The older woman reluctantly let herself be taken away.

'I knew nothing of the notebook's content or any blackmail,' Lianne Roche assured.

'It's time to confess.' Sandrine turned to Sarah Morvan. 'Your lover has already jumped from the boat so as to not be dragged into the deep end by you. Show your cards.'

'Why would you accuse me of murder? I am only the nice, shy cook who jumps when her mother points.'

'I admire how you made everyone around you believe this mask for years. In the beginning, I also did not think you would be capable of murder, but the longer we searched the more evidence indicated against you. The closer I looked, the more your mask cracked.'

'There is no proof of my guilt.'

'You were very clever and careful. That's why I had to set this trap for you. If you had waited to sell the hotel until after your mother's court case, you would have gotten away with three murders. Your greed was your biggest mistake.'

'I had to finish the business while you were interested in my family. Even someone like Kouame would not have dared to murder me or Lianne while the police were watching us.'

'I assumed that Isabelle was the seasoned blackmail champion, but you surpass her by far. Were all the murders just about the sale of the La Baie?'

'How did you get to me? Where did I make a mistake?'

'The barn. That was the first time when the thought occurred to me that you might be behind everything. The car was clean, but you forgot the padlock at the door. We found your fingerprints on it.'

'You didn't have any of my prints to compare them to.'

'That's why I asked you to get your mother's phone and hand it to me.'

'Clever.'

'No, only routine. There was also the motorbike accident. I looked through the old files. It happened on a straight road from the barn to the La Baie. Most likely the night on which you and Daniel killed Carnas.'

'I have no knowledge of the content of the book and didn't know anything of the murders,' Lianne Roche interrupted. 'I only made the contracts. That was all.'

'And who was the one who jostled that idiot Treville from the street?' Sarah snapped at her.

'We'll talk about that later.' Sandrine stopped the fight. 'Let's start from the beginning. Why did you murder Charles Carnas?'

Sarah Morvan rose and went to the bar. Adel stepped in her way, but Sandrine gave him a sign to let her pass. The woman took a bottle of excellent Cognac and a few glasses and returned to the table. She handed one to everyone.

'You too?' she asked the brigadier. 'Or do you not drink alcohol?'

'In measures.' She poured him one.

Sarah Morvan turned her glass between thumb and pointer finger. Lost in thought she looked at her hands.

'Charles came here and stayed with us. He calmed Father down with his drugs, and Mother didn't dare throw the disgusting guy out. She feared for the good reputation of the family should his drug addiction come out. As if anything could be kept secret in such a small town.'

She put the glass to her lips and downed the liquid in one smooth movement.

'Even when he started to lay his hands on her daughter, she kept quiet.' She poured herself another drink. Her hand was shaking ever so slightly. 'I took care of it. The guy drank like there was no tomorrow. A few of his own pills ground into dust, he didn't even notice them.' She tapped her finger against the label on the Cognac.

'Two hundred Euros the bottle and the idiot didn't taste his Oxys.'

'What happened then?'

'He followed me. It wasn't hard to get him into my room. Two, three glasses and he was out before I had to sleep with him. A soft pillow and the weight of the woman whom he wanted to abuse were enough for that pig.' She threw her head back. 'I was generous with the drugs. Most likely they would have been enough to give him a quiet exit, but I had to make sure.'

'How did he get in your boot? I doubt you carried him on your own.'

'Daniel helped me. It was my idea to park the car in the barn. No one had used that thing for years.'

'Carnas had the loot from the robbery. Why didn't you take the chance, steal the money and leave? No one would have suspected you.'

She sighed deeply and nodded.

'We did the dirty work. The guy kept bragging about his money, but I had no idea how much it actually was. Daniel found the bag the next day and couldn't think of anything better than to drag it to Mother's. He fooled her into thinking a rival dealer killed and got rid of Carnas, and she was stupid enough to believe him. Or she didn't want to know the truth. I don't know, we never talked about it. As I said, I parked the car in the barn and rode back on the motorbike with Daniel. His nerves were shattered, and he overlooked this stupid tractor that was driving at night and slammed into us.' She stroked over the knee which she hadn't been able to fully use since the accident. 'I was trapped in a stretch bandage, and the bitch used my money and renovated this shitty hotel. She put every last cent into this place.'

'Your money?'

'I got rid of the guy, so it belonged to me.'

'What happened to your father? Did you also get rid of him?'

'No. In the room and especially in the boot of the car were so many drugs that the problem took care of itself. He took what he could carry, and it is rather hard to avoid an overdose if one literally swims in the stuff. That's what happened.' She stopped for a moment, and Sandrine did not push her. 'Daniel couldn't cope with the whole thing. He was weak. Just after our father's death he packed his things and hid on that old campsite.'

'Who found the book?'

'It was in the glove compartment of the car. I had no idea what the numbers meant or who the people were that were mentioned in it. I left it where it was.'

'Until Isabelle Deschamps found it?'

'Daniel was high as a kite when he decided to get more drugs and took Isabelle along. Instead of waiting in front of the barn she followed him. The bitch must have planned on getting all the drugs. She obviously recognized the car, found Carnas' corpse and the notebook.'

'And she blackmailed you with her boyfriend's murder?'

'She thought she was blackmailing my mother. Her phone is either at reception or behind the bar. I caught the messages, answered them and deleted them afterwards.'

'Not very neat,' noted the brigadier.

Sarah looked at him in surprise.

'Of course not. You were supposed to find them again. I couldn't make it too hard for you.'

'You wanted to get rid of Isabelle. That's why you called Paris. You informed Kouame and told him where to find Isabelle.'

'That felt like the cleanest solution to me. He has a certain reputation of not letting traitors live. I hoped he would do the dirty work for me. However, he sent those two idiots and the bitch escaped. You can imagine how angry I was when her messages practically flew into our house. She was panicking and only wanted one thing, to get away from here.'

'And you met her in the name of your mother?'

'Of course. She would have never believed that I have enough money to pay her.' Sarah smiled. 'She was quite surprised when she saw me. First, she showed off that she would get us for the murder of Carnas if we wouldn't pay an insane amount for her silence.'

'You shot her?'

'What other option did I have? The woman would have spent the money and blackmailed us again. A clean cut was the best solution.'

'I can understand that. But why Daniel?'

'He was weak like all the other men in our family. I gave him the key to our house and killed him there. He had the book from Isabelle. Since the incident with Carnas he knew what I was capable of, and he knew that I had shot that bitch. He didn't want to give me the book but to go to the police. At least then her death would still serve a purpose, he babbled. I could not allow that to happen. He would have ruined everything.'

'You shot him.'

'He didn't leave me a choice,' she answered.

'From your viewpoint probably.'

'I didn't like doing it. You can believe that.'

'And then?'

'It was the chance of a new life, one that I had earned. From the beginning I laid evidence in a way that would lead you to my mother. With her in prison and the notebook in my hand it wasn't hard to convince this criminal to invest into an excellent hotel at the coast.'

'I saw the price. You wanted quite a bit extra.'

'I didn't just give him back his property but also kept him from prison and solved the problem with Isabelle. No one does that for free.'

Sandrine took her glass and held it against the light. The cognac shone like dark honey. She emptied it in one go.

'Adel, get Jenaud's men in from outside, and escort the women to the commissariat. We still have to report what happened.'

Sarah Morvan stood up and stepped to Sandrine.

'The big mistake I made was to not aim good enough in the barn. The other idiots would have never suspected me. You should look out. You won't always have that much luck.'

'I will look for a calmer job.'

'I don't believe it,' Sarah answered. 'You can't escape your calling.'

Sandrine sat down at the table and looked after the two women while they were being helped into the police car. Capitaine Jenaud saluted her, got into his car, and drove off.

Adel Azarou sat down next to her and poured another glass.

'I drive,' he said. 'You earned a drink.'

'Thank you.'

'Sarah Morvan was right,' said Adel.

'With what?'

'This job is your calling. You are a huntress with an excellent instinct.'

'Only training, nothing else.'

'No. Until this morning I was convinced that Florence Morvan committed the murders. I wasn't suspicious enough and pacified too quickly. That's the difference between us.'

She drank the cognac and looked out of the window. The bay was stretching out in front of her. The air was clear, and she could make out the dark line of Normandy on the horizon. The flood was pushing into the harbour as it had done since the beginning of time. Just like the tide, crime would not stop just because she was fighting against it. She was nothing more than a straw in a storm.

'What made you suspicious of Lianne Roche?'

'Female instinct. The air between you two was so charged that I had to find out what happened between you.'

'Inès.'

'She left you because of a woman. Inès didn't know for what woman but as Lianne was making a secret out of it I got curious.'

'It was worth it in the end. In the future, please ask me if it is about my private life.'

She nodded in silence and did not tell him that she had actually done exactly that.

'While we are talking about it ...' He reached into his jacket pocket and pulled out an envelope. 'Inès was very sorry, but she forgot to give the letter to Commissaire Matisse. Maybe you should do that yourself.'

He placed her notice on the table and pushed it towards her.

Sandrine took it and let it disappear into her jacket.

'I should.'

She took her phone and typed a message to Deborah Binet.

Promises had to be kept. She did not mention any names, but a journalist who just happened to be in front of the hotel would see who got arrested.

They stayed seated for a while and enjoyed the silence before they made their way to Saint-Malo. A heap of paperwork was waiting for them.

'Shame. Her croissants were the best ones I had eaten in a while,' she said. She had to start the search once more for a bakery which made croissants just the way she liked them. That might be more difficult than catching a murderer.

Sandrine climbed in the car and left the harbour behind her.

Thanks

I am delighted that you joined Sandrine Perrot and Adel Azarou in their investigation in Brittany and Normandy. Feedback from my readers is very important to me. Critique, praise and ideas are always welcome, and I am happy to answer any questions. My email address is: Author@Christophe-Villain.com

Newsletter: To not miss any new publications you can sign up to the newsletter and get the free novella: Death in Paris - The prequel to the Brittany Mystery Series.

Free Novella

Subscribe to the newsletter and receive a free eBook: Death in Paris.
Sandrine Perrot's back story, her last case in Paris.

Sandrine held the warm coffee cup in her hands and looked out through the café window. The gusty wind drove dark clouds across the sky and swirled leaves along the boulevard. Pedestrians zipped up their jackets and scrambled to keep dry before the impending rain. She wasn't particularly excited about the prospect of having to take her motorbike on the road. Sandrine forgot to shop most of the time and hated to cook. Café Central was her salvation so she wouldn't turn up at work with her stomach growling.

"Would you like anything else to drink?" asked the waitress, who regularly saw Sandrine during her morning shift. She bet the young girl was a student who worked here to earn a few euros. Judging by her distinct accent, she was probably from Provence.

"Thank you but I have to get on the road pretty soon."

"Not a nice day." The young woman took a peek outside and picked up the used plate on which the remains of scrambled eggs and baguette crumbs lay.

"That's why I hold on to my coffee cup for a while and enjoy the warmth in the café before I have to go to work." A bad feeling swept over her that she couldn't pin down to any specific event, but it nagged at her, as if the day could only get worse. The case she was investigating was stuck in her head and she couldn't shake it, which she usually could.

"No hurry," said the waitress, looking around the half-empty café. "It doesn't get crowded again until lunchtime, so until then I don't have much to do."

Sandrine's cell phone, which was lying on the table in front of her, vibrated and she glanced at the display.

"I'm afraid I have to take this call."

The waitress took the hint and took the dirty dishes into the kitchen. "Hello, Martin, what's up?"

She listened to her colleague in silence for a while.

"On the Richard Lenoir Boulevard? I'll be there in fifteen minutes."

Sandrine ended the call and cursed under her breath. Her gut feeling had proved to be right; the day lived up to its promise. She put money on the table, pulled on the waterproof motorcycle jacket and picked up the helmet that was lying on a chair.

She quickly drank the rest of the coffee. The waitress gave her a friendly wave as she left.

Her motorcycle was parked on the wide sidewalk between two trees. She wiped the wet seat with her sleeve before climbing on and pulling on her gloves. She took a deep breath and started the engine. Shortly thereafter, she merged into traffic.

Half a dozen patrol cars and an ambulance were parked by the Saint-Martin Canal. The paramedics were hunkered down in the car and puffs of smoke rose through their slightly ajar windows. They were more comfortable than their police colleagues, who had to go out to cordon off the area. The first onlookers were already gathering on one of the narrow bridges that spanned the watercourse. Sandrine drove through a gap in the metal fence separating the canal from the boulevard and parked the motorcycle on the wide pedestrian promenade. Bollards – stocky

vertical posts – were set at regular intervals, but today no boats were moored here and the lock gate was closed.

"Good morning, Sandrine," a grey-haired man with angular features greeted her. His badge identified him as Major de Police. "Kind of shitty weather to be out on a motorcycle."

"Hello, Martin. It's still a lot quicker than driving a car. Not to mention parking." She stuffed her gloves and scarf into her helmet and stuffed it into one of the panniers. "Is it our guy?"

"The Necktie Killer? Looks like it."

"Is that what they call him now?" She shook her head in disgust. "Far too friendly sounding. He's a sadistic murderer and should be considered and referred to as such."

"I didn't invent it. We owe that to the journalists who needed punchy headlines." He held up his hands defensively.

"I'm sorry. I was thinking of the victims."

"That's all right. Whenever things like that don't get to you anymore, it's time to change careers."

"In there?" she asked, looking toward the entrance to the Saint-Martin Canal, which ran underground for the next few miles. Even on sunny days, this gloomy place seemed ominous to her. "Who from our team is here?"

"Brossault, the medical examiner with the forensic guys and some cops cordoning off the area. The big boys are on their way, it was probably too early in the morning for them."

Sandrine laughed softly. The chief of homicide and the juge d'instruction, the prosecutor in charge of the investigation, would not be long in coming. They were forced to demonstrate that

the police were doing everything they could to take the perpetrator off the street since the series of murders was dominating the front pages of the newspapers. However, they hadn't even come an inch closer to him since they'd found the first victim in the summer. It was now February and two more dead women had joined the list of victims.

"Let's go then," she said, walking towards the scene of the crime.

The rain started, pattering on the dark water of the canal. Major Martin Alary pulled up the collar of his raincoat and walked faster across the slippery pavement. A uniformed cop stepped aside and waved them through the barricade.

"Was it closed?" Sandrine asked, looking at the lock where the water was damming up. The Saint-Martin Canal was just under two-and-a-half-miles long, and connected the Bassin de la Villette in the north with the Seine in the south. It had a total of five locks – enclosures with gates at each end where the water level could be raised or lowered.

"Most people only use the exposed area: a few tourist boats, but mostly paddle boats and small motorboats used for family outings in the Bassin de la Villette. Hardly more than a dozen boats a day traverse the entire length of the canal."

"The less water traffic, the more noticeable things are. Let's hope someone noticed something."

They entered the tunnel through an open metal door guarded by another police officer. Martin Alary wiped raindrops from his shoulders and adjusted his gun holster. A brick path, on which two people could comfortably walk side by side, ran along the length of the canal. The dim light of the rainy day reached only a few feet deep into the tunnel, and the antique-looking lamps that hung at regular intervals on the wall allowed one to see the way, but were useless for forensic

work. The forensics team had already set up blazingly bright spotlights so they wouldn't miss a thing.

A thin man with a pointed beard and a bald head walked towards them.

"Ah. Capitaine Perrot and Major Alary. Already here?" Marcel Carron, the forensics manager, patted Sandrine's companion on the shoulder and gave him a wink before turning to face her. He refrained from giving her a chummy pat on the back.

"How far along are you with securing the crime scene?"

"Almost done. However, there was hardly anything to secure."

"What can you tell me?"

"An employee of the city building department discovered the body during a routine examination. She was floating in the water. He informed us immediately and left the site. Very prudent."

"Is this also the scene of the crime?" the major asked.

"There's no evidence thus far," Carron replied. "We've searched the path for evidence of a struggle, but to no avail. The corpse is unclothed, but we couldn't find clothes anywhere."

"Not surprising."

"I concur."

"Any idea how the body got here?" Alary asked.

"There aren't many options left. There is no current in the canal sufficient enough to move a human body. She would have been spotted within one of the locks."

"Then she was put here," said Sandrine.

"The question is how." The forensic scientist pointed to the metal door at the entrance to the tunnel. "Entry is forbidden and the door is normally locked. However, there's no problem climbing over the door but dragging a corpse of an adult person up and over would be almost impossible without risking being discovered."

"Then there's only one option left," Sandrine said, stepping up to the railing that was too dirty to touch. "The perpetrator threw her off a boat at this point."

"An ideal location," the major agreed. "Nobody would notice since people seldom come in here."

"I'm assuming there's no security camera in the tunnel." Despite saying this, Sandrine looked around.

"Maybe the doctor can tell us more." She wasn't particularly hopeful. So far, the killer had left no usable evidence.

"Good luck."

Sandrine pulled a pair of disposable gloves and shoe covers out of her jacket pocket and put them on. Even though the forensic scientist assumed there wouldn't be anything of interest here, she played it safe.

A few feet away, she found Doctor Brossault standing next to the victim, a blue blanket spread over it.

"Bonjour," she greeted the older man in a dark suit, bow tie and handkerchief in his breast pocket. He turned to face her and used his forefinger to push his rimless glasses up the bridge of his nose. "An ideal place to dump a body, isn't it?"

"Absolutely." He nodded enthusiastically. "The murderer has a soft spot for historical places. You have to give him that."

"The canal dates back from the early 19th century, from what I remember from my history class." "1825 if you want to be exact, but who cares about that anyway?"

Sandrine suppressed a grin. The medical examiner was the type of person who always wanted to be as precise as possible and didn't withhold his knowledge.

"The canal, anyway. The structure built over the canal did not take place until much later: in 1860. At first, it was designed by Haussmann to improve traffic in the city."

"At first?" Sandrine asked. The man loved sharing his knowledge of history and enlightening those around him. It made him happy, so she let him have his fun.

"Naturally. Napoleon III was not exactly a popular head of state. Resistance to his rule simmered particularly in the revolutionary neighbourhoods such as Faubourg-Montmartre and Ménilmontant. So the plan to build over the canal came in handy. A wide swath through the city along which to send cavalry to maintain law and order."

"Interesting," said Major Alary, who Sandrine heard come up behind her. "But it didn't do him any good in the end."

"Fortunately," the doctor agreed.

Sandrine knelt down next to the body and looked inquisitively at the medical examiner. Only when he nodded did she lift the blanket under which the victim lay. A young woman's bloodless face stared at her with lifeless blue eyes. Blonde hair clung damply to pale skin. She wore a silk tie around her neck, where strangulation marks could be seen.

"She was strangled," Sandrine murmured, more to herself than to Doctor Brossault. "Just like the previous two victims," he confirmed.

"What can you tell me?"

"I'd put the woman in her mid-twenties, blonde and attractive like the other victims. She was strangled with the necktie. There are cuts on her wrists. Without wanting to commit myself, I would conclude that plastic restraints were used. The police use those things, too."

"Any other signs that she fought back?"

"I can't imagine that she didn't, but she had no chance of surviving. Not with her hands tied. Of course we are also looking for narcotics."

"Maybe the tie will get us further."

"A silk tie. Quite expensive and downright exclusive. Forensics will confirm that, although I can't imagine Monsieur Carron being an expert on the subject."

She looked up at him probingly.

"Have you ever seen the man properly dressed before?" His brow furrowed as if surprised at her lack of awareness.

"What's so special about these ties?"

"The quality of the silk is impeccable. In terms of design, I would guess mid-century. In addition, our killer is able to tie a perfect Windsor knot, something that is becoming increasingly rare these days. People either forgo a tie completely or fasten it sloppily. I would narrow the circle of perpetrators down to people with style and money."

He finished the sentence and straightened his bow tie.

Sandrine put the blanket back over the woman's face. She would see her again in the medical examiner's office. She'd seen enough for now.

To subscribe to the newsletter, please use the QR code.

Other Books

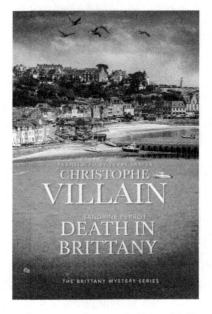

This book is a revised new translation of „Emerald Coast Murder".

Sandrine Perrot's investigation takes her from the picturesque fishing towns to the rural hinterland of Brittany's Emerald Coast.

Police Lieutenant Sandrine Perrot is on leave from her post in Paris and has settled in Cancale, the oyster capital of Brittany. She is temporarily assigned to the Saint-Malo police station for this case. The body of an unidentified woman is discovered on the Brittany coast path along the bay of Mont- Saint-Michel.

With her new assistant, Adel Azarou, she takes on the investigation, which leads them to a cold case from Paris, but also deep into the tragic history of a venerable hotelier family.

Saint-Malo Murder

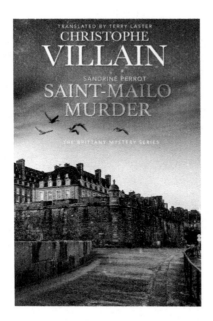

Death of an influencer

The tranquillity of the picturesque old town of Saint-Malo is shattered by a gruesome murder. The dead woman is a well-known influencer and radio presenter who has made many enemies in the region with her controversial opinions and themes. The killer has not only professionally staged the body and crime scene, but also meticulously recorded the crime.

Will she find the perpetrator in the dead woman's private surroundings, or will she have to dig deep into the victim's past?

Deadly Tides at Mont-Saint-Michel

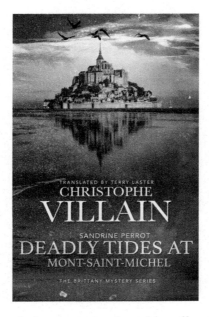

A dead woman loved by all.

Instead of spending a pleasant day with Léon on the coast and at Le Mont-Saint-Michel, Sandrine Perrot is called to a fatal accident in the Saint-Malo marina. The driver's death touches her personally, as she had just met the woman. In the course of the forensic investigation, she discovers that there is more to the alleged accident than she first suspected.

Her investigation leads her into the world of a well-known family in Le Mont-Saint-Michel, a family marked by antiquated traditions but also by conflicts between siblings.

Another person soon disappears without a trace. Was he trying to evade interrogation, or was an unwelcome witness being silenced?

Booklover's Death

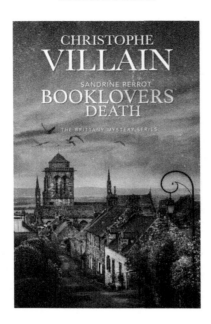

A murdered book collector

A new case takes Sandrine Perrot to Bécherel, the Cité du Livre of Brittany. A place where life revolves around books. The president of a well-known book club has been found murdered in his private library. Did contempt and rivalry among the book lovers lead to murder or does she have to look elsewhere for the motive?

While Sandrine investigates in the city of books, the prosecutor de Chezac builds a case against her. From the sidelines, she has to watch as the situation in Saint-Malo escalates.

Death at the Tidal Mill

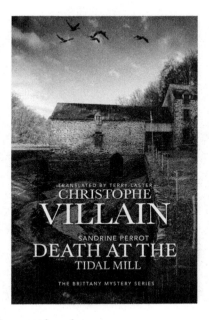

The death of a patriarch.

Their new case leads Sandrine and Adel to an estate on the River Rance. Alexandre de Tréchet, a wealthy landowner, has been found murdered in an old tidal mill.

Were the children, estranged from their father, no longer willing to wait for the considerable inheritance? Or did dodgy business dealings lead to his death?

A dubious private investigator poses mysteries for Sandrine, which she must solve in order to convict the perpetrator.

Shadows from the Past

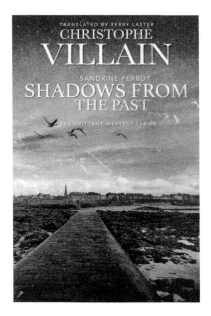

A shadow from her past catches up with Sandrine once again in Saint-Malo.

Sandrine and Adel are called to a crime scene on the beach in Saint-Malo. The body of a young woman has been found below the fortress walls. The perpetrator's methods evoke memories of her last investigation into a serial killer in Paris. A case that remains unsolved to this day.

Is it a coincidence, or has the murderer followed her to Brittany?

A Deadly Challenge

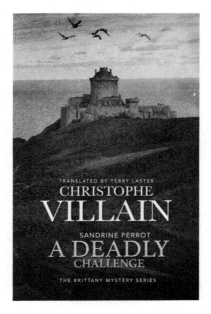

The deep fall of a burglar

It's summer in Brittany and Sandrine is enjoying her last days off before returning to work at the police station in Saint-Malo. On her way to Cap Fréhel, she receives a call from her boss, Commissaire Matisse, asking her to investigate a fatal accident at Fort La Latte.

An uninvited visitor had fallen from the fortress tower during the night. What appears to be a tragic accident caused by overconfidence soon turns out to be a meticulously planned attack on a man who had many enemies.

Her investigation leads her to a group of parkour enthusiasts in Saint-Malo who boast about their illegal exploits on the Internet. Is this the motive for the crime, or will she have to dig deeper into the dead man's criminal past?

Death in the Haunted Forest

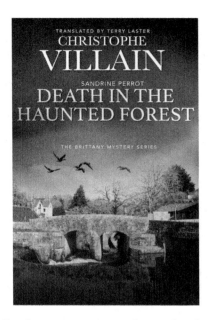

A theatre in the forest, a grotto where the devil lives, and a brutal murder.

It is autumn in Brittany, and Sandrine is visiting the small town of Huelgoat to see the legendary forest where the giant Gargantua once roamed, and where the devil supposedly lives in a cave. Much to her surprise, she encounters Commandant Gérard of the gendarmerie, who is investigating a murder. A male corpse has been found in the forest. After some hesitation, Sandrine agrees to help him with the investigation.

The deceased is an investigative journalist who had retired to Huelgoat. Had someone taken revenge on him for exposing them in his articles? Did his murderer want to prevent the book he was writing from being published? Or had the arrogant man made too many enemies in the village?

Sandrine sets out to uncover the dark secrets the victim had carefully hidden, one by one. She quickly realises that the inhabitants of this seemingly idyllic village have more to hide than meets the eye.

Printed in Dunstable, United Kingdom